Walla Walla
County Libraries

D0088877

THE *Winter* MAN

Also by Diana Palmer

Heartless
Her Kind of Hero
Nora
Heart of Stone
Fearless
Big Sky Winter
Man of the Hour
Trilby
Lawman
Lacy
Hard To Handle
Heart of Winter
Outsider
Night Fever
Before Sunrise
Lawless
Diamond Spur
Desperado
The Texas Ranger
Lord of the Desert
The Cowboy and the Lady
Most Wanted
Fit for a King
Paper Rose
Rage of Passion
Once in Paris
After the Music
Roomful of Roses
Champagne Girl
Passion Flower
Diamond Girl
Friends and Lovers
Cattleman's Choice
Lady Love
The Rawhide Man

THE *Winter* MAN

DIANA PALMER

FIC
PALMER
2009

HQN™

HQN™

Recycling programs
for this product may
not exist in your area.

ISBN-13: 978-0-373-77414-2

THE WINTER MAN

Copyright © 2009 by Harlequin Books S.A.

The publisher acknowledges the copyright holder
of the individual works as follows:

SILENT NIGHT MAN
Copyright © 2008 by Diana Palmer

SUTTON'S WAY
Copyright © 1989 by Diana Palmer

All rights reserved. Except for use in any review, the reproduction or
utilization of this work in whole or in part in any form by any electronic,
mechanical or other means, now known or hereafter invented, including
xerography, photocopying and recording, or in any information storage
or retrieval system, is forbidden without the written permission of the
publisher, Harlequin Enterprises Limited, 225 Duncan Mill Road,
Don Mills, Ontario M3B 3K9, Canada.

This is a work of fiction. Names, characters, places and incidents are
either the product of the author's imagination or are used fictitiously,
and any resemblance to actual persons, living or dead, business
establishments, events or locales is entirely coincidental.

This edition published by arrangement with Harlequin Books S.A.

® and TM are trademarks of the publisher. Trademarks indicated with
® are registered in the United States Patent and Trademark Office, the
Canadian Trade Marks Office and in other countries.

www.HQNBooks.com

Printed in U.S.A.

CONTENTS

SILENT NIGHT MAN   9

SUTTON'S WAY   125

SILENT NIGHT MAN

Chapter One

At the funeral home the friend of the deceased was a big, richly dressed man who looked like a professional wrestler. He was wearing expensive clothing and a cashmere coat. He had olive skin, black eyes and wavy black hair that he wore in a long ponytail. He stood over the casket without saying a word. He looked aloof. He looked dangerous. He hadn't spoken to anyone since he entered the building.

Tony Danzetta stared down at John Hamilton's casket with an expression like stone, although he was raging inside. It was hard to look at the remains of a man he'd known and loved since high school. His best friend was dead. Dead, because of a woman.

Tony's friend, Frank Mariott, had phoned him at the

home of the man he was working for temporarily in Jacobsville, Texas. Tony had planned to stay around for a little longer, take a few weeks off from work before he went back to his real job. But the news about John had sent him rushing home to San Antonio.

Of the three of them, John had been the weak link. The other two were always forced to save him from himself. He fantasized about people and places that he considered were part of his life. Often the people were shocked to learn that he was telling his friends that he was on close terms with them.

Tony and Frank thought that John was harmless. He just wanted to be somebody. He was the son of people who worked for a local clothing manufacturing company. When the company moved outside the United States, they went to work at retail stores. Neither of them finished high school, but John often made up stories to tell classmates about his famous rich parents who had a yacht and their own airplane. Tony and Frank knew better, but they let him spin his yarns. They understood him.

But now John was dead, and that…woman was responsible! He could still see her face from the past, red with embarrassment when she'd asked him about one of their assignments at the adjunct college class they were both taking in criminal justice. That had been six years ago. She couldn't even talk to a man without stammering and shaking. Millie Evans had mousy-brown hair and green eyes. She wore glasses. She was thin and unremarkable. But Tony's adopted foster mother, who had been an archivist at the local library, was Millicent Evans's superior and she liked Millie. She was always talking about her to Tony, pushing her at him, right up until the day she died.

Tony couldn't have told his foster mother, but he knew too much about the girl to be interested in her. John had become fixated on her a couple of years ago and during one of Tony's rare visits home, had told him about her alter ego. In private, he said, Millie was hot. Give her a couple of beers and she'd do anything a man wanted her to do. That prim, nervous pose was just that—a pose. She wasn't shy and retiring. She was a party girl. She'd even done a threesome with him and their friend Frank, he'd told Tony in confidence. Don't mention that to Frank, though, he'd added, because Frank was still embarrassed about it.

What Tony had learned about Millie Evans had turned him right off her. Not that he'd found her attractive before that. She was another in a long line of dull, staid spinsters who'd do anything to get a man. Poor John. He'd felt sorry for his friend, because John was obsessed with Millicent Evans. To John, Millie was the queen of Sheba, the ultimate female. Sometimes she loved him, John moaned, but other times she treated him like a complete stranger. Other times, she complained that he was stalking her. Ridiculous, John had told Tony. As if he had to stalk her, when she was often waiting for him at his apartment, when he got off from work as a night watchman, wearing nothing at all!

John's description of the spinster was incomprehensible to Tony, who'd had beautiful, intelligent, wealthy women after him. He'd never had to chase a woman. Millicent Evans had no looks, no personality and she seemed rather dull witted. He never had been able to understand what John saw in her.

Now John was dead. Millicent Evans had driven him to suicide. Tony stared at the pale, lifeless face and rage built inside him. What sort of woman used a man like that, abused his love to the extent that she caused him to take his own life?

The funeral director had a phone call, which forced him to approach the silent man in the viewing room. He paused beside him. "Would you be Mr. Danzetta?" the man asked respectfully. The caller had identified him as tall and unconventional looking. That was an understatement. Up close, the man was enormous, and those black eyes cut like a diamond.

"I'm Tony Danzetta," he replied in a deep, gravelly voice.

"Your friend Mr. Mariott just phoned to tell us to expect you. He said you had a special request about the burial?"

"Yes," Tony told him. In his cashmere coat, that reached down to his ankles, he looked elegant. "I have two plots in a perpetual care cemetery just outside San Antonio, a short distance from where my foster mother is buried. I'd like you to put John in one of them." He was remembering a hill in Cherokee, North Carolina, where his mother was buried and a cemetery in Atlanta that held the remains of his father and his younger sister. He'd been in San Antonio since junior high school, with his foster mother. He described the plots, one of which he intended for John. "I have a plat of the location in my safe-deposit box. If I could drop it by in the morning?"

"Today would be better," the man replied apologetically. "We have to get our people to open the grave and prepare it for the service on the day after tomorrow, you understand."

He was juggling appointments, one of which was with his banker about a transfer of funds. But he smiled, as if it was of no consequence. He could get the plat out of the box while he was doing business at the bank. "No problem. I'll drop it by on my way to the hotel tonight."

"Thank you. That will save us a bit of bother."

Tony looked down at John. "You did a good job," he said quietly. "He looks…the way he used to look."

The man smiled broadly.

Tony looked at his watch. "I have to go. I'll be back when I've finished my business in town."

"Yes, sir."

"If Frank shows up before I get back, tell him that, will you? And tell him not to go out for food. I'll take him out to eat tonight."

"I will."

"Thanks."

The funeral director walked out of the viewing room, pausing to speak to someone. Tony, his eyes resting sadly on his friend's face, only half noticed the conversation.

He heard soft footsteps come toward the casket and pause beside him. He turned his head. And there she was. The culprit herself. She'd be twenty-six now, he judged, and she was no more attractive than she'd been all those years ago. She dressed better. She was wearing a neat gray suit with a pink blouse and a thick dark coat. Her dark brown hair was in a bun. She was wearing contacts in her green eyes, he imagined, because his foster mother had often mentioned how nearsighted she was. The lack of glasses didn't help her to look any prettier. She had a nice mouth and good skin, but she held no attraction for Tony. Especially after she'd been responsible for his best friend's death.

"I'm very sorry," she said quietly. She looked at John with no visible sign of emotion. "I never meant it to end like this."

"Didn't you?" He turned, his hands in the pockets of his coat, as he glared down at her with piercing dark eyes. "Teasing him for years, playing hard to get, then calling the police to have him arrested as a stalker? And you didn't mean it to end like this?"

She felt cold all over. She knew he'd worked in construction years ago, but there had been rumors about him since, whispers. Dark whispers. John had intimated that Tony was into illegal operations, that he'd killed men. Looking into his black eyes now, she could believe it. He wasn't the man she'd known. What had he said about her teasing John?

"Don't bother to lie," he said icily, cutting off her question even before it got out of her mouth. "John told me all about you."

Her eyebrows arched. What was there to tell, except that his friend John had almost destroyed her life? She drew herself up straighter. "Yes, he was quite good at telling people about me," she began.

"I never could understand what he saw in you," he continued, his voice as pleasant as his eyes were homicidal. "You're nothing to look at. I wouldn't give you a second look if you were dripping diamonds."

That hurt. She tried not to let it show, but it did. God knew what John had told him.

"I…have to go," she stammered. She was no good at confrontations. This big man was looking for a fight. Millie had no weapons against him. Long ago, the spirit had been beaten out of her.

"What, no urge to linger and gloat over your triumph?" He laughed coldly. "The man is dead. You drove him to suicide!"

She turned, her heart breaking, and met the tall man's eyes. "You and Frank could never see it," she replied.

"You wouldn't see it. Other men have infatuations. John had obsessions. He was arrested other times for stalking women—"

"I imagine you put the women up to reporting him," he interrupted. "John said you'd accuse him of stalking and then be waiting for him at his apartment, wearing no clothes at all."

She didn't seem surprised at the comment. He couldn't know that she was used to John's accusations. Much too used to them for comfort.

She moved one shoulder helplessly. "I tried to make him get help. When I finally had him arrested, I spoke to the district attorney myself and requested that they give him a psychiatric evaluation. John refused it."

"Of course he refused it. There was nothing wrong with his mind!" he shot back. "Unless you could call being infatuated with you a psychiatric problem." He raised both eyebrows. "Hell, I'd call it one!"

"Call it whatever you like," she said wearily. She glanced once more at John and turned away from the casket.

"Don't bother coming to the funeral," he said coldly. "You won't be welcome."

"Don't worry, I hadn't planned to," she replied.

He took a quick step toward her, infuriated by her lukewarm attitude, his dark eyes blazing with fury.

She gasped, dropped her purse and jumped back away from him. Her face was white.

Surprised, he stopped in his tracks.

She bent and scrambled for her purse, turned and ran out of the room.

There were murmurs outside the room. He glanced back at John, torn between anger and grief. "God, I'm sorry," he said softly to his friend. "I'm so sorry!"

He forced himself to leave. The funeral director was standing at the front door, looking worried.

"The young lady was very upset," he said uneasily. "White as a sheet and crying."

"I'm sure she was grieving for John," Tony said nonchalantly. "They knew each other a long time."

"Oh. That would explain it, then."

Tony walked to his car and felt better. At least he'd dragged some emotion out of her on behalf of his friend. He got behind the wheel of his expensive sports car and revved it out of the funeral home parking lot, his mind already on his appointment with the bank.

Millie Evans sat at the wheel of her little black VW Beetle and watched Tony drive away, out of her life. She was still crying. His coldness, his fury, had hurt her. She'd had to deal with John's histrionics and threats for two years, watching her life and career go down the drain while he told lies about her to anyone gullible enough to listen. He'd persecuted her, tormented her, made a hell of her daily life. Now he was dead, and Tony wanted to make her pay for driving his poor, helpless friend to suicide.

She wiped at her eyes with a handkerchief. Poor friend, the devil! Perhaps if he and Frank had realized that John was mentally ill years ago, they might have made him get help. He might have straightened out his life and gone on.

Millie was secretly relieved that John hadn't carried out his last, furious threat to end her life. He'd told her that she wouldn't get away with rejecting him. He had friends, he told her, who wouldn't hesitate to kill her for the right amount of money. He had savings, he'd raged; he'd use it all. He'd make sure she didn't live to gloat about pushing him out of her life!

She'd worried about that threat. The news was full of people who'd gone off the deep end and killed others they blamed for their problems, before killing themselves. It was, sadly, a fact of modern life. But she'd never dreamed that she—plain, prim little Millie Evans—would ever have something like that happen to her. Most people never even noticed her.

She'd wanted to be noticed by Tony. She'd loved him forever, it seemed. While his foster mother was alive, she'd coaxed the older woman into talking about her adoptive son. Tony had come a long way from North Carolina. He and his sister, both Cherokee, had lived with their mother and her abusive husband—but not their biological father—in Atlanta just briefly, but the man drank to excess and was brutal to the children. Tony and his sister went into foster homes in Georgia. After his sister, also in foster

care, died, Tony's nurturing foster mother moved him to
San Antonio, where she had family, to get him away from
the grief. She worked as an archivist at the public library
in San Antonio, where Tony was a frequent patron; and
where Millie worked after school and between classes
while she went through college.

Millie had loved hearing stories of Tony as a boy, as a
teenager, as a soldier. Sometimes his foster mother would
bring letters to the library and show them to Millie,
because they were like living history. Tony had a gift for
putting episodes in his life down on paper. He made the
countries where he was stationed come alive, and not
only for his parent.

Millie had hoped that Tony might spend some time at
the library when he came home on leave. But there were
always pretty girls to take on dates. Frank Mariott worked
as a bouncer in a nightclub and he knew cocktail wait-
resses and showgirls. He introduced them to Tony, who
always had a night free for fun.

A library, Millie supposed, wasn't a good place to pick
up girls. She looked in her rearview mirror and laughed.
She saw a plain, sad-faced woman there, with no hopes of
ever attracting a man who'd want to treasure her for the
rest of her life. It was a good thing, she told herself, that
she'd stockpiled so many romance novels to keep her
nights occupied. If she couldn't experience love, at least
she could read about it.

She wiped her eyes, closed up her purse and drove herself back to work. She'd forced herself to go and see John, out of guilt and shame. All she'd accomplished was to find a new enemy and hear more insults about herself. She knew that she'd never meet up with Tony again after this. Perhaps it was just as well. She'd spent enough time eating her heart out over a man who couldn't even see her.

Tony made his funds transfer, got the plat from the safe-deposit box, had the bank copy it for him and replaced the original before he went back to the funeral home.

All the way, in the back of his mind, he kept seeing the fear in Millie's face when he'd moved toward her. That reaction was odd. She might have been surprised by the speed of his movement—a lot of people had been, over the years. But she'd expected him to hit her. It was in her eyes, her face, her whole posture. He wondered what had happened to her in the past that made her so afraid.

Then he chided himself for that ridiculous compassion, when she'd caused John's death. At least he'd made sure that she wouldn't come to the funeral. That would have been the last straw.

He pulled up at the funeral home and locked his car. It was getting colder. Strange weather, he thought. First it was like summer then, in a matter of days, winter arrived. It was normal weather for Texas in late November, he mused.

As he walked into the funeral home, he saw some of

John's family gathered, talking among themselves. Frank spotted Tony and came out into the hall. They shook hands.

"I just have to drop this off," he told Frank, lifting up the copy of the plat. "Then we'll spend a minute talking to John's people before we go out to eat."

The funeral director spotted them and came forward. He took the copy of the plat, smiled at Frank and went back to his office.

"You may get a shock," Frank murmured as they walked into the viewing room.

"What do you mean?" Tony asked, surprised.

John didn't have much family. His parents were long dead. He did have a sister, Ida. She was there, dry-eyed and irritable. She glanced at the doorway and put on a big smile.

"Tony! How nice to see you again!" She ran up to him and hugged him. "You look great!"

"Sorry we have to meet like this," Tony began.

"Yes, the idiot, what a stupid thing to do!" Ida muttered. "He had a life insurance policy worth fifty thousand dollars. I paid the premiums for him, me and Jack, and look what he does! Suicide! We won't get a penny!"

Tony looked as if he'd been hit in the eye.

"Oh, there's Merle. Sorry, honey, I have to talk to her about the flowers. She's giving me a good deal on a wreath..."

John's cousin Ben came forward to shake hands.

"What a mess," he told the two men. He shook his

head. "I bailed him out of jail. He didn't exactly skip bond, but I'll forfeit what I put up," he added heavily. "Two thousand dollars," he grumbled. "He swore he'd pay me back." He wandered off, still shaking his head.

An elderly woman with dyed blond hair and wearing a hideous black dress, peered at Tony. She grinned up at him. "You must be that rich friend of Johnny's," she said. "He said you owned several islands out in the Atlantic and that you were going to give him one and a yacht, too, so he could get to and from this country."

"That's right, Blanche," Frank said, smiling. "Now, you'll have to excuse us, we've got an appointment. We'll see you at the funeral."

"I sure would like to see that yacht," Blanche added.

Frank took Tony by the arm and propelled him out into the lobby.

They were sitting in a good Italian restaurant fifteen minutes later, having given in their order.

"I can't believe it," Tony said furiously. "His own family! Not one of them seems to be sad that he's dead!"

"He was nothing but trouble to them," Frank replied. "He didn't work, you know," he added, shocking Tony, who'd already had a few shocks. "He told the government people that he had a bad back and he fed liquor to two vagrants who signed sworn statements that they'd seen the accident that crippled him. He convinced his doctor and got a statement from him, too, and talked a lawyer into getting him onto partial disability." He shook his head. "But it was barely enough to live on. He pestered his relatives for handouts. When he got arrested for stalking, this last time, he talked Ben into posting his bond. I warned Ben, but he said John had promised that his rich friend would pay Ben back."

"I've known John since high school," he told Frank. "You've known him since junior high. He was a good man."

Frank paused while the waiter served them appetizers and ice water.

"He changed," Frank said quietly. "More than you know. You only saw him on holidays, while your foster mother was still alive, and hardly at all in the past couple of years. I saw him constantly."

"You're trying to say something," Tony murmured, eyeing the other man.

Frank toyed with his salad. "He made friends with some members of a gang a few months ago," he said. "It really thrilled him, that he could kick around with people who weren't afraid of the law. He hated cops, you know," he added. "Ever since the arrest for stalking, when he went after—"

"Yes," Tony interrupted him. "That Millie creature!"

"Creature!" Frank sat back, shocked.

Tony was beginning to feel uncomfortable. "She caused John to kill himself, remember?"

"Who told you that?"

"John did. He sent me a letter. Left me a letter." He pulled it out of his pocket. It had arrived the day he got the news that John was dead, obviously having been mailed in advance of the suicide. "He said she tormented him…hell, read it for yourself." He pushed it across the table.

"I can imagine what's in it," Frank said. He ignored the letter and finished chewing a bite of salad. "He accused women of teasing him when they were only trying to get him to leave them alone. Millie was more kindhearted than most—she kept forgiving him. Then when she refused dates, he started telling tales on her to her coworkers." He glanced at Tony, sitting stiffly, still unbelieving. "You've seen Millie. Now, you tell me, does she really look like the sort of woman who'd lie in wait at John's apartment wearing a French maid's costume with a bottle of champagne in one hand and a champagne flute in the other?"

"It would be tough to imagine," Tony had to admit. "Still, mild-looking women have done crazier things."

"Yes, but Millie's not like that." Frank's face softened. "She sat with your foster mother when she was dying in the hospital, before you could get home. She was there every night after work."

"Sure, you'd defend her, when you did a threesome with her and John!" he snapped.

Frank gaped at him. "I beg your pardon?"

The other man's reaction made Tony even more uncomfortable. He fiddled with his water glass. "John told me about it."

"Oh, for God's sake!" Frank burst out. "I've never done a threesome in my life, much less with Millie!"

"Maybe he made a mistake with the name," Tony mumbled.

"Maybe he made a mistake telling you lies about me," Frank shot back. "I'd give anything to have Millie notice me! Don't you think I know how little I have to give to a woman with her brains? She has a degree in library science. I barely got out of high school. I'm a bouncer," he added heavily. "A nobody."

"Stop that!" Tony said immediately. "You're not just a bouncer. It's a rough job. It takes a hell of a man to do it."

"I'm sure there are guys in New York City who place ads hoping to get hired as bouncers in bars," Frank said sarcastically. "Here in San Antonio, it's not exactly the dream job of most men."

"You're sweet on Millie Evans, so you're defending her."

"I'm sweet on her, all right. If the competition wasn't so stiff, I might even try my luck. That's what made John crazy. He couldn't stand the competition, either. He knew he'd never replace that other guy Millie's been in love with for six years."

"What other guy?" Tony asked carelessly.

"You."

It was as if time stopped and everything went around

in slow motion. Tony put his fork down and looked across at Frank as if he'd gone mad. "Excuse me?"

"Do you think Millie needed courses in criminal justice to be a librarian?" Frank asked drolly. "She took those courses because your foster mother had told her you were taking them, in addition to your regular college classes, so you could get your degree faster. It was an excuse to be around you."

Now, horribly, it made sense. He hadn't even questioned her presence in the classes.

"Great," Tony muttered. "The murderer of my best friend thinks I'm hot!"

"She didn't kill him. But no jury would have convicted her if she had," Frank persisted. "He got her fired, Tony. He went to her boss and told her that Millie was hanging out in bars to have sex with men for an audience. He told that to three of the library's richest patrons, one of whom sat on the board of directors for the library. They demanded that she be fired."

Tony watched the other man warily. "And how do you know it wasn't true?"

"Because I went to a friend of mine at the local precinct and got John's rap sheet and showed it to them."

Tony was feeling ill. "Rap sheet? John had a rap sheet?"

"Yes. For fraud, defamation of character, petty theft, three charges of stalking and a half dozen other charges. I got a statement from the last woman he'd stalked, a receptionist for one of the dentists John went to. She swore in court that John had threatened her life. He convinced a lawyer that she was lying and produced a witness who heard her bragging that she'd get John arrested."

Tony waited for the rest.

"The gang members testified in his favor and got the case thrown out of court. A couple of weeks later, the receptionist was raped. Nobody was ever caught or charged."

Tony leaned forward. "Don't tell me John was mixed up in that!"

"He never admitted it," Frank replied heavily. "But I knew he was. A few months later, one of the gang members was pulled in on a rape charge and he bragged to the arresting officer that he could get away with it anytime he liked. He had alibis, he said. Turned out they were also members of his gang. Sadly for him, on the second rape case, the new gang member he bragged to was wearing a wire. He's doing hard time now."

"But John wasn't like that," Tony protested. "He was a good man!"

"He was sick," Frank said flatly. "He utterly destroyed Millie's life because she didn't want him. Even his relatives apologized to her for what he'd done. There are still people who go to that library who are convinced that Millie has orgies down in the basement, because John told them she did."

"I can't believe it," Tony said to himself.

"Obviously. You didn't know the adult John became. You still saw the kid who played sandlot baseball with you in ninth grade."

"He had a rap sheet. I never knew."

"He was a troubled man. There's something else, too. My friend at the precinct said that when they searched John's room, they found an open bank book on the coffee table. It showed a withdrawal of five thousand dollars in cash—John had apparently sold everything of value that he had. The pawn slips were there, too, neatly arranged. There was a note, addressed to Millie, with only a threat: 'You'll be sorry.' The police haven't told her yet, and they warned me not to say anything. But I'm afraid for her."

"What do you think John did with the money?" Tony asked.

"I don't know."

Tony was frowning. "Any of those gang members ever been suspected of murdering anybody?"

"Yes," came the curt reply. "John had a vindictive nature. It wouldn't surprise me if he didn't put out a contract on Millie."

The John whom Tony knew as a teen wouldn't have been capable of such actions. The man he was only now coming to know might well have done it. He could hardly get his mind to function. He'd come home with clear-cut ideas of the good guy and the bad woman, and now his theories were worthless. He was remembering Millie's tragic expression when he accused her of murdering his friend. He was remembering, too, what Frank had just told him, that Millie had cared about him. It was a good bet that she didn't anymore, he thought cynically.

Frank checked his watch. "I have to get back to the funeral home. Millie said she was coming over to see John. I tried to talk her out of it, but she said that it was something she had to do, that she felt responsible. Even after all John had done to her, she still felt sorry for him."

Tony closed his eyes and groaned. He didn't know how to tell his friend that Millie had already come to see John, and that Tony had treated her like dirt and made her run out of the building in fear of him. It wasn't a revelation he was looking forward to.

Frank actually winced when Tony told him how he'd treated Millie when he'd seen her at the funeral home earlier.

"Good God," Frank said heavily. "That poor woman. How could you, Tony?" he asked accusingly.

Tony grimaced. "I didn't know any better," he defended himself. "All I had to go on was the letter John sent me and the memory of those visits I made home, when he'd cry on my shoulder about how bad she was treating him. I was sure that she'd killed my friend with her heartless behavior."

Frank sighed heavily. "I wish she hadn't gone to the funeral home early."

"Yeah. Me, too," Tony replied. He was never going to be able to forget Millie's mad dash out the door. It would haunt him. "Look, that friend of yours at the precinct," he said. "Could you get him to ask around and see if there's any word on the street about a potential hit?"

"I could do that," Frank said, and brightened a little.

"Maybe John just left a lot of money to an animal shelter and made the threat to scare her," Tony said.

Frank gave him a sour look.

Tony held up both hands. "Sorry."

"It won't matter what he finds out," Frank said. "There's no budget for protective custody on supposition, no matter how educated. They won't be able to assign anybody to protect her."

"I'm off until the new year," Tony said. "I can handle that."

Frank blinked. "I'm sure she'll welcome having you around, after the warm reception you gave her at the funeral home."

Tony flinched. "Yeah. Well, I'll have to apologize, I suppose."

Frank didn't say anything to that. Privately he thought Tony was going to find it difficult to bend enough to convince Millie that he was sorry. His friend had spent most of his life in violent surroundings. His social skills were a bit rusty, especially around women like Millie. Tony's taste was the brassy, forward sort of females he could find in bars. Millie was both refined and reserved. It would be a tough combination to crack for a hard nut like Tony.

* * *

The next morning, a penitent Tony joined Frank at the funeral home for John's last rites. There was a very small group of people there, mostly family. A couple of rough-looking men were sitting in the back, looking around constantly. Tony wondered if they might be John's gang friends.

After the brief service, Tony drove Frank and himself to the cemetery for the graveside service. It was equally brief.

Tony noted that the rough-looking men had also come to the cemetery. One of them was intent on Tony and Frank, as if he found their presence suspicious.

"We're being watched," Tony told his friend as they walked back toward Tony's sports car.

"I noticed," Frank replied. Working as a bouncer had given him a sixth sense about trouble. Tony, in his line of work, also had developed it. They pretended to talk casually, without making it obvious that they saw the two men.

When they got to the car, and were seated and ready to travel, Tony looked in the rearview mirror and noted that one of the men was unobtrusively writing down his license plate number. He started laughing as he pulled the car around two of the family's vehicles and exited the cemetery road.

"What's funny?" Frank asked.

"They're cops," he said.

"What?"

"They're cops," Tony repeated. "Gang members wouldn't give a hoot in hell about my plate number. They want to know who I am, and what my connection is to John." He glanced at his friend. "How about asking your contact in the police department what they want to know about me? I'll phone him with the details."

Frank chuckled. "Fair enough. I'll call him when I get home."

Tony grinned. It amused him to be viewed with suspicion. He mostly was these days. He kept a low profile and never talked about his job.

He dropped Frank off at his apartment, and promised to meet him the following day for lunch. Then he went back to his hotel.

He noted that he was being followed again. He gave his car keys to the valet who handled the parking, walked into the lobby and slowed his pace as he went toward the elevator. He felt eyes on his back. Someone was following him. This was amusing.

He got into the elevator and pretended to be disinterested in his surroundings. A man whom he recognized as one of the two strangers at the funeral got in with him and stood apart, also pretending unconcern.

When Tony got off, on the wrong floor, he noted that the man remained behind but jotted down a number.

He took the staircase down, and was waiting in the

lobby when the man following him got off the elevator. He looked up into Tony's black eyes and actually jumped.

Tony gave him a worldly look. "If you want to know who I am and why I went to John's funeral, come on in the bar and I'll buy you a drink and give you the lowdown."

The man raised his eyebrows, and then started laughing.

"How did you figure it out?" he asked, when they were seated at the bar.

"I've worked with cops before," Tony told him, "in between jobs overseas."

"What sort of jobs overseas?"

Tony chuckled, reached into his pocket for his wallet, flipped it open and displayed his credentials.

The man whistled softly. "I thought about going with them, once, but after six months of being called, interrogated, lie-detected, background-checked and otherwise investigated to death, I gave up and joined the police force. The pay's lousy, but I've only been involved in one shoot-out in ten years." He grinned. "I'll bet you can't say that."

"You'd be right," Tony had to admit. "I'm carrying enough lead in me to fill a revolver. They can't take some of the slugs out because of where they lodged."

"You knew the deceased, I gather."

He nodded. "He was my best friend since high school." He grimaced. "But it turns out I didn't know him at all.

He was stalking a woman we both knew and I thought she was lying about it."

The man pulled out a notepad. "That would be Miss Millicent Evans."

"Yes."

"She wasn't lying," the police detective told him. "She called us in on a 10-16 domestic, physical," he added, using the ten code for a domestic disturbance call. "He'd knocked her around pretty badly."

Tony felt two inches high as he remembered Millie's unexpected reaction when he'd moved so abruptly in the funeral home. He couldn't speak.

"But when it was time to press charges, she wouldn't," the detective said flatly. "We were disappointed. We don't like women beaters. She said he was drinking heavily and had apologized, and it was the first time he'd hit her."

"Was it only the one time?" Tony had to know.

"I think so. She isn't the sort to take that kind of abuse on a routine basis. About a week later, he killed himself." He leaned closer. "We got word that a local gang boss took money to have her killed. That's why we were at the funeral. You got a friend named Frank?"

"Yes."

"He and my lieutenant are best friends," the man told him. "He's got us looking for people who might fit the description of a hit man."

Tony laughed. "And I fit the description."

"I've seen mob hit men who look just like you." He cocked his head. "You Italian?"

Tony grinned. "Cherokee," he said. "My mother's husband adopted me, but he wasn't my father."

"Goes to show," the detective said, "that you can't tell who people are by looking."

"Absolutely."

Tony went by the library the next morning, hoping to apologize to Millie and go from there. But the minute she spotted him in the lobby, she went through a door that had the sign Employees Only and vanished. He asked for her at the desk, as if he hadn't noticed. The clerk on duty went back through the door and reappeared a minute later, red-faced and stuttering.

"I'm sorry, I…couldn't find her," she finished.

Tony smiled sadly. He didn't blame Millie for hating his guts. "It's okay," he said. "Thanks."

He left. Apparently protecting her was going to be done at a distance, unless he could think of a way to get her to listen to him.

He tried calling her at the library when he got back to his hotel. The minute she heard his voice, she hung up. He sighed and called Frank.

"She ran the other way," he told his friend. "I expected it. But I can't convince her that she needs protection if I can't get within speaking distance of her. Any ideas?"

"Yeah," Frank said. "I'll go by her apartment and speak to her."

"Thanks. Tell her I'm sorry. It won't do much good, but I really mean it."

"I know you do."

"I bought one of our tails a drink," Tony told him. "He said they were looking for guys who fit the profile of a hit man. He thinks I do."

Frank burst out laughing. "If the shoe fits…"

"Thanks a lot," he muttered.

"I'll get back to you when I've seen Millie," he promised.

"Okay. I'll be here."

Frank called him the next morning. "She'll talk to you," he told Tony. "But it took a lot of persuading. And she won't believe that John would do anything so drastic as to hire someone to kill her. You're going to have a hard time selling her on the idea of protection," he added.

"Well, I'll work on my people skills," Tony replied.

There was a pause. "I heard a comedian say that you can get a lot more with a smile and a gun than you can with a smile. That about sums up your people skills."

Tony burst out laughing. "You do have a point," he conceded. "I'll try to mellow before I go to see her. Any news from your detective friend?"

"Not yet. He anticipated me, it seems." He chuckled. "He already had his men working on the gang angle, to see if anybody hired a shooter. Maybe he'll turn up something."

"Meanwhile, I'll do what I can to safeguard Millie," Tony replied. "See you."

"Yeah."

Tony dressed casually for the visit to the library, hoping he wouldn't attract too much attention if anyone was watching Millie. He wore jeans and a cotton shirt under a leather jacket. He looked outdoorsy, like a cowboy, but he refused to put on a wide-brimmed hat. He'd never liked to cover his black wavy hair, and he still wore it in a ponytail. He wasn't going to be conservative, no matter what the job called for. He was too much of a renegade.

He walked to the desk and asked for Millie, smiling at the clerk. She smiled back, obviously interested in him. She picked up the phone, pushed a button and told Millie she had a visitor out front.

As she spoke, she was sorting mail. "Oh, and you got a package," she added, still talking to Millie on the phone, her hand reaching toward a flat but lumpy-looking brown envelope with spiky writing on the front.

"Don't touch that," Tony said at once, whipping out his phone. He dialed the emergency services number and requested a squad car and the bomb squad.

The clerk looked at him as if she thought he'd gone nuts.

"Get everybody out of the building," he told her in a

tone bristling with authority. "Don't waste time," he said when she hesitated. "There's enough explosive in there to blow up a city block. Hurry!"

She rushed into the back as Millie came out front. She stopped at the desk, where Tony was still arguing with the dispatcher about the bomb squad.

"Listen, I work for the government," he said in a deep, steady tone. "I've seen letter bombs before. I know what I'm talking about. Do you want to read in the newspapers tomorrow morning that a library blew up because you didn't take the threat seriously? They'll even spell your name right…yes, that's what I said, the bomb squad. And hurry!"

He glanced at Millie, his face hard, his eyes glittering. "We have to get out of here," he told her.

"Out? I've got a package there…"

He caught her hand as she reached for it. "If you like having two hands and a head, you'll do what I tell you. Come on!" he called to the clerk, who was hurrying several patrons and a couple of employees out the front door.

"You are out of your mind," Millie said primly. "I'm not leaving…!"

"Sorry," he said as he whipped her up in his arms and carried her right out the front door, which a grinning patron held open for him. "I don't have time to argue."

A squad car rolled up along with the bomb squad. Tony went to talk to the sergeant in charge.

"It's a letter bomb, on the counter in there," he told the man. "I worked a case in Nairobi with one that looked just like it, but I couldn't get anybody to listen to me. It killed two foreign workers when it went off."

The sergeant sighed. "Okay. We'll check it out. But if you're wrong, you're in a lot of trouble."

"I'm not wrong," Tony told him, and showed his credentials. The sergeant didn't say another word. He went straight to work.

The librarians were skeptical; so were Millie and the patrons. But they all stood patiently in the cold while the bomb squad went hesitantly into the building and looked for the brown envelope Tony had described.

The sergeant came back out, grim-faced. "I'm not completely convinced," he told Tony, "but we'll go by the book. It does look suspicious."

They had a robot with a gripping arm. They sent it into the building to retrieve the package. It took a long time, and many spectators gathered, kept back by two more units of police who arrived to help with crowd control.

There was a camera crew from a local television station on the scene now, and people with camera phones were snapping images to send to the media as well. Some of them were laughing. One man, a grumpy library patron, said he was going to catch cold while the police wasted their time on a bomb threat that would turn out to be a package of photographs or something equally stupid.

As he was speaking, the robot reached the containment bin in which the bomb squad collected suspicious packages. No sooner had it gone in than there was a terrific explosion which knocked the robot onto its back and had spectators screaming and running away.

Tony glanced at the bomb squad sergeant who grimaced. He turned to Millie. She was white-faced and sick at her stomach. If Tony hadn't come in when he did, if she'd opened that package…

He caught her as she slumped to the pavement.

When she came to, she was lying in the backseat of Tony's rented car. He was holding a cold soft drink at her lips, supporting her with one big arm.

"Come on. Take a sip. It will help," he said quietly.

She managed to swallow some of the fizzy liquid. She coughed. "I fainted. I never faint."

"If somebody sent me a bomb, I'd probably faint, too," he replied with a grin. "You're okay. So is everybody else."

She looked up at him quietly. "Why?"

The grin faded. "Some men take possession to the grave with them. John couldn't have you. He wanted to make sure that nobody else ever did. He paid somebody a lot of money to do this. And he almost pulled it off. Now we have to keep you alive while they find out who he hired."

She sat up, breathing heavily. "Surely they won't try again? They'll know that the police are watching now."

"The police don't have the sort of budget they'd need to give you round-the-clock protection. The bomber will know that. Of course he'll try again."

"He's already got the money," she faltered.

"I wouldn't bet on that. More than likely, John set it up so that he can't get it until you're dead and the bomber has proof that you're dead," he told her flatly. "If a gang leader is holding the money, it will be a point of honor with him. Don't look like that, they do have honor among themselves, of a sort. Especially if the leader was John's friend and felt an obligation to him for some reason."

"You knew it was a bomb without touching it," she recalled. "How?"

"It isn't my first bomb," he replied. "I don't do ordinance, but I know guys who do. I learned a lot by watching, the rest by experience."

She frowned. "In the Army? Or working on construction gangs?" she asked.

He hesitated. "I work for the government, in between freelance jobs," he said. "I'm an independent contractor."

"A what?"

"I'm a professional soldier," he told her. "I specialize in counterterrorism."

She was very still. Her pale eyes searched his dark ones. "Did your foster mother ever know?"

He shook his head. "She wouldn't have approved."

"I see."

His eyes narrowed on her averted face. "You don't approve, either, do you?"

She couldn't meet his eyes. She rubbed her cold arms. "My opinion wouldn't mean anything to you."

She climbed out of the car, still a little rocky on her feet. He steadied her.

"You need to get your coat and your purse and come with me," he told her. "We have things to talk about."

"But—" she began.

"Don't argue, Millie," he interrupted. "If you stay in there, you're endangering your coworkers."

That hadn't occurred to her. She looked horrified. "But I have to work," she protested. "I have bills to pay…!"

"You can ask for a leave of absence, can't you?" he persisted. "A few days off won't put you on the streets."

He was making sense, and she knew he was right, but she was afraid that if she asked for time off, she'd lose her job. She'd been at the library all her working life, and she loved what she did. Her superior still hadn't gotten over the gossip John had caused by insinuating that Millie had a wild lifestyle. God knew what she'd say when she heard about the bomb.

"I may not have a job when my boss finds out what happened here today. She's out of town until next Monday," she added sadly.

"Come on. I'll go in with you."

He escorted her back into the building and insisted on seeing her supervisor with her. He explained the situation matter-of-factly, adding that he was certain her colleagues wouldn't like to risk another such incident by insisting that she stay on the job until the culprit was apprehended.

"Certainly not," Barry Hinson said at once. "Millie, we can manage without you for a few days. I'm sure Mrs. Anderson would agree."

Millie sighed. "I don't suppose I have a choice. I'm very sorry," she began.

"It isn't your fault," Barry said firmly. "None of us ever blamed you for what that man did. He should have been locked up," he added, unaware that Tony had been John's friend.

Millie flushed. She didn't look at Tony. "Well, I'll get my things and leave. I'll be back next week."

Barry smiled. "Of course." He glanced warily at Tony. "You won't let anything happen to her?" he asked, assuming that the big man worked for law enforcement.

"No," Tony assured him. "I won't."

Millie didn't want to feel that enveloping warmth that his words caused. She'd risked her heart on this man once before and had been crushed by his rejection. If only, she thought, you could banish feelings and make them leave you alone forever. She went to get her purse and coat and explain to the clerk what she'd been working on before the bomb disrupted their day.

* * *

"Now, what?" Millie asked as she paused by her little black VW in the parking lot. It was used, but clean and well looked after.

"Now, we go somewhere and talk and make decisions."

"There's a cafeteria down the street, where I usually have lunch," she said, naming it.

"I'll meet you there."

She nodded meekly and got into her car.

Ten minutes later, they were having sandwiches and coffee, a late lunch because disposing of the bomb had been a protracted business. Millie ate and drank automatically, but she didn't taste much. It was disconcerting to realize that John actually meant to kill her.

"Stop brooding," Tony said as he sipped coffee. "It won't help."

"I never thought John would want to kill me," she said.

His eyes narrowed. "He beat you up."

She gasped. "How did you know that?"

"Frank."

Her lips made a thin line. "He'd been drinking. He said it was all my fault that his life was falling apart, because I wouldn't marry him. I tried, for the twentieth time, to explain that I didn't love him in that way, but he wouldn't listen. He lost his temper and the next thing I knew, he was slamming me into a wall. Even when it happened, I could hardly believe it. I screamed and screamed, and when he let go of me, I locked myself in the bedroom and called the police."

"You didn't press charges," he muttered.

"He was in tears by the time the police got there. He swore it was the alcohol, that he didn't realize how much he'd had. He said he loved me, he couldn't believe he'd done such a thing. He begged me not to press charges." She shook her head. "I should have. But I felt sorry for him. I always felt sorry for him. He had mental issues, but he wouldn't face that, and he wouldn't get help. I thought I could do something for him."

"You can't fix a broken mind," Tony said heavily. "He was obsessed with you."

His tone intimated that he didn't understand why. She knew what Tony thought of her, because John had told her, time and again. Tony thought she was the most boring woman on earth, and he'd need to be drunk to want to touch her. Looking at his expression now, she was certain that John had been telling the truth. She was plain and prim and unexciting. It was a fact she'd faced long ago.

She pushed back her coffee cup. "After that night, it got to the point that I couldn't walk out of my apartment without running into John. He said he was going to make sure that I didn't have any other man in my life, and he was going to watch me night and day. When he told those lies about me, and then started spending the day in the library, it began jeopardizing my job. I finally decided that I had no other choice than to file stalking charges against him." She ran a hand over the tight bun she kept her long brown hair in. "It was what pushed him over the edge. I even knew that it would—it's why I waited so long to do anything about the problem. He swore he'd get even, no matter what it took." She looked tired, drained of life. "When I knew that he was dead, I was so ashamed, but all I could feel was a sense of relief. I was finally free of him."

"But you came to the funeral home," he commented.

Her face tautened as she recalled Tony's attitude when he'd met her there. "Yes. It was the guilt. I had to see him. I thought it might make amends, somehow."

"And you found me, instead," he replied, grimacing at her expression. "You have to understand, all I had to go on was what John told me. And he told me a lot. He left me a letter, blaming you for his death. I had no reason to doubt him, at the time. Not until Frank told me the truth."

Of course he'd believed his friend, she thought. It wouldn't have occurred to him that Millie wasn't a wild girl. He didn't know Millie. He didn't want to know her. It hurt, realizing that.

"I'm sorry for the way I reacted," he said stiffly. "I didn't know."

She shook her head. "Nobody knew. I was harassed, blackmailed and slandered by him for years, and he made everybody think it was my own fault, that I encouraged him." Her gaze was flat, almost lifeless. "He was the most repulsive man I've ever known."

He frowned. "He was good-looking."

She glanced up at him. "You can't make people love you," she said in a subdued sort of tone. "No matter what you look like. He was coarse and crude, and ugly inside. That's where it counts, you know. The outside might have been attractive. The devil, they say, was beautiful."

"Point taken."

She finished her coffee. "Where do I go now?"

"Back to your apartment. I'm coming with you, to see what I'll need for surveillance."

She frowned. "Surveillance?"

He nodded. "I want cameras and microphones everywhere. It's the only way we can save your life."

And in that moment, she realized, for the first time, just how desperate her situation really was.

Chapter Three

Millie's apartment was on the third floor of a building about ten blocks from the library. She had a small balcony, on which lived many plants during the warm months. Now, the pots contained nothing except dead remnants of the autumn foliage that she'd been too busy to clean out. The past few weeks had been hectic indeed.

Her walls were full of bookcases and books. She was a great reader. Tony noted the titles ranged from history to gardening to languages to true crime. He smiled when he noticed all the romance novels, including several that had to do with professional soldiers. He'd never told her what he did for a living until today, and she hadn't guessed. But apparently she had an adventurous nature that she kept tightly contained, like her hair in that bun.

He noted that she liked pastel colors, and used them in her decorating. The apartment's contents weren't expensive, but they suited the rooms in which she lived. She had good taste for a woman on a budget.

He poked his nose into every nook and cranny of the place, making notes in a small notebook, about entrance, exit and possible avenues of intrusion. Her balcony was a trouble spot. A man with an automatic rifle could see right into the apartment through the glass sliding doors, which had no curtains. The doors had the usual locks, but no dead bolts. The apartment was only feet away from an elevator and a staircase, which gave it easy access. There was no security for the building, and Tony had noticed two or three suspicious-looking men on his way up in the elevator.

He dug his hands into his pockets. It had seemed like a good plan at the time, but now that he'd seen where Millie lived, he knew he couldn't just move in with her and start waiting for an attack to come.

"This won't work," he said flatly.

She turned from the hall closet, where she'd been pulling out a coat and a sweater, and stared at him blankly. "What?"

"This place is a death trap," he said matter-of-factly. "Easy entrance and exit right outside the door, no dead bolts, a perfect line-of-sight aim for anybody with a high-powered rifle with a scope. Add to that a noticeable lack of security and a few shady characters who live in the building, and you've got an impossible situation. You can't stay here."

"But it's where I live," she said plaintively. "I can't just move because some crazy person is trying to kill me. Besides, wouldn't he just follow me?"

"Probably," he had to admit.

"Then what do I do, live out of my car and switch parking lots every night?" she wondered.

He burst out laughing. He hadn't credited her with a sense of humor. "You'd need a bigger car," he agreed.

She let out a long breath. "I guess I could do something illegal and get arrested," she thought aloud. "I'd be safe in jail."

"Not really," he replied. "Gangs operate in every prison in this country, and in other countries. They're like corporations now, Millie—they're international."

"You're kidding," she said, aghast.

"It's the truth. They have a hierarchy, even in prison, and some measure of control and exploitation. They can order hits inside or outside."

She sat down heavily on the arm of her sofa. "Call the U.S. Marshal's office," she said. "Tell them I qualify for the witness protection program. I can be renamed and transplanted."

"Not unless you testify against somebody really evil," he returned. "Sorry."

Her eyebrows arched. "Ouch."

He lifted a huge shoulder. "So we have to look for a different solution. I'll take you back to the hotel with me—"

She flushed and stood up. "I'm not moving in with you."

"Okay. Which one of your coworkers would you like to put into the line of fire?" he asked. "Because that's your choice right now."

She looked worried. "I don't know any of my coworkers that well, and I wouldn't ask them to risk being killed on my account even if I did."

His eyes were curious. "You've worked there for years, and you don't know any of your colleagues well?"

She bit her lower lip. "I don't mix well. I live in another world from most modern people."

"I don't understand."

She laughed. It had a hollow sound. "I go to church, pay my bills on time, obey the law and go to bed with the chickens, alone. I don't fit into a society that rewards permissiveness and degrades virtue. I don't go around with people who think cheating is the best way to get ahead, and money doesn't mean much to me, beyond having enough to get by. Making money seems to be the driving force in the world these days, regardless of what you have to do to get it."

She made him feel uncomfortable. She was describing his own world, into which he fit quite well.

She saw that and sighed. "Sorry. I told you I wasn't normal."

"I haven't said a word," he said defensively.

She searched his dark eyes. "Frank mentioned that you think women are a permissible pleasure, and that the brassier they are, the better you like them."

His jaw tautened. "What's wrong with that?" he asked. "I'm a bachelor and I don't want to settle down."

She lifted her hands. "I didn't mean it as an insult. I'm just pointing out that our views of life are very different. I'm not going to be happy staying in the room, overnight, with a man I barely know."

He could have debated her take on their relationship. They'd known each other for years, even if distantly. But he didn't pursue it. He cocked an eyebrow. "I haven't offered you half my bed," he said curtly. "And I never would. You aren't my type."

"I thought I just said that," she replied.

He made a sound deep in his throat. She made him feel small. He looked around the apartment. "I've got a suite," he said after a minute. "You'll have your own bedroom. The door has a lock." He looked straight into her eyes. "Not that you'll need it."

That was meant as an insult. She understood it. But she'd had years of practice at hiding her feelings from him. She didn't react. She didn't have much of a choice, either. Thinking of her close call at the library was still unsettling. John's criminal friends would see her dead, if they could. Tony was the only thing standing between herself and a funeral parlor, and she was arguing. She pushed back a wisp of brown hair and turned away from him. She was running out of choices.

"Well, I can't stay here," she said to herself.

"No, you can't. And local law enforcement doesn't have the sort of budget they'd need to house and feed you indefinitely. This could go on for weeks, Millie."

"Weeks?" She was staring at him with pure horror. "Surely not! The bomb…"

"May have been a test," he interrupted, "to give your assassin a dry run, show him how quickly local law enforcement reacts to an emergency call."

"I hadn't considered that," she confessed.

"You should. This isn't some petty criminal," he added. "He's a professional. He may not be the best—that plastic explosive he used for the bomb wasn't well concealed or particularly well made. But he knows how to get to you, and that makes him—or her—dangerous. We have to put you someplace where he doesn't have easy access, lure him in and help him make a mistake, so we can nab him."

"How do we do that?" she asked.

"You move in with me," he said simply. "We let the word get around. Then we wait for developments."

"Wait." She tugged at a lock of loose hair. "I can't wait a long time," she worried. "I have to work. I have to support myself."

"You have to be alive in order to do those things," he

reminded her. "I'll call Frank. He can get his contact in the police department to help us out."

"That might be wise," she agreed. She was still debating her options, but she didn't seem to have any left. She wished she could go back in time, to a period in her life when she hadn't known Tony Danzetta. She'd eaten her heart out over him for so many years that it had become a habit. Now here he was, protecting her from danger, for reasons he still hadn't disclosed. He was honest to the point of brutality about his lack of interest in her as a woman. Was it guilt, she wondered, that drove him to help her? Perhaps she'd have the opportunity in the days ahead to learn the answer to that question.

His hotel suite was huge. Millie was fascinated by the glimpse of how the other half lived. She knew what a suite cost in this luxury hotel, and she wondered how Tony's government job made it affordable to him. Maybe, she considered, his father, the contractor, had left him a lot of money. He was obviously used to having the very best of everything.

"Hungry?" he asked when he'd put her suitcase inside what was to be her bedroom.

"Actually, I am," she said. "Could we go somewhere and get a salad?"

He pursed his lips, smiling. "What sort of salad?"

"A Caesar salad would be nice," she said.

"How about a steak to go with it, and a baked potato with real butter and chives and sour cream?"

Her eyes widened. "That sounds wonderful. Coffee, too."

He nodded. He picked up the phone, punched in a number, waited a minute and then proceeded to give an order to someone on the other end of the line. It must be room service, she thought. It fascinated her that he could just pick up the phone and order food. The only time she'd ever done that was when she ordered pizza, and small ones, at that.

"Thirty minutes," he said when he hung up.

"I've never stayed in a hotel and had room service," she confided. "I went on a trip for the library one time, to a conference up in Dallas and stayed in a hotel. It was small, though, and I ate at a McDonald's nearby."

He chuckled. "I couldn't live without room service. I flew in from Iraq late one night, starving to death. I ordered a steak and salad and this huge ice cream split at two o'clock in the morning."

"There's room service then?" she exclaimed.

He didn't mention that he paid a big price for having those items sent up, because room service didn't operate in the wee hours of the morning. He was also friends with the general manager of that particular hotel. "There is in New York City," he told her.

She sat down in one of the big armchairs and he took off his jacket and sprawled over the sofa.

"I guess you've been a lot of places," she said.

He closed his eyes, put his hands under his head and smiled. "A lot."

"I'd like to go to Japan," she said dreamily. "We have this nice old couple who came from Osaka. I love to hear them talk about their home country."

"Japan is beautiful." He rolled over, facing her, tugging a pillow under his head. "I spent a few days in Osaka on a case, and made time to take the bullet train over to Kyoto. There's a samurai fortress there with huge wooden gates. It was built in 1600 and something. They had nightingale floors…"

"What?"

"Nightingale floors. They put nails under the flooring and pieces of metal that would come in contact with the nails if anyone walked on the floor. It made a sound like a nightingale, a pretty sound, but it alerted the samurai inside instantly if ninja assassins were about to attack them. Ninjas were known for their stealth abilities, but the nightingale floors defeated them."

"That's so cool!" she exclaimed.

He studied her with new interest. When she was excited, her face flushed and her eyes shimmered. She looked radiant.

"I've read about Japan for years," he continued. "But little details like that don't usually get into travel books. You have to actually go to a place to learn about it."

"I watch those travel documentaries on TV," she confessed. "I especially like the ones where just plain people go traipsing into the back country of exotic places. I saw one where this guy lived with the Mongols and ate roasted rat."

He chuckled. "I've had my share of those. Not to mention snake and, once, a very old and tough cat."

"A cat?" she asked, horrified. "You *ate* a cat?"

He scowled. "Now, listen, when you're starving to death, you can't be selective! We were in a jungle, hiding from insurgents, and we'd already eaten all the snakes and bugs we could find!"

"But, a cat!" she wailed.

He grimaced. "It was an old cat. It was on its last legs, honest. We used it for stew." He brightened. "We threw up because it tasted so bad!"

"Good!" she exclaimed, outraged.

He rolled onto his back. "Well, the only other thing on offer was a monkey that kept pelting us with coconuts, and I'm not eating any monkeys! Even if they do taste like chicken." He thought about that and laughed out loud.

"What's funny?" she wanted to know.

He glanced at her. "Every time somebody eats something exotic, they always say, 'It tastes just like chicken!'"

She made a face. "I'll bet the cat didn't."

"You got that right. It tasted like…" He got half the word out, flushed and backtracked. "I'd rather have had pemmican, but it's in short supply in the rest of the world. My great-grandmother used to make it. We visited her a couple of times when my stepfather was working in Atlanta and we lived with him. She lived in North Carolina, near the reservation," he recalled thoughtfully. "She was amazing. She knew how to treat all sorts of physical complaints with herbs. She went out every morning, gathering leaves and roots. I wish I'd paid more attention."

"She was Cherokee?" she asked, even though she knew the answer.

He nodded. "Full blooded," he added. His expression grew dark. "Like me. My mother married an Italian contractor. They didn't like it. He was an outsider. They disowned her, everyone except my great-grandmother. She died when I was a kid, and I haven't been back since."

"That's sad. You still have family there, don't you?"

"Yes. An uncle and a few cousins. I heard from my uncle a couple of years ago. He said I should come home and make peace with them."

"But you didn't."

"My mother had a hard life," he said. "When my sister and I went into foster care, it was like the end of the world. Especially when they separated us." His face went taut. "She killed herself."

"Your sister?" she asked, sad for him.

"Yes." He glanced at her. "Didn't my foster mother tell you any of this?"

Millie flushed. The woman had told her quite a lot about Tony, but nothing really personal. She wasn't going to admit that she'd tried to worm things out of her. She averted her eyes. "It must have been hard on you, losing your sister."

"Yeah." He stared at the ceiling. "Some boy in foster care got her pregnant and tried to force her to have an abortion. She wouldn't. She was deeply religious and she saw it as a sin if she went for a termination. She told the boy. So he made threats and she felt that she had nowhere to turn." He sighed, his eyes sad. "She would never have done that if she hadn't been half out of her mind. She thought of suicide as a sin, too. But in the end, she took the only way out she could find."

"I hope he ended up in prison," she muttered. "That boy, I mean."

He made a deep sound. "He did. And shortly afterward, he died mysteriously. Strange things happen to bad people."

She wondered if Tony had any hand in the boy's demise, but she didn't want to ask.

There was a knock at the door. Tony sprang to his feet, grinning. "Food," he guessed.

He peered out the keyhole and saw the trolley, and the waiter. He opened the door and let him in.

Lunch was delicious. Millie had never had food served on a white linen cloth, with heavy utensils and dishes under metal covers. It was a revelation. She munched her salad with obvious enjoyment and went into ecstasies about the tenderness of the steak and the delicious baked potato. Even the coffee was wonderful.

Tony found her obvious delight in the meal humbling. He took fancy food and fancy hotels for granted. He'd long since become blasé about such things. But Millie came from a poor background, and lived on a meager budget. He imagined she'd never stepped into the lobby of a luxury hotel, much less been a guest in one. He pictured taking her out for a spin in his convertible, or taking her sailing on his yacht down in the Bahamas and lying with her in the sun. She had a delightful body. He wondered how it would feel to make love to her on a sandy tropical beach. Then he wondered what the hell he was thinking of. She wasn't his sort of woman. Millie would never go to bed with a man she hadn't married, no matter what her feelings for him were.

That brought back a comment of Frank's, that Millie had once been in love with Tony. He recalled her shy presence at his foster mother's house from time to time as an invited guest, her radiance when he dropped in at the library to see his parent and Millie happened to be around. He must have been blind, he decided, not to have noticed how his presence illuminated the quiet, introverted woman across from him at the table.

Millie stopped eating and stared at him, disconcerted by

his unsmiling, level stare. "Am I…doing something wrong?" she asked at once, her attention diverted to the silverware. "I don't know about fancy place settings—"

"It's just lunch, Millie," he interrupted. "I wasn't studying your eating habits. I was thinking about something, in the past."

"Oh." She was watchful, unconvinced.

He sipped coffee. "Why didn't you tell me what John was doing to you when I came home two years ago?" he asked.

She felt the question keenly. "I knew you wouldn't believe me. You've never liked me."

He frowned. "I didn't know you."

"And didn't want to, either." She laughed hollowly. "I was the invisible woman whenever you came home to visit your foster mother. She'd invite me over sometimes, because she knew I had no life to speak of. You never even noticed that I was around. You only stayed long enough to say a few words and then you were off on some hot date that Frank had fixed up for you, from the bar where he was a bouncer."

That made him feel worse. "I didn't want to get serious about anyone," he said after a minute. "Those glittery women are fine for a good time. You don't plan a future around them."

He was insinuating that they were fine for a one-night stand. The thought embarrassed her, made her uncomfortable. It was one more reminder of the distance between her world and his. She picked at her baked potato and lifted a forkful to her mouth. She wasn't really tasting it now. It was something to do.

"Why didn't you tell John to get a life and get off your back?" he asked suddenly.

She seemed to draw into herself. "It wouldn't have done any good," she told him. "I did try that, repeatedly. It just made him mad."

"Maybe it would have helped drive the point home if you'd stopped forgiving him," he continued doggedly. "Especially after he beat you up. No self-respecting woman would take that sort of behavior from a man."

Her face flushed. She put down her fork and glared at him across the table. "That's so easy for a man to say," she began in a low, angry tone. "You've never been beaten to your knees by an enraged man bent on making you pay for not loving him. I had bruises all over my body and I was terrified that he was actually going to kill me! He yelled at me and called me names and said he'd beat me to death if I didn't give in and agree to marry him." She wrapped her arms around her body, as if she felt a sudden chill. Her eyes went blank. "I believed him. I was sure that he was going to kill me. In the end, I just screamed and screamed. I expected to die. It was a miracle that I got a locked bedroom door between us in time to call for help. The sound of police car sirens was the most beautiful music I'd ever heard," she added in a soft undertone that made Tony feel even worse. "The policewoman who came in first gave John a furious look and when he started toward her, she drew her service pistol and pointed it right at his nose. I knew she'd shoot if he came any closer, and I guess he knew it, too, because he stopped. He sat down on the sofa and started crying. He said it was all my fault because I wouldn't marry him."

"Had he been drinking?"

"Yes. But not enough to make him out of control," she said bitterly. "The policewoman told me that. She asked me to press charges, but John came on his knees to beg me to forgive him. He was sobbing. I felt embarrassed and guilty and I agreed not to have him arrested. It didn't win me any points with the police," she added. "But I don't know that having him arrested again would have done any good. It certainly hadn't stopped him from stalking me, or spreading lies about me. He'd been arrested before, but he was always out in a few days, starting all over again. I got over the beating, but I would never go to his apartment again or let him in if he came to mine. I made sure there were always people around when he came to the library."

Tony felt very small. "Frank said he spread lies about you to your boss."

"Yes. And to the patrons." Her eyes closed in bitter memory. "I thought I'd lose my job forever. I would have, if Frank hadn't talked to a few people. He's been the best friend to me through all this. I don't know what I would have done without him."

"He's sweet on you," he said deliberately. "But he thinks you wouldn't give him the time of day because he works in a low class of job."

"The job wouldn't matter if I could feel that way about him. I wish I could," she added quietly. "But I can't."

The confession made him feel good. He didn't want to know why. He finished his coffee. "Want dessert?" he asked.

She laughed. "I'd have to put it in my pocket," she said. "I'm stuffed."

"So am I. They have a good kitchen staff here."

"I'll say." She finished her own coffee. "Do we push the trolley back down to the kitchen?" she asked.

"Good heavens, no," he exclaimed. "They come and get it."

She flushed. He made her feel like an idiot.

He noticed that and grimaced. "Millie, I wasn't always rich," he said gently. "I had to learn about things like proper table settings and etiquette, too."

She shrugged. "I'm just a country hick, you know," she said with a faint smile. "I live frugally. This—" she waved her hand around "—is like another planet to me."

"Learning new things doesn't hurt," he said. He chuckled. "The first time Jared and I ate in a five-star restaurant, we had to ask the waiter about the utensils and all the courses. Fortunately he was a nice person. He could have made us feel small, but he didn't. Jared tipped him a hundred dollars."

She gasped. That was almost a week's salary for her.

"I know. It was a lot of money to me, at the time," he said. "I'd been a soldier, and before that, a common laborer, working in a construction crew."

"How did you make so much money?" she asked, genuinely curious.

"Hiring out to governments as an independent contractor," he said simply. "Including our own. Jared and I learned counterterrorism skills and for a while, he ran a security company that I worked for. Counterterrorism skills are a valuable commodity in some circles. It's a specialized job and it pays very well."

"Do you go into combat?" she asked.

"If the job calls for it," he replied. "You can't teach in a classroom in a combat zone," he added with a smile. "We teach small forces about incursions and stealth tactics, about IEDs and organizing local militia—stuff like that."

"What's an—" she felt for the word "—IED?"

"You could answer that now." He chuckled. "It's an improvised explosive device. You had one sent to you." The smile faded as he remembered how dangerous her introduction to the world of terror had been. The device, as clumsily built as it was, could have killed her in a heartbeat.

"You said it wasn't well made," she recalled.

"It wasn't. The good ones would pass for a small manuscript," he said. "It's a cowardly way to kill somebody."

She sighed, staring at the carpet. "I can't believe John was this desperate," she said, shaking her head. "To kill somebody, just because they couldn't love you. It's…" She searched for a word.

"Insane," he said through his teeth. "John had mental problems. I'm still shocked that Frank and I didn't see it and you did." It made him uncomfortable for another reason, too, but he wasn't telling her any secrets about his past. Not yet.

She laughed hollowly as she looked up at him. "That's because he wasn't trying to force you to marry him."

He drew in a long breath and looked at his watch. "I've got to meet a man in the lobby about a job," he said. "You stay put, okay?"

She nodded. "Thanks for lunch."

"My pleasure."

He left her sitting on the sofa and went downstairs to see a government agent from his department. There had been a string of kidnappings of rich persons along the Texas border, and Tony's skills might come in handy, they thought. He put Millie out of his mind before he exited the elevator.

She wandered around the suite while he was gone, straying into his bedroom out of curiosity. His suitcase was open on the bed. She picked up a shirt on the carpet that had been hastily discarded, probably when he changed early this morning. She held it to her nostrils and drew in the smell. She smiled, with her eyes closed. People had a personal fragrance, she thought, every one different. She'd know Tony's in a dark room. He smelled of the outdoors, of spice and fir. She loved the smell. She recalled the feeling it gave her to be carried, when he'd taken her out of the library protesting. His arms had been warm and strong and she'd never wanted to leave them. But she was going to have to move on.

She put the shirt down. After a minute she realized that he'd know it had been moved, a man as sharp as Tony. She dropped it back onto the carpet, went out of the bedroom and closed the door.

Chapter Four

It was late when Tony came back. She was watching a movie on television, curled up on the sofa in slacks and a soft yellow knit shirt, with her bare feet under her. He smiled at the picture she made. He thought of a small kitten, cuddly and sweet, and snapped that thought right out of his mind.

"Found something to watch, I gather?" he teased.

She fumbled for the remote control. "Just a movie on regular television," she said quickly, flushing.

He frowned. "You can watch pay-per-view if you want to," he said. "Listen, kid, three or four bucks for a movie isn't going to break the bank."

She flushed even more. "Thanks."

Her embarrassment made him uncomfortable. He was

used to women who didn't mind ordering the most expensive items on the menu, who asked for trips to the most expensive concerts, who wanted jewelry for presents. This one was nervous because he might think she'd watched a movie on the pay channels. He felt odd.

She sat up and worked her feet back into her loafers.

"You want to take in a show or something?" he asked.

She stared at him. "A show?"

"There's a good theater company here. They have a ballet, an orchestra. Somebody's probably doing something Christmasy, even though it isn't quite the holiday season."

She would have loved to go. But she recalled that she didn't have a dress that would do to wear to something fancy. Her clothes closet was bare, except for a few mix and match outfits suitable for work. She didn't even have the sort of shoes she'd need for an evening on the town. Tony probably had a dinner jacket or even a tuxedo packed away in that hanging bag she'd seen on the door to his bathroom.

"Mmm…no," she drawled. "I don't think so. Thank you."

Unaware of her wardrobe difficulties, he took the refusal in stride, thinking she probably didn't care for highbrow entertainment.

"Do you play cards?" he asked.

She shook her head. "Sorry."

He shrugged and sighed. "It's going to be a long week," he murmured. He studied her curiously. "Okay, then. When you're home, what do you do at night?"

She looked uncomfortable. "I read books, mostly, if there's nothing interesting on the military history channel."

His eyelids flickered. "You like military history?"

"I love it," she replied, smiling.

"Which period?"

"Any period," she told him. "I've read everything I could find about Alexander the Great, Julius Caesar, Napoleon, cavalry and Native American battles of the nineteenth century, generals of the Second World War," she rattled off. "I never met a battle I didn't want to read about."

He sat down across from her. "I took my degree in criminal justice," he said. "But I minored in history. My favorite period was World War II, European theater."

She smiled. "I remember. Your foster mother said you were always outlining battle plans to her over dinner."

He chuckled. "She didn't understand a thing I talked about, but she was always patient and kind." The smile faded. He looked down at his shoes. "She convinced me that not all foster parents are bad. I went through several after we moved from the reservation in North Carolina down to Georgia."

This was an experience that had left scars in him. She'd heard his foster mother talk about it. "You said once that your mother died when you were young."

He looked up. His eyes were flat, lifeless. "That's not quite true. I haven't really talked about her in years. About him, either. My stepfather, I mean." His broad shoulders rose and fell. "I tell different stories about them to anybody who asks. I guess I've been running away from the truth all my life."

She didn't speak. She just listened. Waited. Hoped.

He noticed and smiled. "My real father was my mother's second cousin. He lived on the Cherokee reservation in North Carolina where she grew up. But he was married. She got pregnant and she didn't have any money for a termination. So there was this big, loud Italian construction worker doing a project near the res. She started going out with him and by the time she told him she was pregnant, he thought it was his. Then she gave birth to a full-term baby in what he thought was her sixth month, and the jig was up. He hated her. But they stayed together for three more years, until my sister was born. He took a powder and left her with the kids."

"That must have been rough. Was she young?"

"She was nineteen when she had me," he said. "Not terribly young. But my sister was half Cherokee and half white, and my mother couldn't take the constant criticism from her family. When I was seven, she left the reservation and took us on a bus to Atlanta. We didn't know it, but her husband was working there. He found out from her kin where she was. He moved back in with us. She might have tried to run, but he told her that he had legal rights to take the kids if she ran away. So she stayed. And I ended up with an Italian name that has nothing to do with my ancestry."

He laughed. "The only good thing about it is that it saved a few soldiers' lives when I got teased. They didn't make Indian jokes around me, because they thought I was Italian." His eyes glimmered. "I'm proud of my ancestry. Cherokees are still a proud people, even after all the hell the government put us through when they marched us out to Oklahoma in the dead of winter, walking, in 1838."

"I know about that," she said. "It was a tragic episode."

"One of many," he agreed.

She saw the pain on his face. He was talking around his childhood, trying not to remember. She wanted him to deal with it. She might be the only person alive that he'd ever really talked to about it. It would help him. "Your parents didn't have a happy marriage," she prompted.

He shook his head. He traced the back of a big fingernail absently. "My so-called father drank. A lot. And when he drank, he remembered that I wasn't his kid and made me pay for it. I was in the emergency room every few months with bruises and cuts. Once, with a broken bone."

She winced, thinking how hard it must have been for him, at that age, to be so badly treated by a man he considered to be his father. "Didn't your mother do anything to protect you?" she asked, aghast.

"She couldn't. She was a little woman. He knocked her around all the time. He was a big man. She was scared to death of him. She had no place to go. He knew it. He liked that." His face tautened. "But then he started doing things to my little sister, when she was about eight." His whole body seemed to contract. "My mother caught him at it, late one night. She was very calm. She went into the kitchen, got the biggest butcher knife she could find and hid it behind her. She went back into the living room, smiling. She said it was all right, she wouldn't make a fuss. He smirked. He knew she wouldn't do anything. He said so. I can still see her, smiling at him. She went to him like somebody sleepwalking. She stabbed that knife up to the hilt in his stomach, all the way to the heart. He never saw it coming. She was still smiling when he fell down on the floor." His eyes closed. "I never saw so much blood. She didn't move. She stood there, holding the knife, while the life drained out of him. She never stopped smiling, not even when they took her away in the police car."

Millie was horrified. No wonder he wasn't eager to get married and settle down. "What happened to her?" she asked gently.

He drew in a long breath. "They committed her. They said she was insane."

Her heart jumped. "Was she?"

He met her eyes. "I've never been sure, Millie," he said gently. His expression was tormented. "She died long before they had tests that could have backed up their theories." He shifted a little. "Our first set of foster parents told us very little, but they did mention that the psychiatrist said it was schizophrenia. There's a hereditary tendency toward it, I've read."

No wonder he wouldn't reveal his background. He was ashamed. Perhaps he was afraid, too. Maybe he thought he'd go mad himself.

She got up from the sofa and knelt down in front of him, balancing herself with a hand on one big knee. "I've read about mental illness. Some disease processes have a genetic tendency. That doesn't guarantee that anybody else in the family will ever develop the same illness," she said firmly. "You're as sane as I am," she added. "If you'd had mental deficiencies, believe me, they'd have shown up early. Very early."

He looked down at her, scowling. "You think so?" he asked.

"I know so. Did you ever torture an animal for fun? Set fires in your house? Wet the bed when you were in your teens?"

He laughed. "None of those."

"I'm no psychologist," she told him. "But I'm a great reader. Children show signs of mental illness in childhood. Since you were in the child welfare system, I'm sure the caseworkers paid close attention to you, considering your mother's illness. They would have put you in therapy immediately if they'd even suspected you had problems."

He cocked his head and laughed hollowly. "I can tell that you've had no contact with the system," he said with a sigh. "There are people who do their best for foster kids. The woman you knew, who brought me to San Antonio and got me through high school was certainly one of the best foster parents. But I lived with one family in Atlanta who had seven foster kids. They used the money the state gave them to gamble. They went up to Cherokee every month and blew it on the slot machines, hoping to get rich. Meanwhile, the kids went without school clothes, food, attention, you name it. No caseworker ever set foot in the house. Nobody investigated when we went to school dirty. The state did finally get wise, when one of our teachers started asking questions. We were removed from that house. But, you see, there wasn't another family willing to take me and my sister together. That's when we got separated, just before I was fostered to the woman who adopted me and eventually brought me to Texas."

"I'm sorry," she said.

He drew her hands up to his mouth and kissed them. "You always did have the softest heart," he said gently, surprising her. "I remember how you loved kids. You'd tell stories in the library during summer vacation, and they'd gather around you like flies around honey." He laughed softly. "I loved watching your face when you told those stories. You lit up like a Christmas tree."

She was surprised. "When did you see me doing that?"

"Many times," he said surprisingly. The smile faded. "I

thought a lot of you. I was in a dangerous profession and a long way from wanting to settle down. But I used to think that if I ever did, you'd be high on my list of prospects." His face darkened. "And then John started feeding me lies about you. And I listened."

She started to draw away, but he caught her wrists and held her there, his black eyes steady and probing.

"I wish I could take it back," he said. "But I can't. I'm really sorry for the way I treated you. Especially at the funeral home."

The feel of his big, warm hands around her wrists wasn't threatening to her. They were comforting. "You didn't know me," she said.

"I didn't want to know you." He grimaced. "Maybe I won't ever go off the deep end like my mother did. But I've got a past that's going to make it hard for any woman to live with me on a permanent basis. I make my living with guns, Millie," he added, watching her face. "I work for a government agency that sends me in when every other option fails. It's dangerous work. I can't afford any sort of distraction. That's why I don't get involved with nice girls. Girls like you."

It began to make sense. Good time girls didn't expect happy endings. They, like Tony, lived for the moment. He liked his job, had no thought of ever quitting it, and he was telling Millie to back off. In a nice way, but definitely the same message.

She forced a smile. "You're warning me off," she said, trying to sound nonchalant. "Should I be flattered?"

He let go of her wrists. "I don't want to hurt you," he said solemnly. "I could. You're not worldly."

She got to her feet and went back to the sofa and sat down. "I guess I'm not. I'm a librarian," she said philosophically. "Library work isn't Indiana Jones stuff."

"No. But if you read military history, you're an armchair adventurer, at least," he teased.

She smiled, hiding her misery. "What do you like to read?"

"The classics," he said. "But I'm partial to military history myself."

"Do you have a hobby?" she asked, fascinated with what she was learning about him.

He grinned. "I like to cook," he told her. "I can make almost anything, even French pastries."

She laughed. "So can I."

He pursed his lips. "Pity we don't have a kitchen here."

"Isn't it, just?"

He stood up and stretched, powerful muscles rippling in his chest and arms. "It's been a long day. I usually stay up late, but I'm pretty tired. Watch another movie, if you like. It won't disturb me."

She nodded, but she looked uncomfortable.

"What is it?" he asked.

She grimaced. "I was so upset that I forgot to pack anything to sleep in…"

"Now that's a problem I can solve," he told her. He went into his bedroom, rummaged in his suitcase and came back with a round-necked white T-shirt in pristine condition. "It will swallow you whole. As good as a gown, I'd say." He grinned.

She laughed and fought a blush. He really was huge. It would come down to her knees and wrap around her three times. "Thanks."

"Hey. We're bunkmates. We have to share, right?" He winked at her. "Sleep tight."

"You, too."

He went into his room and closed the door. She turned off the television and withdrew into her own room. After she'd put out the light, she lay in the darkness, loving the feel and smell of the T-shirt against her skin. She wondered if she could find some excuse for not giving it back.

She was delighted that he'd told her the true story of his background. She understood him much better. He had good reasons for wanting to stay uninvolved with women. But she wondered if he was beginning to feel the need for companionship, more than just a night's worth. And he'd mentioned watching Millie read to the kids, as if he'd cherished the memory. She felt warm all over at the idea that he'd felt something for her, until John killed it with his lies.

Her heart grew heavy. It was very well to think that she'd touched that cold heart, but he wasn't saying that he loved her or wanted to live with her. He was just looking after her, probably out of guilt because of the way he'd treated her. This wasn't a prelude to a life of happy togetherness. To Tony, it was just another job. She was a job. She'd do well to remember that and get her priorities straight. When the danger was over, she'd go back to her library and Tony would leave and never look back.

She closed her eyes and tried to sleep. It was almost morning by the time she finally managed it.

Two more days passed with no sign of any hired killer. Tony was in contact with both Frank and his detective friend. There was no gossip on the streets about the hit. That bothered Tony. He knew that the killer probably knew where Millie was, and he was biding his time until he saw an opening. This could drag on for weeks. Millie couldn't stay out of work forever, and Tony had a commitment coming up overseas. But there didn't seem to be any way to draw the hired killer out into the open.

Millie was wearing on him. He found himself watching her. She was pretty, in a way, and her figure was tantalizing. He was aroused by her. She didn't dress in a provocative manner, but she had pert little tip-tilted breasts that weren't disguised by her bra or the knit blouses she wore. He spent more and more time thinking how they might feel in his mouth.

It made him ill-tempered. He was used to women who

gave out without reservations. Millie was attracted to him, too. He could see it. Frank had said that she was in love with him. He was tempted to see how far she'd let him go, but he wasn't certain about his own ability to stop in time. He hadn't had a woman in months, and he wasn't a man who could abstain for long periods of time.

Millie noticed his growing irritability and guessed that he didn't like having her cramp his style. Obviously he couldn't cavort with another woman while he was protecting her. She felt guilty. She would have liked to have gone home, and have him smile at her again, even if it meant giving him up to some flashy woman. She was resigned to the fact that he was never going to want her. He'd said several times that she really wasn't his type.

The next night, he paced the floor until he made her uncomfortable enough to go to bed.

"Don't rush off on my account," he said curtly. "I'm just not used to this much inactivity."

"No, I'm really sleepy," she assured him. "Good night."

"Yeah. Good night." He said it with pure sarcasm.

She put on his T-shirt and stretched out on the bed with the lights still on. She was as restless as he was, and probably just as uncomfortable. She ached for something, for kisses, for caresses, for human contact. He hadn't touched her since he'd held her hands while he was talking about his mother. But he'd watched her. His eyes were narrow and covetous. She might be innocent, but she recognized that heat in him. It was in her, too, and she didn't know what to do about it. She'd never felt it so strongly before.

She stretched again, moaning softly as she thought how sweet it would be to lie in Tony's arms and let him kiss her until the aching stopped.

She heard the phone ring. A couple of minutes later, he rapped on her door and opened it without asking if she was decent.

He froze in the doorway, his eyes homing to the sharp peaks of her breasts and the long, uncovered length of her pretty legs. His teeth clenched. "A shark must feel like this, just before he bites," he said in a harsh tone, and he laughed.

"What?" she asked, breathless.

He closed the door behind him, tossed the cell phone he'd been using onto the dresser and made a beeline for the bed.

While she was conferring with herself about what to do next, he moved onto the bed, slid his big, warm hands under the T-shirt, and started kissing her as if he were starved. The combination of the heated, urgent kiss and his warm, enormous hands on her taut breasts was more than her prim scruples could overcome. She arched up into his hands and moaned so hungrily that he swept between her long legs without a second's hesitation, letting her feel what she already knew—that he wanted her.

It was every dream of passion she'd ever had, coming

true. He smelled of rich spice and soap. His long, wavy black hair was unbound, around his shoulders. She gathered it into her hands and savored the silky feel of it, loving its length. She looked down through a heated mist at his mouth on her soft skin, completely covering one small breast. It was so erotic that she arched up off the bed to force his mouth closer. She closed her eyes, shivering with tension that built and built until she thought she might die of the ache.

The T-shirt was on the floor somewhere, along with his pajama bottoms. His mouth was all over her, on her throat, her mouth, her breasts, sliding down with expert cunning to her flat belly and lingering there while his hands teased at the edge of her briefs. He felt her trembling, heard her breathing catch. Just a few more seconds, he thought with pure lust, and she wouldn't be able to stop him. He was on fire, so far gone that his head was spinning with the sweetness of her skin under his mouth.

She felt his hand go under her briefs and when he touched her, instead of completing the arousal, it shocked her into the realization of what they were about to start. He would leave town and go back to work and never even remember what had happened. She would be left with a tarnished dream and a possible pregnancy, because she had nothing to use for birth control.

But when she pushed at his shoulders, he didn't realize she was trying to stop him. He was working the briefs off and she was almost too hungry to argue. But she had to. He'd never forgive her...

"I can't!" she burst out. "Tony, I can't! You have to stop!"

He lifted his head. His eyes were glazed. He was breathing like a distance runner. His broad, muscular, hair-covered chest was heaving with every breath. "What?" he choked.

"I...I can't!" she repeated.

The breathing didn't slow, and his hand was still moving. "Why not?"

"I'm not on the pill!" she burst out.

"Not on the pill." He blinked. "Not on the pill."

"I could get pregnant!" she insisted.

Sanity came back in a cold rush. He took slow breaths until he could control himself. That only made it worse, because he'd been totally helpless and she'd seen it. His eyes grew hot with anger, with condemnation.

With one smooth motion, he bounded away from her and rolled off the bed to his feet. He jerked on his pajama bottoms and turned to face her, still condemning as she scrambled under the bedcover.

"Well, if that doesn't beat all!" he muttered furiously. "You give me a come-hither look, open your arms to me and give it back like a professional. Then at the last minute, when I'm out of my mind, you jerk back and say I have to stop because you could get pregnant! That's just priceless! Priceless!"

"I didn't realize…!" She tried to defend herself.

"Of all the dirty, mean tricks to play on a man, that's the worst," he said in a tone that could have taken rust off. "You were getting even, weren't you? I treated you badly at John's funeral and you wanted payback?"

She flushed and dropped her gaze. She wouldn't cry. She wouldn't cry! She bit her lower lip, hard, as she fought for control. "I didn't do it to get even."

"The hell you didn't!"

"I didn't have anything to use," she protested shakily. "I've never…I haven't…I don't know…"

"You knew all that when I came in here," he said coldly. "You could have said so then."

He was right, of course. She could have. But she'd never been in Tony's arms, held close by him kissed by him, and she'd have died for the experience. It had been like paradise, for those few heated minutes before she came to her senses. She couldn't defend herself. He was probably hurting. She gritted her teeth. She didn't even know how to apologize.

He glared at the picture she made, wrapped up in the cover, only her head showing, her eyes hidden, her face white. If he hadn't been hurting so badly, he might have been less volatile in his treatment of her. But the pain was bad.

He turned and slammed out of the room, leaving the door ajar, fuming and cursing under his breath. His cell phone rang and rang. He finally realized it was on the dresser in Millie's room. She hadn't moved an inch when he scooped it up and opened it.

"Hello," he said furiously.

"Hi, stranger," came a purring, sexy tone. "I heard from Frank that you were in town. How about a little action? I don't have a thing to do tonight."

"Nothing to do?" His voice changed. The tone dropped. He sounded seductive, aware that he was still standing in the doorway of Millie's room and that she could hear every word. "We can't have that. Tell you what, baby, why don't you come over here and we'll have a couple of drinks and see what develops."

"What a nice idea!" she enthused. "Since I already know the name of the hotel, and the room number," she said, "I'll see you in about, ten minutes?"

"Ten minutes will be fine. Just enough time for me to have a shower and get into something comfortable. See you, sweetheart."

He didn't look back. He could imagine Millie's expression, and it made him feel good. She'd given him a nasty surprise, it was fair play for him to give her one. He went right into his own room, swiped up some clean clothes and walked right into the bathroom to shower without a single regret.

Chapter Five

Millie heard Tony's brazen invitation to the other woman with pure anguish. He didn't bother to look her way as he headed toward his own room. Maybe she'd frustrated him, maybe he was angry, but that was no excuse for bringing one of his glittery women over here to seduce her in earshot of Millie.

She might be a disappointment to him, as a woman, but she wasn't a doormat. No way was she staying in here to listen to him cavorting with his girlfriend! No way!

Furious, now, she threw on her clothes and her overcoat, fighting back tears, grabbed her purse, closed the bedroom door and walked right out of the suite. The last thing she heard on the way was the sound of the shower running.

* * *

Tony had on slacks and a blue shirt that flattered his dark complexion. He greeted Angel with a smile and invited her in. She was wearing a sexy pair of black slacks with a lacy blouse, and her long black hair was swinging free. Her black eyes teased him as she walked in front of him to the living room.

"Long time no see." She laughed. "You look good."

"So do you." He bent and kissed her, not passionately, but nicely. He went to pour drinks. "How've you been?"

She told him. He seemed to be listening, but his mind was on what had happened with Millie. Now that he was less stimulated, he recalled that it hadn't been Millie who started things rolling. It had been him. He'd dived on her like a starving shark. She, with her obvious inexperience, hadn't stood a chance. If she'd kept quiet, there wasn't a chance in hell that he'd have stopped in time. By now, they'd be having a conversation about blood tests and babies. His face flushed at just the thought.

"What's wrong?" Angel asked.

"Nothing," he said quickly, pasting on a smile. "Seen Frank lately?"

She let out a loud breath. "Tony, I've just been telling you about Frank. There's a job opening in Dallas and he wants to take it. The manager of the club's offering him advancement into security work, and he'll train him. It pays well."

"You don't say. He didn't tell me anything about it," he added.

"He's been in Dallas, interviewing. He just got back. I saw him at the club when I went off duty tonight. He's going to tell you tomorrow." She sipped her drink, put it down and brazenly slid into Tony's lap. "Don't let's talk about Frank. I'm lonely." She put her mouth against his with a little moan.

In the old days, that would have set the fires burning. But not tonight. Tony was remembering Millie's wretched expression. She'd be sitting in the bedroom hearing him with Angel and probably crying her eyes out over his insensitivity.

He drew away. "We're going to have to put anything past the drinks and conversation on hold," he said gently. "I'm working a job. There's a woman I'm protecting," he added, jerking his head toward the bedroom. "She's asleep, but she might wake up."

"Is she your girl?" Angel asked.

"She's a librarian," he replied flatly.

"Oh, good Lord, you poor man!" She laughed. "A librarian! How did you ever get talked into a job like this?"

He was offended by her attitude toward Millie. "It's not exactly easy to get those jobs," he said, his eyes narrowing. "My foster mother was a research librarian. She went through college to get the job, and even then she had to beat out the competition for it. So did the woman I'm guarding. It takes a good education," he added.

"Well, excuse me." Angel laughed. "Here I am with my little high school diploma making fun of a college graduate!"

He felt uncomfortable. He pushed her away and got to his feet. "It's just a job."

She got up, too. She gave him an amused smile as she picked up her purse. She stopped just in front of him. "Just how old is this bookworm you're taking care of?"

"I don't know. Somewhere in her twenties."

"Pretty?"

He frowned. "Inside, she's pretty," he replied.

"Poor man," she sighed. She reached up and kissed his cheek. "I guess we all meet our Waterloo someday. Looks like this is yours." She chuckled. "Good luck."

That same thought was only beginning to form in his own mind. He smiled sheepishly. "Yeah. Thanks." He bent and kissed her cheek. "It was fun while it lasted."

"Same here. See you around," she added, and winked as she let herself out.

Tony stood, staring at the closed door, with his hands in his slacks pockets and his heart even with his shoes. He'd made a terrible mess of things. Millie was going to hate his guts.

He paused outside her door. He wanted to apologize, to tell her that inviting Angel over was mean-spirited and he was sorry about it. He was sorry for pushing her into a corner and making her feel guilty and cheap, when it was his own fault. He was the one who'd caused the problem and he'd blamed her. It was going to hurt, this apology. With a wistful smile, he knocked gently on the door.

"Millie?" he called.

There was no answer. He tried again, with the same result. She might be in the bathroom and couldn't hear him. Gently he opened the door and peered inside. The bed was empty. Millie's coat and purse were gone. He ran to the bathroom. It was empty, too. She'd gone! She'd walked out, probably while he was in the shower gloating about having Angel come over to show Millie he couldn't care less what she thought of him. Now she was walking into danger. If the contract killer was keeping an eye on her, he'd see her leave the hotel, in the dark, all by herself. He'd have a prime opportunity to kill her, and Tony would be responsible.

He grabbed his cell phone and punched the speed dial for Frank's number. God, he hoped Frank had it turned on!

Sure enough, he had his cell phone on. He answered on the second ring.

"Frank!" Tony said at once. "I need you to call your detective friend and tell him that Millie's on her way back to her apartment, alone. I have to get my car out of the parking garage and it will take precious time. He needs to send somebody to her address right now!"

"She's gone home alone?" Frank was all at sea. "But how did she get out past you? And why did she leave in the middle of the night?"

Tony ground his teeth together. "Tell you later," he gritted. "Do what you can about getting somebody to her apartment, will you? She may be perfectly safe, but I've got a feeling... Never mind. Thanks." He hung up before Frank had the chance to ask any more embarrassing questions. Then he ran down the stairs, foregoing the elevator, on his way to the parking garage. He prayed every step of the way that he wouldn't be too late. That sweet, gentle woman wouldn't stand a chance if the contract killer was anywhere nearby!

He broke speed limits and ran red lights across the city getting to Millie's apartment building, and had the good luck not to be seen by a squad car in the process. He parked in the first spot he came to, got out and ran toward the building. He didn't see another car, or another person, on the way in. Maybe, he thought, just maybe he'd get lucky.

He took the staircase up to the fourth floor and walked cautiously down the hall. He stopped in front of Millie's apartment, looking around carefully. He was relieved not to see any activity. He'd just relaxed and was about to knock on the door when he heard voices inside the apartment. One was male.

Tony almost threw his weight against the door to force it in a moment's panic, but that way would get her killed if the voice he heard was the killer's. So he slipped out of his shoes, picked the lock with ridiculous ease—thanking God that she didn't have a dead bolt lock—and slid his sidearm out of its holster as he silently opened the door.

"...never thought it would be this easy." A male voice chuckled. "So much for your boyfriend's skills."

"Could you just shoot me," Millie asked in a world-weary tone, "and not talk me to death?"

"Well, you've got grit," the man said with reluctant admiration. He raised a pistol with a makeshift silencer—an empty two liter soft drink bottle—duct-taped to the muzzle. "Goodbye from John."

"No. Goodbye from me." Tony had the pistol leveled at the man even as he spoke, his hands steady, his voice calm and cool.

As the hit man turned, shocked, and then lifted his gun again, Tony pulled the trigger. The killer fell to the floor and didn't move.

Tony put away his pistol, checked to make sure the hit man wasn't going to get up again and knelt beside Millie, who was sitting frozen on the edge of her bed. Her face was white. Her eyes were blank with shock. She looked at Tony, but she didn't even see him.

There was an urgent knock at the door. "Miss Evans?" a voice called with deep concern.

"Stay put," Tony said gently. "I'll answer it."

He opened the door, and Frank's detective friend was standing there with a patrol officer.

"We heard a gunshot when we got off the elevator. Is Miss Evans…?" the lieutenant began.

"She's fine," Tony said. "But, sadly for him, the hit man didn't hear me come in."

The lieutenant noted the pistol in its holster. Tony reached for his ID, but the lieutenant waved it away. "No need," he said. "I was on the phone with your boss just this afternoon. Where's the deceased?"

"In here." Tony led them into Millie's bedroom. She was sitting, staring into space. "She's pretty shaken," he told the other men.

"Miss Evans, wouldn't you like to sit in the living room while we process the scene?" the lieutenant asked her.

She looked at him blankly. He grimaced.

Tony bent and lifted her into his arms, cradling her a little too close to his massive chest in the aftermath of fear, and carried her tenderly into the living room. He brushed his mouth over her forehead as he put her on the couch. "It will be all right," he said softly. "I promise."

She didn't make a sound. In the space of minutes, her whole life had been turned upside down. The night had gone from a fulfilled dream to a nightmare. Tony, kissing her. Tony, furious and insulting her. Tony, bringing his girlfriend to the apartment to humiliate her. And now, Tony shooting another man in a space of seconds without hesitation, with eyes so cold they didn't even seem alive. She looked down and saw tiny droplets of blood on her overcoat. The killer's blood.

She took it off, with jerky motions, and dropped it quickly on the floor. She shivered. Tony's job had seemed otherworldly to her until tonight. Now she understood how deadly he was, how dangerous he was. Her eyes went involuntarily to the crumpled human figure on the floor of her bedroom, with dark stains growing around it. She shivered again. She'd only ever seen dead people in caskets. This was sickening. Terrifying. She realized that it could be her own body lying on the floor like that, except for Tony's dark skills.

Tony drew in a quiet breath. "I'm so sorry," he said. He pulled a crocheted afghan off her easy chair and draped it around her. "I never meant tonight to end like this."

She shivered again. She didn't answer Tony, or even look at him.

People came and went. A team of crime scene investigators tramped over the apartment in funny blue pull-on boots, wearing masks and gloves, taking samples of everything, lifting fingerprints, bagging evidence. If Millie hadn't been so shell-shocked, she would have enjoyed watching the process that she'd only ever seen in television dramas.

Through it all, Tony stood with the detective, watching and commenting. At one point, Tony came back in with statement forms and asked if she felt up to writing down what had happened when she got home. She nodded zombielike, took a pen and started writing. Tony filled out his own form from across the room, just to make sure the lieutenant knew he wasn't collaborating on stories with Millie.

Hours later, many hours later, the police and the medical examiner's crew left with the body.

"You can't stay here," Tony told her quietly. "Not after what happened."

There was a tap on the door. Tony opened it and Frank came in. "I just got off work," he said, hesitating when Millie jumped up from the sofa and threw herself into his arms. She cried as if all the tears in the world were suddenly pouring out of her. She clung to Frank, sobbing incoherently. He held her, patting her back, while Tony looked on with anguish. He didn't need to ask why she was suddenly so animated with another man. She'd seen Tony shoot a man. His profession had suddenly become crystal clear to her, and she was afraid of him now. It was a miserable feeling.

"You can't stay here," Frank told her gently. "You can stay with my mother. I already talked to her about it."

"That's so...so kind of her," Millie choked, wiping at her eyes with the back of her hand.

"She likes you. Don't worry about packing anything," he added quickly when she looked, horrified, at her crime-scene-taped bedroom door. "She'll lend you a gown. Come on."

"Okay." She held on to his sleeve. She didn't quite meet

Tony's searching eyes. "Thank you for saving my life," she said, like a child reciting a line her parents has prompted her to say.

"You're welcome," he replied in a cool tone. He was more shaken than he let on. He'd just killed a man. It wasn't the first time. But then he'd never seen himself through the eyes of an innocent. Millie couldn't even look at him anymore. He felt less than human.

Frank saw that. "I'll call you later," he told his friend, knowing that Tony would still be awake however long that was.

Tony drew in a long breath. "Sure."

Frank drew Millie out the door with him. He left it open. Tony stood there watching them until they were out of sight.

He went back to the hotel, but he didn't sleep. He was still awake late in the morning, so he ordered breakfast and sat down to eat it when it came. He called Frank as he made inroads into his second cup of strong black coffee.

"How is she?" he asked his friend.

"Shaken," he replied. "She couldn't stop talking about the way the man got into her apartment so easily, even before she had time to take off her overcoat. She figured he was watching and followed her home."

"That would be my guess, too."

Something in Tony's tone was familiar to the man who'd

known him for so many years. "You never really get used to shooting people, do you?" he asked.

Tony sighed. "No. It goes with the job description, I guess, but in recent years I've been more of a planner than a participant. It's been a long time since I had to throw down on an assailant."

"You've got too much heart, and too much conscience, for the line of work you're in," Frank said flatly. "You need to consider a change, before you get so old that they retire you. Imagine having to live on a government pension," he added, and chuckled softly.

Tony laughed, too, but his heart wasn't in it. "Your friend the lieutenant have anything more to say about last night?" he asked.

"About the killer, you mean? He knew the guy, actually. He'd weaseled out of two homicide charges, just in the past year. In one of them, he shot a pregnant woman, killing her and the child. Funny thing, the two witnesses died in strange accidents, about a week before they were going to testify against him. He said the guy would do anything for money, and it's no loss."

"He was still a human being," Tony said in a dull, quiet tone. "He had family that must have loved him, at least when he was little. He had a mother…"

"He pushed her down a flight of stairs and killed her when he was eight," Frank mused. "It was in his juvy record. The psychiatrist figured it was a terrible accident and shouldn't be held against the poor orphan."

"You're kidding me!"

"The psychiatrist was later sued by the victim's family."

"No wonder."

"So stop beating your conscience to death," Frank counseled. "I'd like to tell you about my new job."

"In Dallas, I guess. Angel was over here—" He stopped dead. That had been a slip he shouldn't have made.

There was a long pause. "So that's why Millie went home alone, huh?" Frank asked, and in a different tone of voice. "Don't tell me—you made a heavy pass at Millie, she ran, you called Angel to come over and soothe you so that Millie could hear it all and see what she'd missed."

"Damn!" Tony muttered. Frank knew him right down to his bones, and he didn't like it.

"She's a virgin, you idiot!" Frank grumbled. "That sort of woman isn't going to go running headlong into a one-night stand. She believes it's a sin."

"Yeah, well, I wasn't exactly thinking clearly at the time!" Tony shot back.

"Now you are, and you've blown it," Frank advised him. "She doesn't want to see you again, ever."

Tony's heart felt as if it were weighed down with bricks. "Yeah. I sort of figured that's how she'd feel."

"Someday, you're going to fall for a woman. I hope for your sake that she doesn't treat you the way you've treated Millie," Frank replied. "She's special."

"I guess she'll marry you and live happily ever after, huh?" Tony asked sarcastically.

"Don't I wish," Frank sighed. "Why do you think I'm moving to Dallas? I'm sick of eating my heart out over Millie."

"You might try candy and flowers and soft music," Tony replied, trying to sound lighthearted.

"I've tried everything. She told me once that you can't make people love you," he added bitterly. "She was right. So I'm cutting my losses."

"She'll have nobody left to talk to," Tony said quietly. "She doesn't mix well. She's never had a real girlfriend that she could confide in. She won't let people get close to her."

"You don't know much about her, do you?" Frank asked.

Tony hesitated. "Not really, no."

"Her father was a roughneck, worked on oil rigs. When he came home, he drank. Excessively. Millie's mother tried to leave him, but he kept Millie with him and threatened to cut her up if her mother didn't come back. She was too scared of him not to do what he said. Millie's whole childhood was one of stark terror, of being afraid to trust anyone. It was almost a relief, she told me, when he died of a heart attack. She and her mother finally had some peace, but it was too late for Millie to reform her character. She doesn't trust anybody these days. And especially not after what John did to her. It was her father all over again, only worse."

Tony felt even smaller. "She never told me."

"Why would she? I'm sure she knew that you weren't interested in her."

"Yeah."

There was another long pause. "What's next on your agenda?" Frank asked.

"What? Oh. I've got an assignment over the border. Very hush-hush."

"Most of them are." Frank chuckled. "Well, I'll leave my forwarding address with Angel. You can come see me up in Dallas after the first of the year."

"I'll do that. I won't have any reason left to come back to San Antonio, once you're gone."

They were both talking around the fact that Millie would still live there.

"Can you tell her I'm sorry?" Tony asked after a minute. "I mean, really sorry. I tried to tell her just after I got the hit man, but she was too scared of me to listen."

"Is that surprising? Most people are scared of you."

"I don't mind it with most people," Tony said gruffly. "She's gone through a lot. More than she should have had to. If I hadn't listened to John, maybe I could have spared her some of it."

"If."

"Yeah. Your lieutenant thinks she's out of the woods, then?"

"He does. One of his men's confidential informants said

that the gang boss who was holding the money for the contract killer decided he needed a nice new car, so he wasn't passing the contract along. Good news for Millie."

"Very good." Tony was relieved. At least she'd be safe now, from John and his postmortem attempts on her life.

"So you can get on with your life now."

"I can."

"Keep in touch," Frank said.

"You know I'll do that. See you around, pal."

"You, too."

Tony leaned back and stared blankly at a painting of Japanese flowers and characters in the frame on the wall. It was all over. He'd go back to his assignments, Millie would go back to work, Frank would take up his new job in Dallas, and nothing would draw the men back to San Antonio ever again. Well, Frank's mother still lived there, so he'd go to see her, probably. But he was willing to bet that Frank wouldn't contact Millie again. Anyway, he consoled himself, he wasn't emotionally attached to Millie. It had been a physical need, brought on by abstinence and proximity. He'd be over it in no time.

He got up and started packing.

Millie was back in her own apartment. Frank had called in a marker and had the people who cleaned the night-club come over and scrub Millie's apartment. He'd paid them out of his own pocket, but he hadn't told her.

When she left Frank's mother's house, Millie was still getting over the trauma. She wasn't looking forward to having to live where a man had died. But when she got inside, she was surprised. The bedroom had been rearranged. It was spotlessly clean. There were new curtains, a new bedspread. It looked brand-new.

"Oh, you shouldn't have done this!" she exclaimed, smiling up at Frank.

He shrugged and grinned. "We're friends. It's for old times' sake. I won't be around for much longer."

"I know." She looked sad. "You'll like Dallas. My mother was from there. We used to go visit my grandmother, until she died."

"I'll like it," he agreed.

"This is great." She looked around, touching the curtains, smoothing the bed. Her eyes were sad. "Tony saved my life, and I barely thanked him," she said in a subdued tone. She looked at Frank, worried. "You know, he never blinked an eye. Tony was ice-cold. He never needed a second shot." She wrapped her arms around herself. "I've never seen anybody shot before."

"It's upsetting, the first time," Frank, a combat veteran, replied.

She cocked her head. "You've shot people."

He nodded. "I was in Iraq, in the early nineties," he reminded her.

She managed a smile. "It's not like they show it on TV

and in the movies," she said. "Or in those spy films, either. This guy didn't have a metal silencer. He'd made one from a soft drink bottle and duct tape."

"Homemade ones still do the job," Frank told her. "He didn't want to attract attention."

"That gun of Tony's sounded like a cannon," she recalled. "The hall was full of people when we left, all trying to get in to see the crime-scene examiners work. I wish I'd paid attention. I was too shaken."

"So was Tony," Frank replied. "Regardless of the contract killer's background, he's still a human being. Tony used to go through some sort of purification thing. He won't go near the res in North Carolina, but he has cousins from his clan in Oklahoma. He hangs out with a couple of them. They build a sweat lodge and help him get through the emotional pangs."

She was fascinated. "I never knew that. Neither did his foster mother, I guess, because she didn't say anything about it."

"She didn't know," he said simply. "He didn't want her to know what his job actually involved. He told her he worked for the government, and she figured that meant he was a desk jockey."

"He protected her," she said.

"Exactly."

She went back into the living room silently, her eyes on the sofa where Tony had placed her so gently after the shooting. He'd been supportive, nurturing, and she'd backed away from him. That must have hurt, especially when he'd shot a man to save her life.

"He said to tell you he was sorry," Frank told her.

She glanced at him. "He didn't need to be."

"About Angel," he emphasized.

She flushed. "Oh. The glittery woman."

He scowled. "Excuse me?"

She drew in a long, resigned breath. "You were always introducing him to girls who worked at the club," she recalled with a sad smile. "Those were his sort of women. He told me so. He didn't want ties, ever."

"He may want them someday."

"Not my business," she said quietly. "He brought her to his room to show me how little I meant to him. It wasn't necessary. I already knew that." She turned to Frank and laughed shortly. "I'm a librarian. Doesn't that just say it all?"

He scowled. "If you'll recall, that girl in the mummy movie was a librarian. She was a two-fisted heroine as well."

"Not me," Millie sighed. "Thanks for everything, Frank," she added, tiptoeing to kiss his tanned cheek. "I'll miss you."

He looked at her with anguished longing that he quickly concealed. He grinned. "I'll miss you, too, kid."

Weeks passed. Thanksgiving went by in a flash, and suddenly it was almost Christmas. Millie stopped by the window of a department store when she got off the city bus at her stop. It was beautifully decorated in an old-fashioned sort of way, with artificial snow and trees and mountains, and a classic Lionel train set running through the scenery. Millie loved electric trains. One day, if she could ever afford a bigger apartment, she promised herself she was going to buy one and run it every Christmas.

It was cold, even in San Antonio. She tugged her coat closer. It was a new coat, an extravagance, but she couldn't bear to wear the old one ever again, even with the blood spatters removed. She'd given the coat to a charity drive.

She wondered how Frank was doing. He'd already moved up to Dallas. He phoned her and said he liked his new colleagues, and thought he was going to enjoy the job. He did miss San Antonio, though, he added. Dallas was brassy and cosmopolitan, a sprawling city with odd, futuristic architecture. San Antonio still retained its historic charm. It was also smaller. But what he really meant was that he missed Millie. She was sorry she couldn't care for him as he cared for her. Despite everything, even after his cruel behavior, it was still Tony who lived in her heart.

Tony. She pulled the coat closer as she walked down the sidewalk toward her apartment building. She imagined he was off in some exotic place with some new glittery woman, having a ball. It was a modern sort of life for most women these days, rushing around from one sex partner to the next with no feeling of obligation or permanence. The movies reflected it. So did television and books. But Millie was a romantic. She lived in a past where men and women both abstained before marriage, where family mattered, where two people got to know each other as individual human beings long before they got to know each other physically. In that world, Millie lived. She devoured romance novels with characters who shared her old-fashioned views on life and society. So what if it was only make-believe. The carnal quality of relationships in real life was as empty as an office trash can on Sunday. Empty and sad. Like Tony's life.

For all his adventures, he would never know the joy of holding a baby in his arms and reading to his child at bedtime; watching him grow and learn and laugh. Millie wanted children so badly that it was almost painful to see them with their parents in stores and know that she would never experience that singular delight. She thought back often to the night in Tony's hotel room when she'd chosen virtue over experience, and she wondered what might have been if she hadn't stopped him. Perhaps there would have been a child, and she could have had it in secret and he'd never have known. It made her sad to think about that. She could have loved the child, even if Tony wouldn't let her love him.

She did enjoy her job. She got to read to children there. In fact, on Christmas Eve the library opened up for an orphan's home. Volunteers gathered to give presents to the children. The volunteers also read stories to the children. It was a new program that the library had only just instituted, and they were hoping that it would be a success. Millie was looking forward to it. She'd wear her red Santa Claus hat and a red dress, and for one night she could pretend that she was a mother. It was the only way, she thought wistfully, that she'd ever be one.

A newspaper reporter had shown up with a camera and a notebook computer to cover the event. Several other people were snapping photos with their cell phone cameras and movie cameras, probably to post on the Web. Millie was having the time of her life with two little girls in her lap. She was reading the story of *The Littlest Angel* to them. It had been her favorite as a child. Judging by the expressions on their faces of these small children, it was becoming a favorite of theirs as well.

She wasn't aware of a movement in the entrance of the library. A big man in a tan cashmere coat and a suit was standing there, watching the activity. The sight of Millie with those little girls only reinforced a thought he'd been harboring for some time now—that she would be a wonderful mother.

"Is it okay for me to be here?" he asked a woman wearing a name tag who was standing next to him.

She looked way up into large black eyes in a darkly tanned face, surrounded by wavy black hair in a ponytail. She smiled. "Of course," she said. "Do you know one of the children?"

He shook his head. "I know the lady who's reading to them," he corrected. "We've been friends for a long time."

"Miss Evans, you mean." She nodded. She smiled sadly. "She's had a very bad time in recent years, you know, especially when that man tried to kill her. She's much better now, though."

"Yes."

"You can go in, if you like," she added. "We've invited

the public to participate. Actually," she added, "we're hoping that the children may form some attachments here that will benefit them. Donors are always welcomed. And there might be an opportunity for adoptions as well."

He frowned. "I hope you've screened the men."

She grimaced. "I know what you mean," she said softly. "No, that wouldn't have been possible, I'm afraid. But there are two undercover police officers in there," she added with a chuckle. "So if anybody has uncomfortable intentions, they'll be in for a big surprise."

He smiled broadly. "Nice thinking!"

She laughed. He was a very pleasant man. "Why don't you go and speak to Miss Evans? She's been very sad the past few weeks. I found her crying in the ladies' room, just after she came back to work. After the shooting, you know. She said she'd been so wrapped up in herself that she'd failed someone who was very close to her." She looked up at his expression. "That wouldn't be you, would it?"

His broad chest rose and fell. "I failed her," he said quietly.

She patted his big arm. "Life is all about redemption," she said softly. "Go make up."

He grinned at her. "You wouldn't be in the market for a husband, I guess?" he teased.

She laughed merrily. She was seventy if she was a day. Her white hair sparkled in the overhead light. "Get out of here, you varmint."

"Yes, ma'am."

He reached Millie just as she ended the story and kissed little cheeks.

"Go get some cake and punch now," she told them, easing them back on their feet.

They laughed and kissed her back. They were pretty little girls. One had jet-black hair and eyes, the other was a redhead. They held hands on the way to the treat table.

Millie was smiling after them when a shadow fell over her. She looked up into Tony's face and caught her breath.

He knelt in front of her chair. "Yeah," he said deeply, searching her green eyes through the lenses of her glasses. She wasn't wearing contacts tonight. "That's how I feel when I see you, too. It takes my breath away."

She didn't have enough time to guard her response. She was so happy to see him that she began to glow. "I didn't expect to see you," she said.

"Didn't you?" His dark eyes smiled. "I stayed away until I thought I'd given you enough time to get over what I did."

"You saved my life," she protested. "I barely thanked you for it."

"You look good with little kids in your lap," he said quietly. "Natural."

"I like children."

"Me, too."

She searched for something to say. "Why are you here?"

"Because you're here, and it's Christmas Eve," he said.

She didn't understand. "But how did you find me?"

"I work for the government," he pointed out. "I know how to find anybody."

That reminded her of the shooting, which brought back disturbing images.

"I'm mostly administrative these days," he said quickly. "I don't have to use a gun. That night…" He looked tormented. "I didn't have a choice," he began.

She put her hand over his mouth. "I'm sorry!" she said huskily. "I'm so sorry. I didn't mean to make you feel guilty over what you did. If you'd hesitated, we wouldn't even be having this conversation!"

He caught her wrist and kissed the palm hungrily.

Her breath caught again at the hunger his touch ignited in her.

He saw it. His dark eyes began to glow.

For long seconds, they just stared at each other, blind to amused looks and muffled conversation.

"Can you come outside and sit in the car with me for a minute?" he asked, clearing his throat.

"I guess so."

He got up and pulled her up with him. He waited while she got into her coat and spoke to the white-haired lady Tony had been flirting with. The elderly woman gave Tony a thumbs-up sign behind Millie's back and he laughed.

"What was that all about?" Millie asked as they went out the front door.

"I'm thinking of having an affair with that lady you were just talking to," he said with a blatant grin. "She's a hoot."

"Mrs. Mims, you mean?" She laughed. "Isn't she, just! She's president of our 'friends of the library.' Before she retired, she was an investigative reporter."

"Well!" He saw something in Millie's face that made him curious. "What does she do now?"

"She writes mystery novels," she told him. "Very successful ones."

"I should talk to her. I know a lot of mysteries." He frowned. "Well, most of them are classified. But I could give her a few hints."

"She'd love that."

He unlocked the door of his rental car, a luxury one, and helped Millie into the passenger seat. She was smoothing the wooden dash when he got in on the other side.

"You do travel in style," she mused.

"I can afford to." He turned on the dome light and pulled something out of his pocket. "I've been doing a lot of thinking, about my life," he said as he faced her, with one arm over the back of her bucket seat. "I've been alone and I've enjoyed it. I've had brief liaisons, and I've enjoyed those, too. But I'm getting older. I'm tired of living alone."

She was hardly breathing as she sat, entranced, staring into his black eyes with breathless hope.

He reached out and touched her soft mouth with his

fingertips, loving the way her eyes closed and her breath jerked out when he did it.

"Oh, hell, the rest can wait a minute. Come here!"

He dragged her over the console into his big arms and kissed her so hungrily that she actually whimpered with smoldering desire.

His breath caught at the sound. His arms contracted. His mouth opened on her lips, his tongue penetrating, his own moan overwhelming hers in the hot, urgent silence that followed.

After a minute, he shuddered and caught her arms. He put her back into her own seat with visible reluctance. He was almost shaking with the force of his need. She was so unsteady that she fell back against the door, her mouth swollen, her eyes wild and soft, all at once.

"My foster mother was like you," he managed. "Old-fashioned and bristling with principles that seem to be a joke in the modern world. But I happen to like it." He fumbled in his pocket for a gray jeweler's box. He put it into Millie's hands and closed them around it. "Open it."

She fumbled trying to get the spring lid to work. Finally he had to help her—not that his hands were much steadier.

There, in the box, was a set of rings. There was a yellow-gold emerald solitaire with diamond accents, and a gold wedding band with alternating diamonds and emeralds.

"They're beautiful," she whispered. Maybe she was dreaming. Yes. That was probably it. She pinched her own arm and jumped.

"You're not dreaming," he said, amused. "But I've done my share of that, since I messed up things in my hotel room." He made a whistling sound. "That was a closer call than you'll ever know, girl. If you hadn't started protesting, I couldn't have stopped. I'd never lost control like that in my whole life, even when I was in my teens."

Everything went over her head except the last sentence. "Really?"

"Really. You are one hot experience."

"Me?" she asked, surprised. "But I don't know anything."

He grinned slowly. "Yeah. That's the exciting thing."

She blushed. He laughed when he saw the color in her cheeks. He was thinking how rare a thing that was. He couldn't stop thinking about how it had been with her, on that hotel bed. Even in memory, it made his blood run hot.

"I've done bad things in my life," he said then, very solemnly. "I like to think I did them in the service of my country, to protect our way of life. It was exciting work, and profitable. But I've put a lot of money away, and I've gotten the wild streak in me tamed somewhat." He hesitated. It was hard work, putting this into words. "What I'm trying to say…I mean, what I'm trying to ask…"

"I'd marry you if we had to live in a mud hut in a swamp with ten million mosquitos!" she interrupted.

He caught his breath. "Millie!"

He scooped her up again and kissed her so long, and so hard, that the windows all fogged up. Which was probably a good thing. Because when the tap at the window came, they weren't in any condition to be seen.

They scrambled apart, rearranging clothing, trying to look normal.

Tony buzzed the window down, with a carefully calm expression that didn't go well at all with the smear of lipstick across his mouth and face, and his hopelessly stained white shirt and half-undone tie and unbuttoned shirt. "Yes?" he said politely.

The white-haired woman doubled up laughing.

He scowled, trying to neaten himself up. In future years, the story would be told and retold by both partners.

"I just wanted to say…" she choked, trying to stop laughing long enough to be coherent, "that we're opening the presents, and the little girls…would like Millie to help them open theirs."

"We'll be right in. We were just getting rings out of boxes and stuff," he said, ruffled.

She murmured that it looked to her that it was a good idea to get the rings on and the words said in some legal fashion, and pretty quickly. Then she laughed some more and left.

Tony slid the engagement ring onto Millie's finger and kissed her. "So much for surprising your colleagues," he mused. "I imagine Ms. Perry Mason there will have tipped off the whole bunch by the time we get back inside."

"I don't mind," she said shyly.

He was lost in her smile. "Me, neither," he said.

Then he had to kiss her again. But they managed to get back into the library before all the presents were opened, to an unconcealed round of laughter that only the adults in the group truly understood.

They spent Christmas Day together talking about the future in between kisses. Tony offered her a church wedding, but they both decided that it could probably wait until they had more than one friend to ask to attend it. Meanwhile the local probate judge's office did nicely, with an attorney who was looking for a birth certificate and a judge's clerk for witnesses.

It had been Tony who refused to go past some energetic petting before the wedding. He wanted Millie to have things just the way she wanted them, he explained. So they'd wait.

However, the minute they reached Millie's apartment, which was closer than his hotel room, they were undressing even as Tony locked her door. They didn't even make it to the bedroom. Millie had her first intensely intimate experience on the carpeted floor of her apartment, and she never felt the carpet burns until she and Tony were lying in a tangled, sweaty heap under the soft hall-ceiling light.

"Wow," he managed.

"Oh, yes," she whispered while her heartbeat threatened to pound her into the floor.

He stretched his tired muscles, laughing when they cramped. "Hell!" he muttered. "I really tried to make it to the bedroom…"

"I don't care," she said in a tone that almost purred with satisfaction. "On a floor, standing up, in the bathroom…I never dreamed it would feel like that!"

He rolled over, so that he could look down into her soft green eyes. Her glasses and her clothing were strewn around them. "It hurt, at first."

"Did it?" she asked, surprised. "I didn't even notice."

"You flinched," he mused, brushing his warm mouth over her swollen lips. He chuckled softly. "But I knew what to do about that."

She blushed as she recalled exactly what he'd done about that.

His mouth smoothed down over soft, smooth, warm flesh. "I'm still vibrating," he murmured. "It was like swallowing fireworks!"

"Yes." She reached up and pulled him down to her, loving the feel of his muscular, hairy chest over her bare breasts. The contact electrified her. She arched up, catching his legs with hers, curling them around, tugging hopefully.

"It may hurt," he whispered.

"It may not," she whispered back, touching him shyly, but boldly.

He groaned. After that, he wasn't in any condition to protest.

She had to sit down very carefully. He noticed and his pursed lips smiled, reminding her of the restraint he'd tried to exercise.

"You insisted," he charged.

She grimaced. "Yes, but now I know better." She grinned at him anyway. "It was worth it."

He laughed out loud. "Yes, it was. Are you hungry?"

Her eyebrows arched. "I am."

He went into the kitchen and started looking through cabinets and the refrigerator. He laughed. "I can see that you're not impartial to Italian cooking."

"I love it. But you're not Italian."

"Not hardly. I just have that last name, since my mother married the devil." He frowned. "I should have had it changed, I guess. But that SOB who got her pregnant would never have let her use his name, and I don't want it, either." He shrugged. "Nothing wrong with an Italian name. It confuses people who think they know my background." He glanced at her. "I like confusing people," he said.

She got up and went to him, sliding her arms around his middle, pressing her cheek against all that warm strength. "I love you so much," she whispered. "I thought I'd die of it."

His own arms contracted. He kissed her hair. "I didn't say the words," he whispered. "But you must know that I feel them, right to my soul. These past few weeks without you have been pure hell!" He bent and kissed her soft mouth with something like anguish. "God, I love you!"

Tears welled up in her eyes and overflowed. Afterward,

he stood just holding her, rocking her in his big arms, while they savored the belonging.

"It's a few days too late, now, but I just remembered that I didn't get you anything for Christmas," he said suddenly, disturbed.

"Yes, you did," she argued. She looked up at him with clear green eyes. "I got you for Christmas." She kissed his chin and grinned. "You're the best belated present I ever had! My very own Silent Night Man." She cuddled close and added impishly, "My very own CIA agent! But I promise not to tell a soul."

He laughed wholeheartedly and wrapped her up close with a sigh. "You're the best present I ever had, too, precious. Merry Christmas."

"Merry Christmas, my darling," she whispered. She closed her eyes. Under her ear she heard the deep, steady beat of his heart. She remembered the instant she'd looked up into his eyes on Christmas Eve, and the glorious happiness she'd felt. It had only gotten better in the days that followed. This had been, she decided, the best Christmas of her whole life. She was holding her happiness in her arms.

* * * * *

SUTTON'S WAY

Chapter One

The noise outside the cabin was there again, and Amanda shifted restlessly with the novel in her lap, curled up in a big armchair by the open fireplace in an Indian rug. Until now, the cabin had been paradise. There was three feet of new snow outside, she had all the supplies she needed to get her through the next few wintery weeks of Wyoming weather, and there wasn't a telephone in the place. Best of all, there wasn't a neighbor.

Well, there was, actually. But nobody in their right mind would refer to that man on the mountain as a neighbor. Amanda had only seen him once and once was enough.

She'd met him, if their head-on encounter could be referred to as a meeting, on a snowy Saturday last week.

Quinn Sutton's majestic ranch house overlooked this cabin nestled against the mountainside. He'd been out in the snow on a horse-drawn sled that contained huge square bales of hay, and he was heaving them like feather pillows to a small herd of red-and-white cattle. The sight had touched Amanda, because it indicated concern. The tall, wiry rancher out in a blizzard feeding his starving cattle. She'd even smiled at the tender picture it made.

And then she'd stopped her four-wheel-drive vehicle and stuck her blond head out the window to ask directions to the Blalock Durning place, which was the cabin one of her aunt's friends was loaning her. And the tender picture dissolved into stark hostility.

The tall rancher turned toward her with the coldest black eyes and the hardest face she'd ever seen in her life. He had a day's growth of stubble, but the stubble didn't begin to cover up the frank homeliness of his lean face. He had amazingly high cheekbones, a broad forehead and a jutting chin, and he looked as if someone had taken a straight razor to one side of his face, which had a wide scratch. None of that bothered Amanda because Hank Shoeman and the other three men who made music with her group were even uglier than Quinn Sutton. But at least Hank and the boys could smile. This man looked as if he invented the black scowl.

"I said," she'd repeated with growing nervousness, "can you tell me how to get to Blalock Durning's cabin?"

Above the sheepskin coat, under the battered gray ranch hat, Quinn Sutton's tanned face didn't move a muscle. "Follow the road, turn left at the lodgepoles," he'd said tersely, his voice as deep as a rumble of thunder.

"Lodgepoles?" she'd faltered. "You mean Indian lodgepoles? What do they look like?"

"Lady," he said with exaggerated patience, "a lodgepole is a pine tree. It's tall and piney, and there are a stand of them at the next fork in the road."

"You don't need to be rude, Mr...?"

"Sutton," he said tersely. "Quinn Sutton."

"Nice to meet you," she murmured politely. "I'm Amanda." She wondered if anyone might accidentally recognize her here in the back of beyond, and on the off chance, she gave her mother's maiden name instead of her own last name. "Amanda Corrie," she added untruthfully. "I'm going to stay in the cabin for a few weeks."

"This isn't the tourist season," he'd said without the slightest pretense at friendliness. His black eyes cut her like swords.

"Good, because I'm not a tourist," she said.

"Don't look to me for help if you run out of wood or start hearing things in the dark," he added coldly. "Somebody will tell you eventually that I have no use whatsoever for women."

While she was thinking up a reply to that, a young boy of about twelve had come running up behind the sled.

"Dad!" he called, amazingly enough to Quinn Sutton. "There's a cow in calf down in the next pasture. I think it's a breech!"

"Okay, son, hop on," he told the boy, and his voice had become fleetingly soft, almost tender. He looked back at Amanda, though, and the softness left him. "Keep your door locked at night," he'd said. "Unless you're expecting Durning to join you," he added with a mocking smile.

She'd stared at him from eyes as black as his own and started to tell him that she didn't even know Mr. Durning, who was her aunt's friend, not hers. But she bit her tongue. It wouldn't do to give this man an opening. "I'll do that little thing," she agreed. She glanced at the boy, who was eyeing her curiously from his perch on the sled. "And it seems that you do have at least one use for women," she added with a vacant smile. "My condolences to your wife, Mr. Sutton."

She'd rolled up the window before he could speak and she'd whipped the four-wheel-drive down the road with little regard for safety, sliding all over the place on the slick and rutted country road.

She glared into the flames, consigning Quinn Sutton to them with all her angry heart. She hoped and prayed that there wouldn't ever be an accident or a reason she'd have to seek out his company. She'd rather have asked help from a passing timber wolf. His son hadn't seemed at all like him, she recalled. Sutton was as dangerous looking as a timber wolf, with a face like the side of a bombed mountain and eyes that were coal-black and cruel. In the sheepskin coat he'd been wearing with that raunchy Stetson that day, he'd looked like one of the old mountain men might have back in Wyoming's early days. He'd given Amanda some bad moments and she'd hated him after that uncomfortable confrontation. But the boy had been kind. He was redheaded and blue-eyed, nothing like his father, not a bit of resemblance.

She knew the rancher's name only because her aunt had mentioned him, and cautioned Amanda about going near the Sutton ranch. The ranch was called Ricochet, and Amanda had immediately thought of a bullet going awry. Probably one of Sutton's ancestors had thrown some lead now and again. Mr. Sutton looked a lot more like a bandit than he did a rancher, with his face unshaven, that wide, awful scrape on his cheek and his crooked nose. It was an unforgettable face all around, especially those eyes....

She pulled the Indian rug closer and gave the book in her slender hand a careless glance. She wasn't really in the mood to read. Memories kept tearing her heart. She leaned her blond head back against the chair and her dark eyes studied the flames with idle appreciation of their beauty.

The nightmare of the past few weeks had finally caught up with her. She'd stood onstage, with the lights beating down on her long blond hair and outlining the beige leather dress that was her trademark, and her voice had simply refused to cooperate. The shock of being unable to produce a single note had caused her to faint, to the shock and horror of the audience.

She came to in a hospital, where she'd been given what seemed to be every test known to medical science. But nothing would produce her singing voice, even though she could talk. It was, the doctor told her, purely a psychological problem, caused by the trauma of what had happened. She needed rest.

So Hank, who was the leader of the group, had called her aunt Bess and convinced her to arrange for Amanda to get away from it all. Her aunt's rich boyfriend had this holiday cabin in Wyoming's Grand Teton Mountains and was more than willing to let Amanda recuperate there. Amanda had protested, but Hank and the boys and her aunt had insisted. So here she was, in the middle of winter, in several feet of snow, with no television, no telephone and facilities that barely worked. Roughing it, the big, bearded bandleader had told her, would do her good.

She smiled when she remembered how caring and kind the guys had been. Her group was called Desperado, and her leather costume was its trademark. The four men who made up the rest of it were fine musicians, but they looked like the Hell's Angels on stage in denim and leather with thick black beards and mustaches and untrimmed hair. They were really pussycats under that rough exterior, but nobody had ever been game enough to try to find out if they were.

Hank and Deke and Jack and Johnson had been trying to get work at a Virginia night spot when they'd run into Amanda Corrie Callaway, who was also trying to get work there. The club needed a singer and a band, so it was a match made in heaven, although Amanda with her sheltered upbringing had been a little afraid of her new backup band. They, on the other hand, had been nervous around her because she was such a far cry from the usual singers they'd worked with. The shy, introverted young blonde made them self-conscious about their appearance. But their first performance together had been a phenomenal hit, and they'd been together four years now.

They were famous, now. Desperado had been on the music videos for two years, they'd done television shows and magazine interviews, and they were recognized everywhere they went. Especially Amanda, who went by the stage name of Mandy Callaway. It wasn't a bad life, and it was making them rich. But there wasn't much rest or time for a personal life. None of the group was married except Hank, and he was already getting a divorce. It was hard for a homebound spouse to accept the frequent absences that road tours required.

She still shivered from the look Quinn Sutton had given her, and now she was worried about her aunt Bess, though the woman was more liberal minded and should know the score. But Sutton had convinced Amanda that she wasn't the first woman to be at Blalock's cabin. She should have told that arrogant rancher what her real relationship with Blalock Durning was, but he probably wouldn't have believed her.

Of course, she could have put him in touch with Jerry and proved it. Jerry Allen, their road manager, was one of the best in the business. He'd kept them from starving during the beginning, and they had an expert crew of electricians and carpenters who made up the rest of the retinue. It took a huge bus to carry the people and equipment, appropriately called the "Outlaw Express."

Amanda had pleaded with Jerry to give them a few weeks' rest after the tragedy that had cost her her nerve, but he'd refused. Get back on the horse, he'd advised. And she'd tried. But the memories were just too horrible.

So finally he'd agreed to Hank's suggestion and she was officially on hiatus, as were the other members of the group, for a month. Maybe in that length of time she could come to grips with it, face it.

It had been a week and she felt better already. Or she would, if those strange noises outside the cabin would just stop! She had horrible visions of wolves breaking in and eating her.

"Hello?"

The small voice startled her. It sounded like a boy's. She got up, clutching the fire poker in her hand and went to the front door. "Who's there?" she called out tersely.

"It's just me. Elliot," he said. "Elliot Sutton."

She let out a breath between her teeth. Oh, no, she thought miserably, what was he doing here? His father would come looking for him, and she couldn't bear to have that...that savage anywhere around!

"What do you want?" she groaned.

"I brought you something."

It would be discourteous to refuse the gift, she guessed, especially since he'd apparently come through several feet of snow to bring it. Which brought to mind a really interesting question: where was his father?

She opened the door. He grinned at her from under a thick cap that covered his red hair.

"Hi," he said. "I thought you might like to have some roasted peanuts. I did them myself. They're nice on a cold night."

Her eyes went past him to a sled hitched to a sturdy draft horse. "Did you come in that?" she asked, recognizing the sled he and his father had been riding the day she'd met them.

"Sure," he said. "That's how we get around in winter, what with the snow and all. We take hay out to the livestock on it. You remember, you saw us. Well, we usually take hay out on it, that is. When Dad's not laid up," he added pointedly, and his blue eyes said more than his voice did.

She knew she was going to regret asking the question before she opened her mouth. She didn't want to ask. But no young boy came to a stranger's house in the middle of a snowy night just to deliver a bag of roasted peanuts.

"What's wrong?" she asked with resigned perception.

He blinked. "What?"

"I said, what's wrong?" She made her tone gentler. He couldn't help it that his father was a savage, and he was worried under that false grin. "Come on, you might as well tell me."

He bit his lower lip and looked down at his snow-covered boots. "It's my dad," he said. "He's bad sick and he won't let me get the doctor."

So there it was. She knew she shouldn't have asked. "Can't your mother do something?" she asked hopefully.

"My mom ran off with Mr. Jackson from the livestock association when I was just a little feller," he replied, registering Amanda's shocked expression. "She and Dad got divorced and she died some years ago, but Dad doesn't talk about her. Will you come, miss?"

"I'm not a doctor," she said, hesitating.

"Oh, sure, I know that," he agreed eagerly, "but you're a girl. And girls know how to take care of sick folks, don't they?" The confidence slid away and he looked like what he was—a terrified little boy with nobody to turn to. "Please, lady," he added. "I'm scared. He's hot and shaking all over and—!"

"I'll get my boots on," she said. She gathered them from beside the fireplace and tugged them on, and then she went for a coat and stuffed her long blond hair under a stocking cap. "Do you have cough syrup, aspirins, throat lozenges—that sort of thing?"

"Yes, ma'am," he said eagerly, then sighed. "Dad won't take them, but we have them."

"Is he suicidal?" Amanda asked angrily as she went out the door behind him and locked the cabin before she climbed on the sled with the boy.

"Well sometimes things get to him," he ventured. "But he doesn't ever get sick, and he won't admit that he is. But he's out of his head and I'm scared. He's all I got."

"We'll take care of him," she promised, and hoped she could deliver on the promise. "Let's go."

"Do you know Mr. Durning well?" he asked as he called to the draft horse and started him back down the road and up the mountain toward the Sutton house.

"He's sort of a friend of a relative of mine," she said evasively. The sled ride was fun, and she was enjoying the cold wind and snow in her face, the delicious mountain air. "I'm only staying at the cabin for a few weeks. Just time to…get over something."

"Have you been sick, too?" he asked curiously.

"In a way," she said noncommittally.

The sled went jerkily up the road, around the steep hill. She held on tight and hoped the big draft horse had steady feet. It was a harrowing ride at the last, and then they were up, and the huge redwood ranch house came into sight, blazing with light from its long, wide front porch to the gabled roof.

"It's a beautiful house," Amanda said.

"My dad added on to it for my mom, before they married," he told her. He shrugged. "I don't remember much about her, except she was redheaded. Dad sure hates women." He glanced at her apologetically. "He's not going to like me bringing you...."

"I can take care of myself," she returned, and smiled reassuringly. "Let's go see how bad it is."

"I'll get Harry to put up the horse and sled," he said, yelling toward the lighted barn until a grizzled old man appeared. After a brief introduction to Amanda, Harry left and took the horse away.

"Harry's been here since Dad was a boy," Elliot told her as he led her down a bare-wood hall and up a steep staircase to the second storey of the house. "He does most everything, even cooks for the men." He paused outside a closed door, and gave Amanda a worried look. "He'll yell for sure."

"Let's get it over with, then."

She let Elliot open the door and look in first, to make sure his father had something on.

"He's still in his jeans," he told her, smiling as she blushed. "It's okay."

She cleared her throat. So much for pretended sophistication, she thought, and here she was twenty-four years old. She avoided Elliot's grin and walked into the room.

Quinn Sutton was sprawled on his stomach, his bare muscular arms stretched toward the headboard. His back gleamed with sweat, and his thick, black hair was damp with moisture. Since it wasn't hot in the room, Amanda decided that he must have a high fever. He was moaning and talking unintelligibly.

"Elliot, can you get me a basin and some hot water?" she asked. She took off her coat and rolled up the sleeves of her cotton blouse.

"Sure thing," Elliot told her, and rushed out of the room.

"Mr. Sutton, can you hear me?" Amanda asked softly. She sat down beside him on the bed, and lightly touched his bare shoulder. He was hot, all right—burning up. "Mr. Sutton," she called again.

"No," he moaned. "No, you can't do it…!"

"Mr. Sutton…"

He rolled over and his black eyes opened, glazed with fever, but Amanda barely noticed. Her eyes were on the rest of him, male perfection from shoulder to narrow hips. He was darkly tanned, too, and thick, black hair wedged from his chest down his flat stomach to the wide belt at his hips. Amanda, who was remarkably innocent not only for her age, but for her profession as well, stared like a star-struck girl. He was beautiful, she thought, amazed at the elegant lines of his body, at the ripple of muscle and the smooth, glistening skin.

"What the hell do you want?" he rasped.

So much for hero worship, she thought dryly. She lifted her eyes back to his. "Elliot was worried," she said quietly. "He came and got me. Please don't fuss at him. You're raging with fever."

"Damn the fever, get out," he said in a tone that might have stopped a charging wolf.

"I can't do that," she said. She turned her head toward the door where Elliot appeared with a basin full of hot water and a towel and washcloth over one arm.

"Here you are, lady," he said. "Hi, Dad," he added with a wan smile at his furious father. "You can beat me when you're able again."

"Don't think I won't," Quinn growled.

"There, there, you're just feverish and sick, Mr. Sutton," Amanda soothed.

"Get Harry and have him throw her off my land," Quinn told Elliot in a furious voice.

"How about some aspirin, Elliot, and something for him to drink? A small whiskey and something hot—"

"I don't drink whiskey," Quinn said harshly.

"He has a glass of wine now and then," Elliot ventured.

"Wine, then." She soaked the cloth in the basin. "And you might turn up the heat. We don't want him to catch a chill when I sponge him down."

"You damned well aren't sponging me down!" Quinn raged.

She ignored him. "Go and get those things, please, Elliot, and the cough syrup, too."

"You bet, lady!" he said grinning.

"My name is Amanda," she said absently.

"Amanda," the boy repeated, and went back down-stairs.

"God help you when I get back on my feet," Quinn said with fury. He laid back on the pillow, shivering when she touched him with the cloth. "Don't…!"

"I could fry an egg on you. I have to get the fever down. Elliot said you were delirious."

"Elliot's delirious to let you in here," he shuddered. Her fingers accidentally brushed his flat stomach and he arched, shivering. "For God's sake, don't," he groaned.

"Does your stomach hurt?" she asked, concerned. "I'm sorry." She soaked the cloth again and rubbed it against his shoulders, his arms, his face.

His black eyes opened. He was breathing roughly, and his face was taut. The fever, she imagined. She brushed back her long hair, and wished she'd tied it up. It kept flowing down onto his damp chest.

"Damn you," he growled.

"Damn you, too, Mr. Sutton." She smiled sweetly. She finished bathing his face and put the cloth and basin aside. "Do you have a long-sleeved shirt?"

"Get out!"

Elliot came back with the medicine and a small glass of wine. "Harry's making hot chocolate," he said with a smile. "He'll bring it up. Here's the other stuff."

"Good," she said. "Does your father have a pajama jacket or something long-sleeved?"

"Sure!"

"Traitor," Quinn groaned at his son.

"Here you go." Elliot handed her a flannel top, which she proceeded to put on the protesting and very angry Mr. Sutton.

"I hate you," Quinn snapped at her with his last ounce of venom.

"I hate you, too," she agreed. She had to reach around him to get the jacket on, and it brought her into much too close proximity to him. She could feel the hair on his chest rubbing against her soft cheek, she could feel her own hair smoothing over his bare shoulder and chest. Odd, that shivery feeling she got from contact with him. She ignored it forcibly and got his other arm into the pajama jacket. She fastened it, trying to keep her fingers from touching his chest any more than necessary because the feel of that pelt of hair disturbed her. He shivered violently at the touch of her hands and her long, silky hair, and she assumed it was because of his fever.

"Are you finished?" Quinn asked harshly.

"Almost." She pulled the covers over him, found the electric-blanket control and turned it on. Then she ladled cough syrup into him, gave him aspirin and had him take a sip of wine, hoping that she wasn't overdosing him in the process. But the caffeine in the hot chocolate would probably counteract the wine and keep it from doing any damage in combination with the medicine. A sip of wine wasn't likely to be that dangerous anyway, and it might help the sore throat she was sure he had.

"Here's the cocoa," Harry said, joining them with a tray of mugs filled with hot chocolate and topped with whipped cream.

"That looks delicious. Thank you so much," Amanda said, and smiled shyly at the old man.

He grinned back. "Nice to be appreciated." He glared at Quinn. "Nobody else ever says so much as a thank-you!"

"It's hard to thank a man for food poisoning," Quinn rejoined weakly.

"He ain't going to die," Harry said as he left. "He's too damned mean."

"That's a fact," Quinn said and closed his eyes.

He was asleep almost instantly. Amanda drew up a chair and sat down beside him. He'd still need looking after, and presumably the boy went to school. It was past the Christmas holidays.

"You go to school, don't you?" she asked Elliot.

He nodded. "I ride the horse out to catch the bus and then turn him loose. He comes to the barn by himself. You're staying?"

"I'd better, I guess," she said. "I'll sit with him. He may get worse in the night. He's got to see a doctor tomorrow. Is there one around here?"

"There's Dr. James in town, in Holman that is," he said. "He'll come out if Dad's bad enough. He has a cancer patient down the road and he comes to check on her every few days. He could stop by then."

"We'll see how your father is feeling. You'd better get to bed," she said and smiled at him.

"Thank you for coming, Miss...Amanda," Elliot said. He sighed. "I don't think I've ever been so scared."

"It's okay," she said. "I didn't mind. Good night, Elliot."

He smiled at her. "Good night."

He went out and closed the door. Amanda sat back in her chair and looked at the sleeping face of the wild man. He seemed vulnerable like this, with his black eyes closed. He had the thickest lashes she'd ever seen, and his eyebrows were thick and well shaped above his deep-set eyes. His mouth was rather thin, but it was perfectly shaped, and the full lower lip was sensuous. She liked that jutting chin, with its hint of stubbornness. His nose was formidable and straight, and he wasn't that bad looking...asleep. Perhaps it was the coldness of his eyes that made him seem so much rougher when he was awake. Not that he looked that unintimidating even now. He had so many coarse edges....

She waited a few minutes and touched his forehead. It was a little cooler, thank God, so maybe he was going to be better by morning. She went into the bathroom and washed her face and went back to sit by him. Somewhere in the night, she fell asleep with her blond head pillowed on the big arm of the chair. Voices woke her.

"Has she been there all night, Harry?" Quinn was asking.

"Looks like. Poor little critter, she's worn out."

"I'll shoot Elliot!"

"Now, boss, that's no way to treat the kid. He got scared, and I didn't know what to do. Women know things about illness. Why, my mama could doctor people and she never had no medical training. She used herbs and things."

Amanda blinked, feeling eyes on her. She found Quinn Sutton gazing steadily at her from a sitting position on the bed.

"How do you feel?" she asked without lifting her sleepy head.

"Like hell," he replied. "But I'm a bit better."

"Would you like some breakfast, ma'am?" Harry asked with a smile. "And some coffee?"

"Coffee. Heavenly. But no breakfast, thanks, I won't impose," she said drowsily, yawning and stretching uninhibitedly as she sat up, her full breasts beautifully outlined against the cotton blouse in the process.

Quinn felt his body tautening again, as it had the night before so unexpectedly and painfully when her hands had touched him. He could still feel them, and the brush of her long, silky soft hair against his skin. She smelled of gardenias and the whole outdoors, and he hated her more than ever because he'd been briefly vulnerable.

"Why did you come with Elliot?" Quinn asked her when Harry had gone.

She pushed back her disheveled hair and tried not to think how bad she must look without makeup and with her hair uncombed. She usually kept it in a tight braid on top of her head when she wasn't performing. It made her feel vulnerable to have its unusual length on display for a man like Quinn Sutton.

"Your son is only twelve," she answered him belatedly. "That's too much responsibility for a kid," she added. "I know. I had my dad to look after at that age, and no mother. My dad drank," she added with a bitter smile. "Excessively. When he drank he got into trouble. I can remember knowing how to call a bail bondsman at the age of thirteen. I never dated, I never took friends home with me. When I was eighteen, I ran away from home. I don't even know if he's still alive, and I don't care."

"That's one problem Elliot won't ever have," he replied quietly. "Tough girl, aren't you?" he added, and his black eyes were frankly curious.

She hadn't meant to tell him so much. It embarrassed her, so she gave him her most belligerent glare. "Tough enough, thanks," she said. She got out of the chair. "If you're well enough to argue, you ought to be able to take care of yourself. But if that fever goes up again, you'll need to see the doctor."

"I'll decide that," he said tersely. "Go home."

"Thanks, I'll do that little thing." She got her coat and put it on without taking time to button it. She pushed her hair up under the stocking cap, aware of his eyes on her the whole time.

"You don't fit the image of a typical hanger-on," he said unexpectedly.

She glanced at him, blinking with surprise. "I beg your pardon?"

"A hanger-on," he repeated. He lifted his chin and studied her with mocking thoroughness. "You're Durning's latest lover, I gather. Well, if it's money you're after, he's the perfect choice. A pretty little tramp could go far with him… Damn!"

She stood over him with the remains of his cup of hot chocolate all over his chest, shivering with rage.

"I'm sorry," she said curtly. "That was a despicable thing to do to a sick man, but what you said to me was inexcusable."

She turned and went to the door, ignoring his muffled curses as he threw off the cover and sat up.

"I'd cuss, too," she said agreeably as she glanced back at him one last time, her eyes running helplessly over the broad expanse of hair-roughened skin. "All that sticky hot chocolate in that thicket on your chest," she mused. "It will probably take steam cleaning to remove it. Too bad you can't attract a 'hanger-on' to help you bathe it out. But, then, you aren't as rich as Mr. Durning, are you?" And she walked out, her nose in the air. As she went toward the stairs, she imagined that she heard laughter. But of course, that couldn't have been possible.

Amanda regretted the hot-chocolate incident once she was back in the cabin, even though Quinn Sutton had deserved every drop of it. How dare he call her such a name!

Amanda was old-fashioned in her ideas. A real country girl from Mississippi who'd had no example to follow except a liberated aunt and an alcoholic parent, and she was like neither of them. She hardly even dated these days. Her working gear wasn't the kind of clothing that told men how conventional her ideals were. They saw the glitter and sexy outfit and figured that Amanda, or just "Mandy" as she was known onstage, lived like her alter ego looked. There were times when she rued the day she'd ever signed on with Desperado, but she was too famous and making too much money to quit now.

She put her hair in its usual braid and kept it there for the rest of the week, wondering from time to time about Quinn Sutton and whether or not he'd survived his illness. Not that she cared, she kept telling herself. It didn't matter to her if he turned up his toes.

There was no phone in the cabin, and no piano. She couldn't play solitaire, she didn't have a television. There was only the radio and the cassette player for company, and Mr. Durning's taste in music was really extreme. He liked opera and nothing else. She'd have died for some soft rock, or just an instrument to practice on. She could play drums as well as the synthesizer and piano, and she wound up in the kitchen banging on the counter with two stainless-steel knives out of sheer boredom.

When the electricity went haywire in the wake of two inches of freezing rain on Sunday night, it was almost a relief. She sat in the darkness laughing. She was trapped in a house without heat, without light, and the only thing she knew about fireplaces was that they required wood. The logs that were cut outside were frozen solid under the sleet and there were none in the house. There wasn't even a pack of matches.

She wrapped up in her coat and shivered, hating the solitude and the weather and feeling the nightmares coming back in the icy night. She didn't want to think about the reason her voice had quit on her, but if she spent enough time alone, she was surely going to go crazy reliving that night onstage.

Lost in thought, in nightmarish memories of screams and her own loss of consciousness, she didn't hear the first knock on the door until it came again.

"Miss Corrie!" a familiar angry voice shouted above the wind.

She got up, feeling her way to the door. "Keep your shirt on," she muttered as she threw it open.

Quinn Sutton glared down at her. "Get whatever you'll need for a couple of days and come on. The power's out. If you stay here you'll freeze to death. It's going below zero tonight. My ranch has an extra generator, so we've still got the power going."

She glared back. "I'd rather freeze to death than go anywhere with you, thanks just the same."

He took a slow breath. "Look, your morals are your own business. I just thought—"

She slammed the door in his face and turned, just in time to have him kick in the door and come after her.

"I said you're coming with me, lady," he said shortly. He bent and picked her up bodily and started out the door. "And to hell with what you'll need for a couple of days."

"Mr....Sutton!" she gasped, stunned by the unexpected contact with his hard, fit body as he carried her easily out the door and closed it behind them.

"Hold on," he said tautly and without looking at her. "The snow's pretty heavy right through this drift."

In fact, it was almost waist-deep. She hadn't been

outside in two days, so she hadn't noticed how high it had gotten. Her hands clung to the old sheepskin coat he was wearing. It smelled of leather and tobacco and whatever soap he used, and the furry collar was warm against her cold cheek. He made her feel small and helpless, and she wasn't sure she liked it.

"I don't like your tactics," she said through her teeth as the wind howled around them and sleet bit into her face like tiny nails.

"They get results. Hop on." He put her up on the sled, climbed beside her, grasped the reins and turned the horse back toward the mountain.

She wanted to protest, to tell him to take his offer and go to hell. But it was bitterly cold and she was shivering too badly to argue. He was right, and that was the hell of it. She could freeze to death in that cabin easily enough, and nobody would have found her until spring came or until her aunt persuaded Mr. Durning to come and see about her.

"I don't want to impose," she said curtly.

"We're past that now," he replied. "It's either this or bury you."

"I'm sure I know which you'd prefer," she muttered, huddling in her heavy coat.

"Do you?" he asked, turning his head. In the daylight glare of snow and sleet, she saw an odd twinkle in his black eyes. "Try digging a hole out there."

She gave him a speaking glance and resigned herself to going with him.

He drove the sled right into the barn and left her to wander through the aisle, looking at the horses and the two new calves in the various stalls while he dealt with unhitching and stalling the horse.

"What's wrong with these little things?" she asked, her hands in her pockets and her ears freezing as she nodded toward the two calves.

"Their mamas starved out in the pasture," he said quietly. "I couldn't get to them in time."

He sounded as if that mattered to him. She looked up at his dark face, seeing new character in it. "I didn't think a cow or two would matter," she said absently.

"I lost everything I had a few months back," he said matter-of-factly. "I'm trying to pull out of bankruptcy, and right now it's a toss-up as to whether I'll even come close. Every cow counts." He looked down at her. "But it isn't just the money. It disturbs me to see anything die from lack of attention. Even a cow."

"Or a mere woman?" she said with a faint smile. "Don't worry, I know you don't want me here. I'm…grateful to you for coming to my rescue. Most of the firewood was frozen and Mr. Durning apparently doesn't smoke, because there weren't a lot of matches around."

He scowled faintly. "No, Durning doesn't smoke. Didn't you know?"

She shrugged. "I never had reason to ask," she said, without telling him that it was her aunt, not herself, who would know about Mr. Durning's habits. Let him enjoy his disgusting opinion of her.

"Elliot said you'd been sick."

She lifted a face carefully kept blank. "Sort of," she replied.

"Didn't Durning care enough to come with you?"

"Mr. Sutton, my personal life is none of your business," she said firmly. "You can think whatever you want to about me. I don't care. But for what it's worth, I hate men probably as much as you hate women, so you won't have to hold me off with a stick."

His face went hard at the remark, but he didn't say anything. He searched her eyes for one long moment and then turned toward the house, gesturing her to follow.

Elliot was overjoyed with their new houseguest. Quinn Sutton had a television and all sorts of tapes, and there was, surprisingly enough, a brand-new keyboard on a living-room table.

She touched it lovingly, and Elliot grinned at her. "Like it?" he asked proudly. "Dad gave it to me for Christmas. It's not an expensive one, you know, but it's nice to practice on. Listen."

He turned it on and flipped switches, and gave a pretty decent rendition of a tune by Genesis.

Amanda, who was formally taught in piano, smiled at his efforts. "Very good," she praised. "But try a B-flat instead of a B at the end of that last measure and see if it doesn't give you a better sound."

Elliot cocked his head. "I play by ear," he faltered.

"Sorry." She reached over and touched the key she wanted. "That one." She fingered the whole chord. "You have a very good ear."

"But I can't read music," he sighed. His blue eyes searched her face. "You can, can't you?"

She nodded, smiling wistfully. "I used to long for piano lessons. I took them in spurts and then begged a…friend to let me use her piano to practice on. It took me a long time to learn just the basics, but I do all right."

"All right" meant that she and the boys had won a Grammy award for their last album and it had been one of her own songs that had headlined it. But she couldn't tell Elliot that. She was convinced that Quinn Sutton would have thrown her out the front door if he'd known what she did for a living. He didn't seem like a rock fan, and once he got a look at her stage costume and her group, he'd probably accuse her of a lot worse than being his neighbor's live-in lover. She shivered. Well, at least she didn't like Quinn Sutton, and that was a good thing. She might get out of here without having him find out who she really was, but just in case, it wouldn't do to let herself become interested in him.

"I don't suppose you'd consider teaching me how to read music?" Elliot asked. "For something to do, you know, since we're going to be snowed in for a while, the way it looks."

"Sure, I'll teach you," she murmured, smiling at him. "If your dad doesn't mind," she added with a quick glance at the doorway.

Quinn Sutton was standing there, in jeans and a red-checked flannel shirt with a cup of black coffee in one hand, watching them.

"None of that rock stuff," he said shortly. "That's a bad influence on kids."

"Bad influence?" Amanda was almost shocked, despite the fact that she'd gauged his tastes very well.

"Those raucous lyrics and suggestive costumes, and satanism," he muttered. "I confiscated his tapes and put them away. It's indecent."

"Some of it is, yes," she agreed quietly. "But you can't lump it all into one category, Mr. Sutton. And these days, a lot of the groups are even encouraging chastity and going to war on drug use..."

"You don't really believe that bull, do you?" he asked coldly.

"It's true, Dad," Elliot piped up.

"You can shut up," he told his son. He turned. "I've got a lot of paperwork to get through. Don't turn that thing on high, will you? Harry will show you to your room when you're ready to bed down, Miss Corrie," he added, and looked as if he'd like to have shown her to a room underwater. "Or Elliot can."

"Thanks again," she said, but she didn't look up. He made her feel totally inadequate and guilty. In a small way, it was like going back to that night...

"Don't stay up past nine, Elliot," Quinn told his son.

"Okay, Dad."

Amanda looked after the tall man with her jaw hanging loose. "What did he say?" she asked.

"He said not to stay up past nine," Elliot replied. "We all go to bed at nine," he added with a grin at her expression. "There, there, you'll get used to it. Ranch life, you know. Here, now, what was that about a B-flat? What's a B-flat?"

She was obviously expected to go to bed with the chickens and probably get up with them, too. Absently she picked up the keyboard and began to explain the basics of music to Elliot.

"Did he really hide all your tapes?" she asked curiously.

"Yes, he did," Elliot chuckled, glancing toward the stairs. "But I know where he hid them." He studied her with pursed lips. "You know, you look awfully familiar somehow."

Amanda managed to keep a calm expression on her face, despite her twinge of fear. Her picture, along with that of the men in the group, was on all their albums and tapes. God forbid that Elliot should be a fan and have one of them, but they were popular with young people his age. "They say we all have a counterpart, don't they?" she asked and smiled. "Maybe you saw somebody who looked like me. Here, this is how you run a C scale...."

She successfully changed the subject and Elliot didn't bring it up again. They went upstairs a half hour later, and she breathed a sigh of relief. Since the autocratic Mr. Sutton hadn't given her time to pack, she wound up sleeping in her clothes under the spotless white sheets. She only hoped that she wasn't going to have the nightmares here. She couldn't bear the thought of having Quinn Sutton ask her about them. He'd probably say that she'd gotten just what she deserved.

But the nightmares didn't come. She slept with delicious abandon and didn't dream at all. She woke up the next morning oddly refreshed just as the sun was coming up, even before Elliot knocked on her door to tell her that Harry had breakfast ready downstairs.

She combed out her hair and rebraided it, wrapping it around the crown of her head and pinning it there as she'd had it last night. She tidied herself after she'd washed up, and went downstairs with a lively step.

Quinn Sutton and Elliot were already making great inroads into huge, fluffy pancakes smothered in syrup when she joined them.

Harry brought in a fresh pot of coffee and grinned at her. "How about some hotcakes and sausage?" he asked.

"Just a hotcake and a sausage, please," she said and grinned back. "I'm not much of a breakfast person."

"You'll learn if you stay in these mountains long," Quinn said, sparing her a speaking glance. "You need more meat on those bones. Fix her three, Harry."

"Now, listen…" she began.

"No, you listen," Quinn said imperturbably, sipping black coffee. "My house, my rules."

She sighed. It was just like old times at the orphanage, during one of her father's binges when she'd had to live with Mrs. Brim's rules. "Yes, sir," she said absently.

He glared at her. "I'm thirty-four, and you aren't young enough to call me 'sir.'"

She lifted startled dark eyes to his. "I'm twenty-four," she said. "Are you really just thirty-four?" She flushed even as she said it. He did look so much older, but she hadn't meant to say anything. "I'm sorry. That sounded terrible."

"I look older than I am," he said easily. "I've got a friend down in Texas who thought I was in my late thirties, and he's known me for years. No need to apologize." He didn't add that he had a lot of mileage on him, thanks to his ex-wife. "You look younger than twenty-four," he did add.

He pushed away his empty plate and sipped coffee, staring at her through the steam rising from it. He was wearing a blue-checked flannel shirt this morning, buttoned up to his throat, with jeans that were well fitting but not overly tight. He didn't dress like the men in Amanda's world, but then, the men she knew weren't the same breed as this Teton man.

"Amanda taught me all about scales last night," Elliot said excitedly. "She really knows music."

"How did you manage to learn?" Quinn asked her, and she saw in his eyes that he was remembering what she'd told him about her alcoholic father.

She lifted her eyes from her plate. "During my dad's binges, I stayed at the local orphanage. There was a lady there who played for her church. She taught me."

"No sisters or brothers?" he asked quietly.

She shook her head. "Nobody in the world, except an aunt." She lifted her coffee cup. "She's an artist, and she's been living with her latest lover—"

"You'd better get to school, son," Quinn interrupted tersely, nodding at Elliot.

"I sure had, or I'll be late. See you!"

He grabbed his books and his coat and was gone in a flash, and Harry gathered the plates with a smile and vanished into the kitchen.

"Don't talk about things like that around Elliot," Quinn said shortly. "He understands more than you think. I don't want him corrupted."

"Don't you realize that most twelve-year-old boys know more about life than grown-ups these days?" she asked with a faint smile.

"In your world, maybe. Not in mine."

She could have told him that she was discussing the way things were, not the way she preferred them, but she knew it would be useless. He was so certain that she was wildly liberated. She sighed. "Maybe so," she murmured.

"I'm old-fashioned," he added. His dark eyes narrowed on her face. "I don't want Elliot exposed to the liberated outlook of the so-called modern world until he's old enough to understand that he has a choice. I don't like a society that ridicules honor and fidelity and innocence. So I fight back in the only way I can. I go to church on Sunday, Miss Corrie," he mused, smiling at her curious expression. "Elliot goes, too. You might not know it from watching television or going to movies, but there are still a few people in America who also go to church on Sunday, who work hard all week and find their relaxation in ways that don't involve drugs, booze or casual sex. How's that for a shocking revelation?"

"Nobody ever accused Hollywood of portraying real life," she replied with a smile. "But if you want my honest opinion, I'm pretty sick of gratuitous sex, filthy language and graphic violence in the newer movies. In fact, I'm so sick of it that I've gone back to watching the old-time movies from the 1940s." She laughed at his expression. "Let me tell you, these old movies had real handicaps—the actors all had to keep their clothes on and they couldn't swear. The writers were equally limited, so they created some of the most gripping dramas ever produced. I love them. And best of all, you can even watch them with kids."

He pursed his lips, his dark eyes holding hers. "I like George Brent, George Sanders, Humphrey Bogart, Bette Davis and Cary Grant best," he confessed. "Yes, I watch them, too."

"I'm not really all that modern myself," she confessed, toying with the tablecloth. "I live in the city, but not in the fast lane." She put down her coffee cup. "I can understand why you feel the way you do, about taking Elliot to church and all. Elliot told me a little about his mother..."

He closed up like a plant. "I don't talk to outsiders about my personal life," he said without apology and got up, towering over her. "If you'd like to watch television or listen to music, you're welcome. I've got work to do."

"Can I help?" she asked.

His heavy eyebrows lifted. "This isn't the city."

"I know how to cut open a bale of hay," she said. "The orphanage was on a big farm. I grew up doing chores. I can even milk a cow."

"You won't milk the kind of cows I keep," he returned. His dark eyes narrowed. "You can feed those calves in the barn, if you like. Harry can show you where the bottle is."

Which meant that he wasn't going to waste his time on her. She nodded, trying not to feel like an unwanted guest. Just for a few minutes she'd managed to get under that hard reserve. Maybe that was good enough for a start. "Okay."

His black eyes glanced over her hair. "You haven't worn it down since the night Elliot brought you here," he said absently.

"I don't ever wear it down at home, as a rule," she said quietly. "It…gets in my way." It got recognized, too, she thought, which was why she didn't dare let it loose around Elliot too often.

His eyes narrowed for an instant before he turned and shouldered into his jacket.

"Don't leave the perimeter of the yard," he said as he stuck his weather-beaten Stetson on his dark, thick hair. "This is wild country. We have bears and wolves, and a neighbor who still sets traps."

"I know my limitations, thanks," she said. "Do you have help, besides yourself?"

He turned, thrusting his big, lean hands into work gloves. "Yes, I have four cowboys who work around the place. They're all married."

She blushed. "Thank you for your sterling assessment of my character."

"You may like old movies," he said with a penetrating stare. "But no woman with your kind of looks is a virgin at twenty-four," he said quietly, mindful of Harry's sharp ears. "And I'm a backcountry man, but I've been married and I'm not stupid about women. You won't play me for a fool."

She wondered what he'd say if he knew the whole truth

about her. But it didn't make her smile to reflect on that. She lowered her eyes to the thick white mug. "Think what you like, Mr. Sutton. You will anyway."

"Damned straight."

He walked out without looking back, and Amanda felt a vicious chill even before he opened the door and went out into the cold white yard.

She waited for Harry to finish his chores and then went with him to the barn, where the little calves were curled up in their stalls of hay.

"They're only days old," Harry said, smiling as he brought the enormous bottles they were fed from. In fact, the nipples were stretched across the top of buckets and filled with warm mash and milk. "But they'll grow. Sit down, now. You may get a bit dirty…"

"Clothes wash," Amanda said easily, smiling. But this outfit was all she had. She was going to have to get the elusive Mr. Sutton to take her back to the cabin to get more clothes, or she'd be washing out her things in the sink tonight.

She knelt down in a clean patch of hay and coaxed the calf to take the nipple into its mouth. Once it got a taste of the warm liquid, it wasn't difficult to get it to drink. Amanda loved the feel of its silky red-and-white coat under her fingers as she stroked it. The animal was a Hereford, and its big eyes were pink rimmed and soulful. The calf watched her while it nursed.

"Poor little thing," she murmured softly, rubbing between its eyes. "Poor little orphan."

"They're tough critters, for all that," Harry said as he fed the other calf. "Like the boss."

"How did he lose everything, if you don't mind me asking?"

He glanced at her and read the sincerity in her expression. "I don't guess he'd mind if I told you. He was accused of selling contaminated beef."

"Contaminated...how?"

"It's a long story. The herd came to us from down in the Southwest. They had measles. Not," he added when he saw her puzzled expression, "the kind humans get. Cattle don't break out in spots, but they do develop cysts in the muscle tissue and if it's bad enough, it means that the carcasses have to be destroyed." He shrugged. "You can't spot it, because there are no definite symptoms, and you can't treat it because there isn't a drug that cures it. These cattle had it and contaminated the rest of our herd. It was like the end of the world. Quinn had sold the beef cattle to the packing-plant operator. When the meat was ordered destroyed, he came back on Quinn to recover his money, but Quinn had already spent it to buy new cattle. We went to court... Anyway, to make a long story short, they cleared Quinn of any criminal charges and gave him the opportunity to make restitution. In turn, he sued the people who sold him the contaminated herd in the first place." He smiled ruefully. "We just about broke even, but it meant starting over from scratch. That was last year. Things are still rough, but Quinn's a tough customer and he's got a good business head. He'll get through it. I'd bet on him."

Amanda pondered that, thinking that Quinn's recent life had been as difficult as her own. At least he had Elliot. That must have been a comfort to him. She said as much to Harry.

He gave her a strange look. "Well, yes, Elliot's special to him," he said, as if there were things she didn't know. Probably there were.

"Will these little guys make it?" she asked when the calf had finished his bottle.

"I think so," Harry said. "Here, give me that bottle and I'll take care of it for you."

She sighed, petting the calf gently. She liked farms and ranches. They were so real, compared to the artificial life she'd known since she was old enough to leave home. She loved her work and she'd always enjoyed performing, but it seemed sometimes as if she lived in another world. Values were nebulous, if they even existed, in the world where she worked. Old-fashioned ideas like morality, honor, chastity were laughed at or ignored. Amanda kept hers to herself, just as she kept her privacy intact. She didn't discuss her inner feelings with anyone. Probably her friends and associates would have died laughing if they'd known just how many hang-ups she had, and how distant her outlook on life was from theirs.

"Here's another one," Quinn said from the front of the barn.

Amanda turned her head, surprised to see him because he'd ridden out minutes ago. He was carrying another small calf, but this one looked worse than the younger ones did.

"He's very thin," she commented.

"He's got scours." He laid the calf down next to her. "Harry, fix another bottle."

"Coming up, boss."

Amanda touched the wiry little head with its rough hide. "He's not in good shape," she murmured quietly.

Quinn saw the concern on her face and was surprised by it. He shouldn't have been, he reasoned. Why would she have come with Elliot in the middle of the night to nurse a man she didn't even like, if she wasn't a kind woman?

"He probably won't make it," he agreed, his dark eyes searching hers. "He'd been out there by himself for a long time. It's a big property, and he's a very small calf," he defended when she gave him a meaningful look. "It wouldn't be the first time we missed one, I'm sorry to say."

"I know." She looked up as Harry produced a third bottle, and her hand reached for it just as Quinn's did. She released it, feeling odd little tingles at the brief contact with his lean, sure hand.

"Here goes," he murmured curtly. He reached under the calf's chin and pulled its mouth up to slide the nipple in. The calf could barely nurse, but after a minute it seemed to rally and then it fed hungrily.

"Thank goodness," Amanda murmured. She smiled at Quinn, and his eyes flashed as they met hers, searching, dark, full of secrets. They narrowed and then abruptly fell to her soft mouth, where they lingered with a kind of questioning irritation, as if he wanted very much to kiss her and hated himself for it. Her heart leaped at the knowledge. She seemed to have a new, built-in insight about this standoffish man, and she didn't understand either it or her attitude toward him. He was domineering and hardheaded and unpredictable and she should have disliked him. But she sensed a sensitivity in him that touched her heart. She wanted to get to know him.

"I can do this," he said curtly. "Why don't you go inside?"

She was getting to him, she thought with fascination. He was interested in her, but he didn't want to be. She watched the way he avoided looking directly at her again, the angry glance of his eyes.

Well, it certainly wouldn't do any good to make him furious at her, especially when she was going to be his unwanted houseguest for several more days, from the look of the weather.

"Okay," she said, giving in. She got to her feet slowly. "I'll see if I can find something to do."

"Harry might like some company while he works in the kitchen. Wouldn't you, Harry?" he added, giving the older man a look that said he'd damned sure better like some company.

"Of course I would, boss," Harry agreed instantly.

Amanda pushed her hands into her pockets with a last glance at the calves. She smiled down at them. "Can I help feed them while I'm here?" she asked gently.

"If you want to," Quinn said readily, but without looking up.

"Thanks." She hesitated, but he made her feel shy and tongue-tied. She turned away nervously and walked back to the house.

Since Harry had the kitchen well in hand, she volunteered to iron some of Quinn's cotton shirts. Harry had the ironing board set up, but not the iron, so she went into the closet and produced one. It looked old, but maybe it would do, except that it seemed to have a lot of something caked on it.

She'd just started to plug it in when Harry came into the room and gasped.

"Not that one!" he exclaimed, gently taking it away from her. "That's Quinn's!"

She opened her mouth to make a remark, when Harry started chuckling.

"It's for his skis," he explained patiently.

She nodded. "Right. He irons his skis. I can see that."

"He does. Don't you know anything about skiing?"

"Well, you get behind a speedboat with them on..."

"Not waterskiing. *Snow* skiing," he emphasized.

She shrugged. "I come from southern Mississippi." She grinned at him. "We don't do much business in snow, you see."

"Sorry. Well, Quinn was an Olympic contender in giant slalom when he was in his late teens and early twenties. He would have made the team, but he got married and Elliot was on the way, so he gave it up. He still gets in plenty of practice," he added, shuddering. "On old Ironside peak, too. Nobody, but nobody, skis it except Quinn and a couple of other experts from Larry's Lodge over in Jackson Hole."

"I haven't seen that one on a map..." she began, because she'd done plenty of map reading before she came here.

"Oh, that isn't its official name, it's what Quinn calls it." He grinned. "Anyway, Quinn uses this iron to put wax on the bottom of his skis. Don't feel bad, I didn't know any better, either, at first, and I waxed a couple of shirts. Here's the right iron."

He handed it to her, and she plugged it in and got started. The elusive Mr. Sutton had hidden qualities, it seemed. She'd watched the winter Olympics every four years on television, and downhill skiing fascinated her.

But it seemed to Amanda that giant slalom called for a kind of reckless skill and speed that would require ruthlessness and single-minded determination. Considering that, it wasn't at all surprising to her that Quinn Sutton had been good at it.

Amanda helped Harry do dishes and start a load of clothes in the washer. But when she took them out of the dryer, she discovered that several of Quinn's shirts were missing buttons and had loose seams.

Harry produced a needle and some thread, and Amanda set to work mending them. It gave her something to do while she watched a years-old police drama on television.

Quinn came in with Elliot a few hours later.

"Boy, the snow's bad," Elliot remarked as he rubbed his hands in front of the fire Harry had lit in the big stone fireplace. "Dad had to bring the sled out to get me, because the bus couldn't get off the main highway."

"Speaking of the sled," Amanda said, glancing at Quinn,

"I've got to have a few things from the cabin. I'm really sorry, but I'm limited to what I'm wearing…."

"I'll run you down right now, before I go out again."

She put the mending aside. "I'll get my coat."

"Elliot, you can come, too. Put your coat back on," Quinn said unexpectedly, ignoring his son's surprised glance.

Amanda didn't look at him, but she understood why he wanted Elliot along. She made Quinn nervous. He was attracted to her and he was going to fight it to the bitter end. She wondered why he considered her such a threat.

He paused to pick up the shirt she'd been working on, and his expression got even harder as he glared at her. "You don't need to do that kind of thing," he said curtly.

"I've got to earn my keep somehow." She sighed. "I can feed the calves and help with the housework, at least. I'm not used to sitting around doing nothing," she added. "It makes me nervous."

He hesitated. An odd look rippled over his face as he studied the neat stitches in his shirtsleeve where the rip had been. He held it for a minute before he laid it gently back on the sofa. He didn't look at Amanda as he led the way out the door.

It didn't take her long to get her things together. Elliot wandered around the cabin. "There are knives all over the counter," he remarked. "Want me to put them in the sink?"

"Go ahead. I was using them for drumsticks," she called as she closed her suitcase.

"They don't look like they'd taste very good." Elliot chuckled.

She came out of the bedroom and gave him an amused glance. "Not that kind of drumsticks, you turkey. Here." She put down the suitcase and took the blunt stainless-steel knives from him. She glanced around to make sure Quinn hadn't come into the house and then she broke into an impromptu drum routine that made Elliot grin even more.

"Say, you're pretty good," he said.

She bowed. "Just one of my minor talents," she said. "But I'm better with a keyboard. Ready to go?"

"Whenever you are."

She started to pick up her suitcase, but Elliot reached down and got it before she could, a big grin on his freckled face. She wondered again why he looked so little like his father. She knew that his mother had been a redhead, too, but it was odd that he didn't resemble Quinn in any way at all.

Quinn was waiting on the sled, his expression unreadable, impatiently smoking his cigarette. He let them get on and turned the draft horse back toward his own house. It was snowing lightly and the wind was blowing, not fiercely but with a nip in it. Amanda sighed, lifting her face to the snow, not caring that her hood had fallen back to reveal the coiled softness of her blond hair. She felt alive out here as she never had in the city, or even back East. There was something about the wilderness that made her feel at peace with herself for the first time since the tragedy that had sent her retreating here.

"Enjoying yourself?" Quinn asked unexpectedly.

"More than I can tell you," she replied. "It's like no other place on earth."

He nodded. His dark eyes slid over her face, her cheeks flushed with cold and excitement, and they lingered there for one long moment before he forced his gaze back to the trail. Amanda saw that look and it brought a sense of foreboding. He seemed almost angry.

In fact, he was. Before the day was out, it was pretty apparent that he'd withdrawn somewhere inside himself and had no intention of coming out again. He barely said two words to Amanda before bedtime.

"He's gone broody," Elliot mused before he and Amanda called it a night. "He doesn't do it often, and not for a long time, but when he's got something on his mind, it's best not to get on his nerves."

"Oh, I'll do my best," Amanda promised, and crossed her heart.

But that apparently didn't do much good, in her case, because he glared at her over breakfast the next morning and over lunch, and by the time she finished mending a window curtain in the kitchen and helped Harry bake a cake for dessert, she was feeling like a very unwelcome guest.

She went out to feed the calves, the nicest of her daily chores, just before Quinn was due home for supper. Elliot had lessons and he was holed up in his room trying to get them done in time for a science-fiction movie he wanted to watch after supper. Quinn insisted that homework came first.

She fed two of the three calves and Harry volunteered to feed the third, the little one that Quinn had brought home with scours, while she cut the cake and laid the table. She was just finishing the place settings when she heard the sled draw up outside the door.

Her heart quickened at the sound of Quinn's firm, measured stride on the porch. The door opened and he came in, along with a few snowflakes.

He stopped short at the sight of her in an old white apron with wisps of blond hair hanging around her flushed face, a bowl of whipped potatoes in her hands.

"Don't you look domestic?" he asked with sudden, bitter sarcasm.

The attack was unexpected, although it shouldn't have been. He'd been irritable ever since the day before, when he'd noticed her mending his shirt.

"I'm just helping Harry," she said. "He's feeding the calves while I do this."

"So I noticed."

She put down the potatoes, watching him hang up his hat and coat with eyes that approved his tall, fit physique, the way the red-checked flannel shirt clung to his muscular torso and long back. He was such a lonely man, she

thought, watching him. So alone, even with Elliot and
Harry here. He turned unexpectedly, catching her staring
and his dark eyes glittered.

He went to the sink to wash his hands, almost vibrating with pent-up anger. She sensed it, but it only piqued
her curiosity. He was reacting to her. She felt it, knew it,
as she picked up a dish towel and went close to him to
wrap it gently over his wet hands. Her big black eyes
searched his, and she let her fingers linger on his while
time seemed to end in the warm kitchen.

His dark eyes narrowed, and he seemed to have stopped
breathing. He was aware of so many sensations. Hunger.
Anger. Loneliness. Lust. His head spun with them, and the
scent of her was pure, soft woman, drifting up into his
nostrils, cocooning him in the smell of cologne and
shampoo. His gaze fell helplessly to her soft bow of a
mouth and he wondered how it would feel to bend those
few inches and take it roughly under his own. It had been
so long since he'd kissed a woman, held a woman.
Amanda was particularly feminine, and she appealed to
everything that was masculine in him. He almost vibrated
with the need to reach out to her.

But that way lay disaster, he told himself firmly. She was
just another treacherous woman, probably bored with
confinement, just keeping her hand in with attracting
men. He probably seemed like a pushover, and she was
going to use her charms to make a fool of him. He took a

deep, slow breath and the glitter in his eyes became even more pronounced as he jerked the towel out of her hands and moved away.

"Sorry," she mumbled. She felt her cheeks go hot, because there had been a cold kind of violence in the action that warned her his emotions weren't quite under control. She moved away from him. Violence was the one thing she did expect from men. She'd lived with it for most of her life until she'd run away from home.

She went back to the stove, stirring the sauce she'd made to go with the boiled dumpling.

"Don't get too comfortable in the kitchen," he warned her. "This is Harry's private domain and he doesn't like trespassers. You're just passing through."

"I haven't forgotten that, Mr. Sutton," she replied, and her eyes kindled with dark fire as she looked at him. There was no reason to make her feel so unwelcome. "Just as soon as the thaw comes, I'll be out of your way for good."

"I can hardly wait," he said, biting off the words.

Amanda sighed wearily. It wasn't her idea of the perfect rest spot. She'd come away from the concert stage needing healing, and all she'd found was another battle to fight.

"You make me feel so at home, Mr. Sutton," she said wistfully. "Like part of the family. Thanks so much for your gracious hospitality, and do you happen to have a jar of rat poison…?"

Quinn had to bite hard to keep from laughing. He turned and went out of the kitchen as if he were being chased.

After supper, Amanda volunteered to wash dishes, but Harry shooed her off. Quinn apparently did book work every night, because he went into his study and closed the door, leaving Elliot with Amanda for company. They'd watched the science-fiction movie Elliot had been so eager to see and now they were working on the keyboard.

"I think I've got the hang of C major," Elliot announced, and ran the scale, complete with turned under thumb on the key of F.

"Very good," she enthused. "Okay, let's go on to G major."

She taught him the scale and watched him play it, her mind on Quinn Sutton's antagonism.

"Something bothering you?" Elliot asked suspiciously.

She shrugged. "Your dad doesn't want me here."

"He hates women," he said. "You knew that, didn't you?"

"Yes. But why?"

He shook his head. "It's because of my mother. She did something really terrible to him, and he never talks about her. He never has. I've got one picture of her, in my room."

"I guess you look like her," she said speculatively.

He handed her the keyboard. "I've got red hair and freckles like she had," he confessed. "I'm just sorry that I…well, that I don't look anything like Dad. I'm glad he cares about me, though, in spite of everything. Isn't it great that he likes me?"

What an odd way to talk about his father, Amanda

thought as she studied him. She wanted to say something else, to ask about that wording, but it was too soon. She hid her curiosity in humor.

"There are more things in heaven and earth, Horatio, than are dreamt of in your philosophy,'" she intoned deeply.

He chuckled. "Hamlet," he said. "Shakespeare. We did that in English class last month."

"Culture in the high country." She applauded. "Very good, Elliot."

"I like rock culture best," he said in a stage whisper. "Play something."

She glanced toward Quinn's closed study door with a grimace. "Something soft."

"No!" he protested, and grinned. "Come on, give him hell."

"Elliot!" she chided.

"He needs shaking up, I tell you, he's going to die an old maid. He gets all funny and red when unmarried ladies talk to him at church, and just look at how grumpy he's been since you've been around. We've got to save him, Amanda," he said solemnly.

She sighed. "Okay. It's your funeral." She flicked switches, turning on the auto rhythm, the auto chords, and moved the volume to maximum. With a mischievous glance at Elliot, she swung into one of the newest rock songs, by a rival group, instantly recognizable by the reggae rhythm and sweet harmony.

"Good God!" came a muffled roar from the study.

Amanda cut off the keyboard and handed it to Elliot.

"No!" Elliot gasped.

But it was too late. His father came out of the study and saw Elliot holding the keyboard and started smoldering.

"It was her!" Elliot accused, pointing his finger at her.

She peered at Quinn over her drawn-up knees. "Would I play a keyboard that loud in your house, after you warned me not to?" she asked in her best meek voice.

Quinn's eyes narrowed. They went back to Elliot.

"She's lying," Elliot said. "Just like the guy in those truck commercials on TV…!"

"Keep it down," Quinn said without cracking a smile. "Or I'll give that thing the decent burial it really needs. And no more damned rock music in my house! That thing has earphones. Use them!"

"Yes, sir," Elliot groaned.

Amanda saluted him. "We hear and obey, excellency!" she said with a deplorable Spanish accent. "Your wish is our command. We live only to serve…!"

The slamming of the study door cut her off. She burst into laughter while Elliot hit her with a sofa cushion.

"You animal," he accused mirthfully. "Lying to Dad, accusing me of doing something I never did! How could you?"

"Temporary insanity," she gasped for breath. "I couldn't help myself."

"We're both going to die," he assured her. "He'll lie awake all night thinking of ways to get even and when we least expect it, pow!"

"He's welcome. Here. Run that G major scale again."

He let her turn the keyboard back on, but he was careful to move the volume switch down as far as it would go.

It was almost nine when Quinn came out of the study and turned out the light.

"Time for bed," he said.

Amanda had wanted to watch a movie that was coming on, but she knew better than to ask. Presumably they did occasionally watch television at night. She'd have to ask one of these days.

"Good night, Dad. Amanda," Elliot said, grinning as he went upstairs with a bound.

"Did you do your homework?" Quinn called up after him.

"Almost."

"What the hell does that mean?" he demanded.

"It means I'll do it first thing in the morning! 'Night, Dad!"

A door closed.

Quinn glared at Amanda. "That won't do," he said tersely. "His homework comes first. Music is a nice hobby, but it's not going to make a living for him."

Why not, she almost retorted, it makes a six-figure annual income for me, but she kept her mouth shut.

"I'll make sure he's done his homework before I offer to show him anything else on the keyboard. Okay?"

He sighed angrily. "All right. Come on. Let's go to bed."

She put her hands over her chest and gasped, her eyes wide and astonished. "Together? Mr. Sutton, really!"

His dark eyes narrowed in a veiled threat. "Hell will freeze over before I wind up in bed with you," he said icily. "I told you, I don't want used goods."

"Your loss," she sighed, ignoring the impulse to lay a lamp across his thick skull. "Experience is a valuable commodity in my world." She deliberately smoothed her hands down her waist and over her hips, her eyes faintly coquettish as she watched him watching her movements. "And I'm very experienced," she drawled. In music, she was.

His jaw tautened. "Yes, it does show," he said. "Kindly keep your attitudes to yourself. I don't want my son corrupted."

"If you really meant that, you'd let him watch movies and listen to rock music and trust him to make up his own mind about things."

"He's only twelve."

"You aren't preparing him to live in the real world," she protested.

"This," he said, "is the real world for him. Not some fancy apartment in a city where women like you lounge around in bars picking up men."

"Now you wait just a minute," she said. "I don't lounge around in bars to pick up men." She shifted her stance. "I hang out in zoos and flash elderly men in my trench coat."

He threw up his hands. "I give up."

"Good! Your room or mine?"

He whirled, his dark eyes flashing. Her smile was purely provocative and she was deliberately baiting him, he could sense it. His jaw tautened and he wanted to pick her up and shake her for the effect her teasing was having on him.

"Okay, I quit," Amanda said, because she could see that he'd reached the limits of his control and she wasn't quite brave enough to test the other side of it. "Good night. Sweet dreams."

He didn't answer her. He followed her up the stairs and watched her go into her room and close the door. After a minute, he went into his own room and locked the door. He laughed mirthlessly at his own rash action, but he hoped she could hear the bolt being thrown.

She could. It shocked her, until she realized that he'd done it deliberately, probably trying to hurt her. She laid back on her bed with a long sigh. She didn't know what to do about Mr. Sutton. He was beginning to get to her in a very real way. She had to keep her perspective. This was only temporary. It would help to keep it in mind.

Quinn was thinking the same thing. But when he turned out the light and closed his eyes, he kept feeling Amanda's loosened hair brushing down his chest, over his flat stomach, his loins. He shuddered and woke up sweating in the middle of the night. It was the worst and longest night of his life.

The next morning, Quinn glared at Amanda across the breakfast table after Elliot had left for school.

"Leave my shirts alone," he said curtly. "If you find any more tears, Harry can mend them."

Her eyebrows lifted. "I don't have germs," she pointed out. "I couldn't contaminate them just by stitching them up."

"Leave them alone," he said harshly.

"Okay. Suit yourself." She sighed. "I'll just busy myself making lacy pillows for your bed."

He said something expressive and obscene; her lips fell open and she gaped at him. She'd never heard him use language like that.

It seemed to bother him that he had. He put down his fork, left his eggs and went out the door as if leopards were stalking him.

Amanda stirred her eggs around on the plate, feeling vaguely guilty that she'd given him such a hard time that he'd gone without half his breakfast. She didn't know why she needled him. It seemed to be a new habit, maybe to keep him at bay, to keep him from noticing how attracted she was to him.

"I'm going out to feed the calves, Harry," she said after a minute.

"Dress warm. It's snowing again," he called from upstairs.

"Okay."

She put on her coat and hat and wandered out to the barn through the path Quinn had made in the deep snow. She'd never again grumble at little two- and three-foot drifts in the city, she promised herself. Now that she knew what real snow was, she felt guilty for all her past complaints.

The barn was warmer than the great outdoors. She pushed snowflakes out of her eyes and face and went to fix the bottles as Harry had shown her, but Quinn was already there and had it done.

"No need to follow me around trying to get my attention," Amanda murmured with a wicked smile. "I've already noticed how sexy and handsome you are."

He drew in a furious breath, but just as he was about to speak she moved closer and put her fingers against his cold mouth.

"You'll break my heart if you use ungentlemanly language, Mr. Sutton," she told him firmly. "I'll just feed the calves and admire you from afar, if you don't mind. It seems safer than trying to throw myself at you."

He looked torn between shaking her and kissing her. She stood very still where he towered above her, even bigger than usual in that thick shepherd's coat and his tall, gray Stetson. He looked down at her quietly, his narrowed eyes lingering on her flushed cheeks and her soft, parted mouth.

Her hands were resting against the coat, and his were on her arms, pulling. She could hardly breathe as she realized that he'd actually touched her voluntarily. He jerked her face up under his, and she could see anger and something like bitterness in the dark eyes that held hers until she blushed.

"Just what are you after, city girl?" he asked coldly.

"A smile, a kind word and, dare I say it, a round of hearty laughter?" she essayed with wide eyes, trying not to let him see how powerfully he affected her.

His dark eyes fell to her mouth. "Is that right? And nothing more?"

Her breath came jerkily through her lips. "I…have to feed the calves."

His eyes narrowed. "Yes, you do." His fingers on her arms contracted, so that she could feel them even through the sleeves of her coat. "Be careful what you offer me," he said in a voice as light and cold as the snow outside the barn. "I've been without a woman for one hell of a long time, and I'm alone up here. If you're not what you're making yourself out to be, you could be letting yourself in for some trouble."

She stared up at him only half comprehending what he was saying. As his meaning began to filter into her consciousness, her cheeks heated and her breath caught in her throat.

"You…make it sound like a threat," she breathed.

"It is a threat, Amanda," he replied, using her name for the first time. "You could start something you might not want to finish with me, even with Elliot and Harry around."

She bit her lower lip nervously. She hadn't considered that. He looked more mature and formidable than he ever had before, and she could feel the banked-down fires in him kindling even as he held her.

"Okay," she said after a minute.

He let her go and moved away from her to get the bottles. He handed them to her with a long, speculative look.

"It's all right," she muttered, embarrassed. "I won't attack you while your back is turned. I almost never rape men."

He lifted an eyebrow, but he didn't smile. "You crazed female sex maniac," he murmured.

"Goody Two-Shoes," she shot back.

A corner of his mouth actually turned up. "You've got that one right," he agreed. "Stay close to the house while it's snowing like this. We wouldn't want to lose you."

"I'll just bet we wouldn't," she muttered and stuck her tongue out at his retreating back.

She knelt down to feed the calves, still shaken by her confrontation with Quinn. He was an enigma. She was almost certain that he'd been joking with her at the end of the exchange, but it was hard to tell from his poker face. He didn't look like a man who'd laughed often or enough.

The littlest calf wasn't responding as well as he had earlier. She cuddled him and coaxed him to drink, but he did it without any spirit. She laid him back down with a sigh. He didn't look good at all. She worried about him for the rest of the evening, and she didn't argue when the television was cut off at nine o'clock. She went straight to bed, with Quinn and Elliot giving her odd looks.

Chapter Four

Amanda was subdued at the breakfast table, more so when Quinn started watching her with dark, accusing eyes. She knew she'd deliberately needled him for the past two days, and now she was sorry. He'd hinted that her behavior was about to start something, and she was anxious not to make things any worse than they already were.

The problem was that she was attracted to him. The more she saw of him, the more she liked him. He was different from the superficial, materialistic men in her own world. He was hardheaded and stubborn. He had values, and he spoke out for them. He lived by a rigid code of ethics, and honor was a word that had great meaning for him. Under all that, he was sensitive and caring. Amanda couldn't help the way she was beginning to feel about him. She only wished that she hadn't started off on the wrong foot with him.

She set out to win him over, acting more like her real self. She was polite and courteous and caring, but without the rough edges she'd had in the beginning. She still did the mending, despite his grumbling, and she made cushions for the sofa out of some cloth Harry had put away. But all her domestic actions only made things worse. Quinn glared at her openly now, and his lack of politeness raised even Harry's eyebrows.

Amanda had a sneaking hunch that it was attraction to her that was making him so ill humored. He didn't act at all like an experienced man, despite his marriage, and the way he looked at her was intense. If she could bring him out into the open, she thought, it might ease the tension a little.

She did her chores, including feeding the calves, worrying even more about the littlest one because he wasn't responding as well today as he had the day before. When Elliot came home, she refused to help him with the keyboard until he did his homework. With a rueful smile and a knowing glance at his dad, he went up to his room to get it over with.

Meanwhile, Harry went out to get more firewood and Amanda was left in the living room with Quinn watching an early newscast.

The news was, as usual, all bad. Quinn put out his

cigarette half angrily, his dark eyes lingering on Amanda's soft face.

"Don't you miss the city?" he asked.

She smiled. "Sure. I miss the excitement and my friends. But it's nice here, too." She moved toward the big armchair he was sitting in, nervously contemplating her next move. "You don't mind all that much, do you? Having me around, I mean?"

He glared up at her. He was wearing a blue-checked flannel shirt, buttoned up to the throat, and the hard muscles of his chest strained against it. He looked twice as big as usual, his dark hair unruly on his broad forehead as he stared up into her eyes.

"I'm getting used to you, I guess," he said stiffly. "Just don't get too comfortable."

"You really don't want me here, do you?" she asked quietly.

He sighed angrily. "I don't like women," he muttered.

"I know." She sat down on the arm of his chair, facing him. "Why not?" she asked gently.

His body went taut at the proximity. She was too close. Too female. The scent of her got into his nostrils and made him shift restlessly in the chair. "It's none of your damned business why not," he said evasively. "Will you get up from there?"

She warmed at the tone of his voice. So she did disturb him! Amanda smiled gently as she leaned forward. "Are you sure you want me to?" she asked and suddenly threw caution to the wind and slid down into his lap, putting her soft mouth hungrily on his.

He stiffened. He jerked. His big hands bit into her arms so hard they bruised. But for just one long, sweet moment, his hard mouth gave in to hers and he gave her back the kiss, his lips rough and warm, the pressure bruising, and he groaned as if all his dreams had come true at once.

He tasted of smoke for the brief second that he allowed the kiss. Then he was all bristling indignation and cold fury. He slammed to his feet, taking her with him, and literally threw her away, so hard that she fell against and onto the sofa.

"Damn you," he ground out. His fists clenched at his sides. His big body vibrated with outrage. "You cheap little tart!"

She lay trembling, frightened of the violence in his now white face and blazing dark eyes. "I'm not," she defended feebly.

"Can't you live without it for a few days, or are you desperate enough to try to seduce me?" he hissed. His eyes slid over her with icy contempt. "It won't work. I've told you already, I don't want something that any man can have! I don't want any part of you, least of all your overused body!"

She got to her feet on legs that threatened to give way under her, backing away from his anger. She couldn't even speak. Her father had been like that when he drank too much, white-faced, icy hot, totally out of control. And when he got that way, he hit. She cringed away from Quinn as he moved toward her and suddenly, she whirled and ran out of the room.

He checked his instinctive move to go after her. So she was scared, was she? He frowned, trying to understand why. He'd only spoken the truth; did she not like hearing what she was? The possibility that he'd been wrong, that she wasn't a cheap little tart, he wouldn't admit even to himself.

He sat back down and concentrated on the television without any real interest. When Elliot came downstairs, Quinn barely looked up.

"Where's Amanda going?" he asked his father.

Quinn raised an eyebrow. "What?"

"Where's Amanda going in such a rush?" Elliot asked again. "I saw her out the window, tramping through waist-deep snow. Doesn't she remember what you told her about old McNaber's traps? She's headed straight for them if she keeps on the way she's headed... Where are you going?"

Quinn was already on his feet and headed for the back door. He got into his shepherd's coat and hat without speaking, his face pale, his eyes blazing with mingled fear and anger.

"She was crying," Harry muttered, sparing him a glance. "I don't know what you said to her, but—"

"Shut up," Quinn said coldly. He stared the older man down and went out the back door and around the house, following in the wake Amanda's body had made. She was already out of sight, and those traps would be buried under several feet of snow. Bear traps, and she wouldn't see them until she felt them. The thought of that merciless metal biting her soft flesh didn't bear thinking about, and it would be his fault because he'd hurt her.

Several meters ahead, into the woods now, Amanda was cursing silently as she plowed through the snowdrifts, her black eyes fierce even through the tears. Damn Quinn Sutton, she panted. She hoped he got eaten by moths during the winter, she hoped his horse stood on his foot, she hoped the sled ran over him and packed him into the snow and nobody found him until spring. It was only a kiss, after all, and he'd kissed her back just for a few seconds.

She felt the tears burning coldly down her cheeks as they started again. Damn him. He hadn't had to make her feel like such an animal, just because she'd kissed him. She cared about him. She'd only wanted to get on a friendlier footing with him. But now she'd done it. He hated her for sure, she'd seen it in his eyes, in his face, when he'd called her those names. Cheap little tart, indeed! Well, Goody Two-Shoes Sutton could just hold his breath until she kissed him again, so there!

She stopped to catch her breath and then plowed on. The cabin was somewhere down here. She'd stay in it even if she did freeze to death. She'd shack up with a grizzly bear before she'd spend one more night under Quinn Sutton's roof. She frowned. Were there grizzly bears in this part of the country?

"Amanda, stop!"

She paused, wondering if she'd heard someone call her name, or if it had just been the wind. She was in a break of lodgepole pines now, and a cabin was just below in the valley. But it wasn't Mr. Durning's cabin. Could that be McNaber's...?

"Amanda!"

That was definitely her name. She glanced over her shoulder and saw the familiar shepherd's coat and dark worn Stetson atop that arrogant head.

"Eat snow, Goody Two-Shoes!" she yelled back. "I'm going home!"

She started ahead, pushing hard now. But he had the edge, because he was walking in the path she'd made. He was bigger and faster, and he had twice her stamina. Before she got five more feet, he had her by the waist.

She fought him, kicking and hitting, but he simply wrapped both arms around her and held on until she finally ran out of strength.

"I hate you," she panted, shivering as the cold and the exertion got to her. "I hate you!"

"You'd hate me more if I hadn't stopped you," he said, breathing hard. "McNaber lives down there. He's got bear traps all over the place. Just a few more steps, and you'd have been up to your knees in them, you little fool! You can't even see them in snow this deep!"

"What would you care?" she groaned. "You don't want

me around. I don't want to stay with you anymore. I'll take my chances at the cabin!"

"No, you won't, Amanda," he said. His embrace didn't even loosen. He whipped her around, his big hands rough on her sleeves as he shook her. "You're coming back with me, if I have to carry you!"

She flinched, the violence in him frightening her. She swallowed, her lower lip trembling and pulled feebly against his hands.

"Let go of me," she whispered. Her voice shook, and she hated her own cowardice.

He scowled. She was paper-white. Belatedly he realized what was wrong and his hands released her. She backed away as far as the snow would allow and stood like a young doe at bay, her eyes dark and frightened.

"Did he hit you?" he asked quietly.

She didn't have to ask who. She shivered. "Only when he drank," she said, her voice faltering. "But he always drank." She laughed bitterly. "Just…don't come any closer until you cool down, if you please."

He took a slow, steadying breath. "I'm sorry," he said, shocking her. "No, I mean it. I'm really sorry. I wouldn't have hit you, if that's what you're thinking. Only a coward would raise his hand to a woman," he said with cold conviction.

She wrapped her arms around herself and stood, just breathing, shivering in the cold.

"We'd better get back before you freeze," he said tautly.

Her very defensiveness disarmed him. He felt guilty and protective all at once. He wanted to take her to his heart and comfort her, but even as he stepped toward her, she backed away. He hadn't imagined how much that would hurt until it happened. He stopped and stood where he was, raising his hands in an odd gesture of helplessness. "I won't touch you," he promised. "Come on, honey. You can go first."

Tears filmed her dark eyes. It was the first endearment she'd ever heard from him and it touched her deeply. But she knew it was only casual. Her behavior had shocked him and he didn't know what to do. She let out a long breath.

Without a quip or comeback, she eased past him warily and started back the way they'd come. He followed her, giving thanks that he'd been in time, that she hadn't run afoul of old McNaber's traps. But now he'd really done it. He'd managed to make her afraid of him.

She went ahead of him into the house. Elliot and Harry took one look at her face and Quinn's and didn't ask a single question.

She sat at the supper table like a statue. She didn't speak, even when Elliot tried to bring her into the conversation. And afterward, she curled up in a chair in the living room and sat like a mouse watching television.

Quinn couldn't know the memories he'd brought back, the searing fear of her childhood. Her father had been a big man, and he was always violent when he drank. He was sorry afterward, sometimes he even cried when he saw the bruises he'd put on her. But it never stopped him. She'd run away because it was more than she could bear, and fortunately there'd been a place for runaways that took her in. She'd learned volumes about human kindness from those people. But the memories were bitter and Quinn's bridled violence had brought them sweeping in like storm clouds.

Elliot didn't ask her about music lessons. He excused himself a half hour early and went up to bed. Harry had long since gone to his own room.

Quinn sat in his big chair, smoking his cigarette, but he started when Amanda put her feet on the floor and glanced warily at him.

"Don't go yet," he said quietly. "I want to talk to you."

"We don't have anything to say to each other," she said quietly. "I'm very sorry for what I did this afternoon. It was impulsive and stupid, and I promise I'll never do it again. If you can just put up with me until it thaws a little, you'll never have to see me again."

He sighed wearily. "Is that what you think I want?" he asked, searching her face.

"Of course it is," she replied simply. "You've hated having me here ever since I came."

"Maybe I have. I've got more reason to hate and distrust women than you'll ever know. But that isn't what I want to talk about," he said, averting his gaze from her wan face. He didn't like thinking about that kiss and how disturbing it had been. "I want to know why you thought I might hit you."

She dropped her eyes to her lap. "You're big, like my father," she said. "When he lost his temper, he always hit."

"I'm not your father," Quinn pointed out, his dark eyes narrowing. "And I've never hit anyone in a temper, except maybe another man from time to time when it was called for. I never raised my hand to Elliot's mother, although I felt like it a time or two, in all honesty. I never lifted a hand to her even when she told me she was pregnant with Elliot."

"Why should you have?" she asked absently. "He's your son."

He laughed coldly. "No, he isn't."

She stared at him openly. "Elliot isn't yours?" she asked softly.

He shook his head. "His mother was having an affair with a married man and she got caught out." He shrugged. "I was twenty-two and grass green and she mounted a campaign to marry me. I guess I was pretty much a sitting duck. She was beautiful and stacked and she had me eating out of her hand in no time. We got married and right after the ceremony, she told me what she'd done. She laughed at how clumsy I'd been during the courtship, how she'd had to steel herself not to be sick when I'd kissed her. She told me about Elliot's father and how much she loved him, then she dared me to tell people the truth about how easy it had been to make me marry her."

He blew out a cloud of smoke, his eyes cold with memory. "She had me over a barrel. I was twice as proud back then as I am now. I couldn't bear to have the whole community laughing at me. So I stuck it out. Until Elliot was born, and she and his father took off for parts unknown for a weekend of love. Unfortunately for them, he wrecked the car in his haste to get to a motel and killed both of them outright."

"Does Elliot know?" she asked, her voice quiet as she glanced toward the staircase.

"Sure," he said. "I couldn't lie to him about it. But I took care of him from the time he was a baby, and I raised him. That makes me his father just as surely as if I'd put the seed he grew from into his mother's body. He's my son, and I'm his father. I love him."

She studied his hard face, seeing behind it to the pain he must have suffered. "You loved her, didn't you?"

"Calf love," he said. "She came up on my blind side and I needed somebody to love. I'd always been shy and clumsy around girls. I couldn't even get a date when I was in school because I was so rough-edged. She paid me a lot of attention. I was lonely." His big shoulders shrugged. "Like I said, a sitting duck. She taught me some hard lessons about your sex," he added, his narrowed eyes on her face. "I've never forgotten them. And nobody's had a second chance at me."

Her breath came out as a sigh. "That's what you thought

this afternoon, when I kissed you," she murmured, reddening at her own forwardness. "I'm sorry. I didn't realize you might think I was playing you for a sucker."

He frowned. "Why did you kiss me, Amanda?"

"Would you believe, because I wanted to?" she asked with a quiet smile. "You're a very attractive man, and something about you makes me weak in the knees. But you don't have to worry about me coming on to you again," she added, getting to her feet. "You teach a pretty tough lesson yourself. Good night, Mr. Sutton. I appreciate your telling me about Elliot. You needn't worry that I'll say anything to him or to anybody else. I don't carry tales, and I don't gossip."

She turned toward the staircase, and Quinn's dark eyes followed her. She had an elegance of carriage that touched him, full of pride and grace. He was sorry now that he'd slapped her down so hard with cruel words. He really hadn't meant to. He'd been afraid that she was going to let him down, that she was playing. It hadn't occurred to him that she found him attractive or that she'd kissed him because she'd really wanted to.

He'd made a bad mistake with Amanda. He'd hurt her and sent her running, and now he wished he could take back the things he'd said. She wasn't like any woman he'd ever been exposed to. She actually seemed unaware of her beauty, as if she didn't think much of it. Maybe he'd gotten it all wrong and she wasn't much more experienced than he was. He wished he could ask her. She disturbed him very much, and now he wondered if it wasn't mutual.

Amanda was lying in bed, crying. The day had been horrible, and she hated Quinn for the way he'd treated her. It wasn't until she remembered what he'd told her that she stopped crying and started thinking. He'd said that he'd never slept with Elliot's mother, and that he hadn't been able to get dates in high school. Presumably that meant that his only experience with women had been after Elliot's mother died. She frowned. There hadn't been many women, she was willing to bet. He seemed to know relatively nothing about her sex. She frowned. If he still hated women, how had he gotten any experience? Finally her mind grew tired of trying to work it out and she went to sleep.

Amanda was up helping Harry in the kitchen the next morning when Quinn came downstairs after a wild, erotic dream that left him sweating and swearing when he woke up. Amanda had figured largely in it, with her blond hair loose and down to her lower spine, his hands twined in it while he made love to her in the stillness of his own bedroom. The dream had been so vivid that he could almost see the pink perfection of her breasts through the bulky, white knit sweater she was wearing, and he almost groaned as his eyes fell to the rise and fall of her chest under it.

She glanced at Quinn and actually flushed before she

dragged her eyes back down to the pan of biscuits she was putting into the oven.

"I didn't know you could make biscuits," Quinn murmured.

"Harry taught me," she said evasively. Her eyes went back to him again and flitted away.

He frowned at that shy look until he realized why he was getting it. He usually kept his shirts buttoned up to his throat, but this morning he'd left it open halfway down his chest because he was still sweating from that dream. He pursed his lips and gave her a speculative stare. He wondered if it were possible that he disturbed her as much as she disturbed him. He was going to make it his business to find out before she left here. If for no other reason than to salve his bruised ego.

He went out behind Elliot, pausing in the doorway. "How's the calf?" he asked Amanda.

"He wasn't doing very well yesterday," she said with a sigh. "Maybe he's better this morning."

"I'll have a look at him before I go out." He glanced out at the snow. "Don't try to get back to the cabin again, will you? You can't get through McNaber's traps without knowing where they are."

He actually sounded worried. She studied his hard face quietly. That was nice. Unless, of course, he was only worried that she might get laid up and he'd have to put up with her for even longer.

"Is the snow ever going to stop?" she asked.

"Hard to say," he told her. "I've seen it worse than this even earlier in the year. But we'll manage, I suppose."

"I suppose." She glared at him.

He pulled on his coat and buttoned it, propping his hat over one eye. "In a temper this morning, are we?" he mused.

His eyes were actually twinkling. She shifted back against the counter, grateful that Harry had gone off to clean the bedrooms. "I'm not in a temper. Cheap little tarts don't have tempers."

One eyebrow went up. "I called you that, didn't I?" He let his eyes run slowly down her body. "You shouldn't have kissed me like that. I'm not used to aggressive women."

"Rest assured that I'll never attack you again, Goody Two-Shoes."

He chuckled softly. "Won't you? Well, disappointment is a man's lot, I suppose."

Her eyes widened. She wasn't sure she'd even heard him. "You were horrible to me!"

"I guess I was." His dark eyes held hers, making little chills up and down her spine at the intensity of the gaze. "I thought you were playing games. You know, a little harmless fun at the hick's expense."

"I don't know how to play games with men," she said stiffly, "and nobody, anywhere, could call you a hick with a straight face. You're a very masculine man with a keen mind and an overworked sense of responsibility. I wouldn't make fun of you even if I could."

His dark eyes smiled into hers. "In that case, we might call a truce for the time being."

"Do you think you could stand being nice to me?" she asked sourly. "I mean, it would be a strain, I'm sure."

"I'm not a bad man," he pointed out. "I just don't know much about women, or hadn't that thought occurred?"

She searched his eyes. "No."

"We'll have to have a long talk about it one of these days." He pulled the hat down over his eyes. "I'll check on the calves for you."

"Thanks." She watched him go, her heart racing at the look in his eyes just before he closed the door. She was more nervous of him now than ever, but she didn't know what to do about it. She was hoping that the chinook would come before she had to start worrying too much. She was too confused to know what to do anymore.

Chapter Five

Amanda finished the breakfast dishes before she went out to the barn. Quinn was still there, his dark eyes quiet on the smallest of the three calves. It didn't take a fortune-teller to see that something was badly wrong. The small animal lay on its side, its dull, lackluster red-and-white coat showing its ribs, its eyes glazed and unseeing while it fought to breathe.

She knelt beside Quinn and he glanced at her with concern.

"You'd better go back in the house, honey," he said.

Her eyes slid over the small calf. She'd seen pets die over the years, and now she knew the signs. The calf was dying. Quinn knew it, too, and was trying to shield her.

That touched her, oddly, more than anything he'd said or done since she'd been on Ricochet. She looked up at him. "You're a nice man, Quinn Sutton," she said softly.

He drew in a slow breath. "When I'm not taking bites out of you, you mean?" he replied. "It hurts like hell when you back away from me. You'll never know how sorry I am for what happened yesterday."

One shock after another. At least it took her mind off the poor, laboring creature beside them. "I'm sorry, too," she said. "I shouldn't have been so..." She stopped, averting her eyes. "I don't know much about men, Quinn," she said finally. "I've spent my whole adult life backing away from involvement, emotional or physical. I know how to flirt, but not much more." She risked a glance at him, and relaxed when she saw his face. "My aunt is Mr. Durning's lover, you know. She's an artist. A little flighty, but nice. I've...never had a lover."

He nodded quietly. "I've been getting that idea since we wound up near McNaber's cabin yesterday. You reacted pretty violently for an experienced woman." He looked away from her. That vulnerability in her pretty face was working on him again. "Go inside now. I can deal with this."

"I'm not afraid of death," she returned. "I saw my mother die. It wasn't scary at all. She just closed her eyes."

His dark eyes met hers and locked. "My father went the same way." He looked back down at the calf. "It won't be long now."

She sat down in the hay beside him and slid her small hand into his big one. He held it for a long moment. Finally his voice broke the silence. "It's over. Go have a cup of coffee. I'll take care of him."

She hadn't meant to cry, but the calf had been so little and helpless. Quinn pulled her close, holding her with quiet comfort, while she cried. Then he wiped the tears away with his thumbs and smiled gently. "You'll do," he murmured, thinking that sensitivity and courage was a nice combination in a woman.

She was thinking the exact same thing about him. She managed a watery smile and with one last, pitying look at the calf, she went into the house.

Elliot would miss it, as would she, she thought. Even Quinn had seemed to care about it, because she saw him occasionally sitting by it, petting it, talking to it. He loved little things. It was evident in all the kittens and puppies around the place, and in the tender care he took of all his cattle and calves. And although Quinn cursed old man McNaber's traps, Elliot had told her that he stopped by every week to check on the dour old man and make sure he had enough chopped wood and supplies. For a taciturn iceman, he had a surprisingly warm center.

She told Harry what had happened and sniffed a little while she drank black coffee. "Is there anything I can do?" she asked.

He smiled. "You do enough," he murmured. "Nice to have some help around the place."

"Quinn hasn't exactly thought so," she said dryly.

"Oh, yes he has," he said firmly as he cleared away the dishes they'd eaten his homemade soup and corn bread in. "Quinn could have taken you to Mrs. Pearson down the mountain if he'd had a mind to. He doesn't have to let you stay here. Mrs. Pearson would be glad of the company." He glanced at her and grinned at her perplexed expression. "He's been watching you lately. Sees the way you sew up his shirts and make curtains and patch pillows. It's new to him, having a woman about. He has a hard time with change."

"Don't we all?" Amanda said softly, remembering how clear her own life had been until that tragic night. But it was nice to know that Quinn had been watching her. Certainly she'd been watching him. And this morning, everything seemed to have changed between them. "When will it thaw?" she asked, and now she was dreading it, not anticipating it. She didn't want to leave Ricochet. Or Quinn.

Harry shrugged. "Hard to tell. Days. Weeks. This is raw mountain country. Can't predict a chinook. Plenty think they can, though," he added, and proceeded to tell her about a Blackfoot who predicted the weather with jars of bear grease.

She was much calmer but still sad when Quinn finally came back inside.

He spared her a glance before he shucked his coat,

washed his hands and brawny forearms and dried them on a towel.

He didn't say anything to her, and Harry, sensing the atmosphere, made himself scarce after he'd poured two cups of coffee for them.

"Are you all right?" he asked her after a minute, staring down at her bent head.

"Sure." She forced a smile. "He was so little, Quinn." She stopped when her voice broke and lowered her eyes to the table. "I guess you think I'm a wimp."

"Not really." Without taking time to think about the consequences, his lean hands pulled her up by the arms, holding her in front of him so that her eyes were on a level with his deep blue, plaid flannel shirt. The sleeves were rolled up, and it was open at the throat, where thick, dark hair curled out of it. He looked and smelled fiercely masculine and Amanda's knees weakened at the unexpected proximity. His big hands bit into her soft flesh, and she wondered absently if he realized just how strong he was.

The feel of him so close was new and terribly exciting, especially since he'd reached for her for the first time. She didn't know what to expect, and her heart was going wild. She raised her eyes to his throat. His pulse was jumping and she stared at it curiously, only half aware of his hold and the sudden increase of his breathing.

He was having hell just getting a breath. The scent of

her was in his nostrils, drowning him. Woman smell. Sweet and warm. His teeth clenched. It was bad enough having to look at her, but this close, she made his blood run hot and wild as it hadn't since he was a young man. He didn't know what he was doing, but the need for her had haunted him for days. He wanted so badly to kiss her, the way she'd kissed him the day before, but in a different way. He wasn't quite sure how to go about it.

"You smell of flowers," he said roughly.

That was an interesting comment from a nonpoetic man. She smiled a little to herself. "It's my shampoo," she murmured.

He drew in a steadying breath. "You don't wear your hair down at all, do you?"

"Just at night," she replied, aware that his face was closer than it had been, because she could feel his breath on her forehead. He was so tall and overwhelming this close. He made her feel tiny and very feminine.

"I'm sorry about the calf, Amanda," he said. "We lose a few every winter. It's part of ranching."

The shock of her name on his lips made her lift her head. She stared up at him curiously, searching his dark, quiet eyes. "I suppose so. I shouldn't have gotten so upset, though. I guess men don't react to things the way women do."

"You don't know what kind of man I am," he replied. His hands felt vaguely tremulous. He wondered if she knew the effect she had on him. "As it happens, I get attached to the damned things, too." He sighed heavily. "Little things don't have much choice in this world. They're at the mercy of everything and everybody."

Her eyes softened as they searched his. He sounded different when he spoke that way. Vulnerable. Almost tender. And so alone.

"You aren't really afraid of me, are you?" he asked, as if the thought was actually painful.

She grimaced. "No. Of course not. I was ashamed of what I'd done, and a little nervous of the way you reacted to it, that's all. I know you wouldn't hurt me." She drew in a soft breath. "I know you resent having me here," she confessed. "I resented having to depend on you for shelter. But the snow will melt soon, and I'll leave."

"I thought you'd had lovers," he confessed quietly. "The way you acted...well, it just made all those suspicions worse. I took you at face value."

Amanda smiled. "It was all put-on. I don't even know why I did it. I guess I was trying to live up to your image of me."

He loved the sensation her sultry black eyes aroused in him. Unconsciously his hands tightened on her arms. "You haven't had a man, ever?" he asked huskily.

The odd shadow of dusky color along his cheekbones fascinated her. She wondered about the embarrassment asking the question had caused. "No. Not ever," she stammered.

"The way you look?" he asked, his eyes eloquent.

"What do you mean, the way I look?" she said, bristling.

"You know you're beautiful," he returned. His eyes darkened. "A woman who looks like you do could have her pick of men."

"Maybe," she agreed without conceit. "But I've never wanted a man in my life, to be dominated by a man. I've made my own way in the world. I'm a musician," she told him, because that didn't give away very much. "I support myself by playing a keyboard."

"Yes, Elliot told me. I've heard you play for him. You're good." He felt his heartbeat increasing as he looked at her. She smelled so good. He looked down at her mouth and remembered how it had felt for those few seconds when he'd given in to her playful kiss. Would she let him do it? He knew so little about those subtle messages women were supposed to send out when they wanted a man's lovemaking. He couldn't read Amanda's eyes. But her lips were parted and her breath was coming rather fast from between them. Her face was flushed, but that could have been from the cold.

She gazed up into his eyes and couldn't look away. He wasn't handsome. His face really seemed as if it had been chipped away from the side of the Rockies, all craggy angles and hard lines. His mouth was thin and faintly cruel looking. She wondered if it would feel as hard as it looked if he was in control, dominating her lips. It had been different when she'd kissed him….

"What are you thinking?" he asked huskily, because her eyes were quite frankly on his mouth.

"I…was wondering," she whispered hesitantly, "how hard your mouth would be if you kissed me."

His heart stopped and then began to slam against his chest. "Don't you know already?" he asked, his voice deeper, harsher. "You kissed me."

"Not…properly."

He wondered what she meant by properly. His wife had only kissed him when she had to, and only in the very beginning of their courtship. She always pushed him away and murmured something about mussing her makeup. He couldn't remember one time when he'd kissed anyone with passion, or when he'd ever been kissed by anyone else like that.

His warm, rough hands let go of her arms and came up to frame her soft oval face. His breath shuddered out of his chest when she didn't protest as he bent his dark head.

"Show me what you mean…by properly," he whispered.

He had to know, she thought dizzily. But his lips touched hers and she tasted the wind and the sun on them. Her hands clenched the thick flannel shirt and she resisted searching for buttons, but she wanted very much to touch that thicket of black, curling hair that covered his broad chest. She went on her tiptoes and pushed her mouth against his, the force of the action parting his lips as well as her own, and she felt him stiffen and heard him groan as their open mouths met.

She dropped back onto her feet, her wide, curious eyes meeting his stormy ones.

"Like that?" he whispered gruffly, bending to repeat the action with his own mouth. "I've never done it… with my mouth open," he said, biting off the words against her open lips.

She couldn't believe he'd said that. She couldn't believe, either, the sensations rippling down to her toes when she gave in to the force of his ardor and let him kiss her that way, his mouth rough and demanding as one big hand slid to the back of her head to press her even closer.

A soft sound passed her lips, a faint moan, because she couldn't get close enough to him. Her breasts were flattened against his hard chest, and she felt his heartbeat against them. But she wanted to be closer than that, enveloped, crushed to him.

"Did I hurt you?" he asked in a shaky whisper that touched her lips.

"What?" she whispered back dizzily.

"You made a sound."

Her eyes searched his, her own misty and half closed and rapt. "I moaned," she whispered. Her nails stroked him through the shirt and she liked the faint tautness of his body as he reacted to it. "I like being kissed like that."

She rubbed her forehead against him, smelling soap and detergent and pure man. "Could we take your shirt off?" she whispered.

Her hands were driving him nuts, and he was wondering the same thing himself. But somewhere in the back of his mind he remembered that Harry was around, and that it might look compromising if he let her touch him that way. In fact, it might get compromising, because he felt his body harden in a way it hadn't since his marriage. And because it made him vulnerable and he didn't want her to feel it, he took her gently by the arms and moved her away from him with a muffled curse.

"Harry," he said, his breath coming deep and rough.

She colored. "Oh, yes." She moved back, her eyes a little wild.

"You don't have to look so threatened. I won't do it again," he said, misunderstanding her retreat. Had he frightened her again?

"Oh, it's not that. You didn't frighten me." She lowered her eyes to the floor. "I'm just wondering if you'll think I'm easy...."

He scowled. "Easy?"

"I don't usually come on to men," she said softly. "And I've never asked anybody to take his shirt off before." She glanced up at him, fascinated by the expression on his face. "Well, I haven't," she said belligerently. "And you don't have to worry; I won't throw myself at you anymore, either. I just got carried away in the heat of the moment...."

His eyebrows arched. None of what she was saying made sense. "Like you did yesterday?" he mused, liking the color that came and went in her face. "I did accuse you of throwing yourself at me," he said on a long sigh.

"Yes. You seem to think I'm some sort of liberated sex maniac."

His lips curled involuntarily. "Are you?" he asked, and sounded interested.

She stamped her foot. "Stop that. I don't want to stay here anymore!"

"I'm not sure it's a good idea myself," he mused, watching her eyes glitter with rage. God, she was pretty! "I mean, if you tried to seduce me, things could get sticky."

The red in her cheeks got darker. "I don't have any plans to seduce you."

"Well, if you get any, you'd better tell me in advance," he said, pulling a cigarette from his shirt pocket. "Just so I can be prepared to fight you off."

That dry drawl confused her. Suddenly he was a different man, full of male arrogance and amusement. Things had shifted between them during that long, hard kiss. The distance had shortened, and he was looking at her with an expression she couldn't quite understand.

"How did you get to the age you are without winding up in someone's bed?" Quinn asked then. He'd wondered at her shyness with him and then at the way she blushed all the time. He didn't know much about women, but he wanted to know everything about her.

Amanda wrapped her arms around herself and shrugged. When he lit his cigarette and still stood there waiting for an answer, she gave in and replied. "I couldn't give up control," she said simply. "All my life I'd been dominated and pushed around by my father. Giving in to a man seemed like throwing away my rights as a person. Especially giving in to a man in bed," she stammered, averting her gaze. "I don't think there's anyplace in the world where a man is more the master than in a bedroom, despite all the liberation and freedom of modern life."

"And you think that women should dominate there."

She looked up. "Well, not dominate." She hesitated. "But a woman shouldn't be used just because she's a woman."

His thin mouth curled slightly. "Neither should a man."

"I wasn't using you," she shot back.

"Did I accuse you?" he returned innocently.

She swallowed. "No, I guess not." She folded her arms over her breasts, wincing because the tips were hard and unexpectedly tender.

"That hardness means you feel desire," he said, grinning when she gaped and then glared at him. She made him feel about ten feet tall. "I read this book about sex," he continued. "It didn't make much sense to me at the time, but it's beginning to."

"I am not available as a living model for sex education!"

He shrugged. "Suit yourself. But it's a hell of a loss to my education."

"You don't need educating," she muttered. "You were married."

He nodded. "Sure I was." He pursed his lips and let his eyes run lazily over her body. "Except that she never wanted me, before or after I married her."

Amanda's lips parted. "Oh, Quinn," she said softly. "I'm sorry."

"So was I, at the time." He shook his head. "I used to wonder at first why she pulled back every time I kissed her. I guess she was suffering it until she could get me to put the ring on her finger. Up until then, I thought it was her scruples that kept me at arm's length. But she never had many morals." He stared at Amanda curiously, surprised at how easy it was to tell her things he'd never shared with another human being. "After I found out what she really was, I couldn't have cared less about sharing her bed."

"No, I don't suppose so," she agreed.

He lifted the cigarette to his lips and his eyes narrowed as he studied her. "Elliot's almost thirteen," he said. "He's been my whole life. I've taken care of him and done for him. He knows there's no blood tie between us, but I love him and he loves me. In all the important ways, I'm his father and he's my son."

"He loves you very much," she said with a smile. "He talks about you all the time."

"He's a good boy." He moved a little closer, noticing how she tensed when he came close. He liked that reaction a lot. It told him that she was aware of him, but shy and reticent. "You don't have men," he said softly. "Well, I don't have women."

"Not for…a few months?" she stammered, because she couldn't imagine that he was telling the truth.

He shrugged his powerful shoulders. "Well, not for a bit longer than that. Not much opportunity up here. And I can't go off and leave Elliot while I tomcat around town. It's been a bit longer than thirteen years."

"A bit?"

He looked down at her with a curious, mocking smile. "When I was a boy, I didn't know how to get girls. I was big and clumsy and shy, so it was the other boys who scored." He took another draw, a slightly jerky one, from his cigarette. "I still have the same problem around most women. It's not so much hatred as a lack of ability, and shyness. I don't know how to come on to a woman," he confessed with a faint smile.

Amanda felt as if the sun had just come out. She smiled back. "Don't you, really?" she asked softly. "I thought it was just that you found me lacking, or that I wasn't woman enough to interest you."

He could have laughed out loud at that assumption. "Is

that why you called me Goody Two-Shoes?" he asked pleasantly.

She laughed softly. "Well, that was sort of sour grapes." She lowered her eyes to his chest. "It hurt my feelings that you thought I didn't have any morals, when I'd never made one single move toward any other man in my whole life."

He felt warm all over from that shy confession. It took down the final brick in his wall of reserve. She wasn't like any woman he'd ever known. "I'm glad to know that. But you and I have more in common than a lack of technique," he said, hesitating.

"We do?" she asked. Her soft eyes held his. "What do you mean?"

He turned and deliberately put out his cigarette in the ashtray on the table beside them. He straightened and looked down at her speculatively for a few seconds before he went for broke. "Well, what I mean, Amanda," he replied finally, "is that you aren't the only virgin on the place."

Chapter Six

"I didn't hear that," Amanda said, because she knew she hadn't. Quinn Sutton couldn't have told her that he was a virgin.

"Yes, you did," he replied. "And it's not all that far-fetched. Old McNaber down the hill's never had a woman, and he's in his seventies. There are all sorts of reasons why men don't get experience. Morals, scruples, isolation, or even plain shyness. Just like women," he added with a meaningful look at Amanda. "I couldn't go to bed with somebody just to say I'd had sex. I'd have to care about her, want her, and I'd want her to care about me. There are idealistic people all over the world who never find that particular combination, so they stay celibate. And really, I think that people who sleep around indiscriminately are in the minority even in these liberated times. Only a fool takes that sort of risk with the health dangers what they are."

"Yes, I know." She watched him with fascinated eyes. "Haven't you ever…wanted to?" she asked.

"Well, that's the problem, you see," he replied, his dark eyes steady on her face.

"What is?"

"I have…wanted to. With you."

She leaned back against the counter, just to make sure she didn't fall down. "With me?"

"That first night you came here, when I was so sick, and your hair drifted down over my naked chest. I shivered, and you thought it was with fever," he mused. "It was a fever, all right, but it didn't have anything to do with the virus."

Her fingers clenched the counter. She'd wondered about his violent reaction at the time, but it seemed so unlikely that a cold man like Quinn Sutton would feel that way about a woman. He was human, she thought absently, watching him.

"That's why I've given you such a hard time," he confessed with narrowed, quiet eyes. "I don't know how to handle desire. I can't throw you over my shoulder and carry you upstairs, not with Elliot and Harry around, even if you were the kind of woman I thought at first you were. The fact that you're as innocent as I am only makes it more complicated."

She looked at him with new understanding, as fascinated by him as he seemed to be by her. He wasn't that bad looking, she mused. And he was terribly strong, and sexy in an earthy kind of way. She especially liked his eyes. They were much more expressive than that poker face.

"Fortunately for you, I'm kind of shy, too," she murmured.

"Except when you're asking men to take their clothes off," Quinn said, nodding.

Harry froze in the doorway with one foot lifted while Amanda gaped at him and turned red.

"Put your foot down and get busy," Quinn muttered irritably. "Why were you standing there?"

"I was getting educated." Harry chuckled. "I didn't know Amanda asked people to take their clothes off!"

"Only me," Quinn said, defending her. "And just my shirt. She's not a bad girl."

"Will you stop!" Amanda buried her face in her hands. "Go away!"

"I can't. I live here," Quinn pointed out. "Did I smell brandy on your breath?" he asked suddenly.

Harry grimaced even as Amanda's eyes widened. "Well, yes you do," he confessed. "She was upset and crying and all…"

"How much did you give her?" Quinn persisted.

"Only a few drops," Harry promised. "In her coffee, to calm her."

"Harry, how could you!" Amanda laughed. The coffee had tasted funny, but she'd been too upset to wonder why.

"Sorry," Harry murmured dryly. "But it seemed the thing to do."

"It backfired," Quinn murmured and actually smiled.

"You stop that!" Amanda told him. She sat down at the table. "I'm not tipsy. Harry, I'll peel those apples for the pie if I can have a knife."

"Let me get out of the room first, if you please," Quinn said, glancing at her dryly. "I saw her measuring my back for a place to put it."

"I almost never stab men with knives," she promised impishly.

He chuckled. He reached for his hat and slanted it over his brow, buttoning his old shepherd's coat because it was snowing outside again.

Amanda looked past him, the reason for all the upset coming back now as she calmed down. Her expression became sad.

"If you stay busy, you won't think about it so much," Quinn said quietly. "It's part of life, you know."

"I know." She managed a smile. "I'm fine. Despite Harry," she added with a chuckle, watching Harry squirm before he grinned back.

Quinn's dark eyes met hers warmly for longer than he meant, so that she blushed. He tore his eyes away finally, and went outside.

Harry didn't say anything, but his smile was speculative.

Elliot came home from school and persuaded Amanda

to get out the keyboard and give him some more pointers. He admitted that he'd been bragging about her to his classmates and that she was a professional musician.

"Where do you play, Amanda?" Elliot asked curiously, and he stared at her with open puzzlement. "You look so familiar somehow."

She sat very still on the sofa and tried to stay calm. Elliot had already told her that he liked rock music and she knew Quinn had hidden his tapes. If there was a tape in his collection by Desperado, it would have her picture on the cover along with that of her group.

"Do I really look familiar?" she asked with a smile. "Maybe I just have that kind of face."

"Have you played with orchestras?" he persisted.

"No. Just by myself, sort of. In nightclubs," she improvised. Well, she had once sung in a nightclub, to fill in for a friend. "Mostly I do backup. You know, I play with groups for people who make tapes and records."

"Wow!" he exclaimed. "I guess you know a lot of famous singers and musicians?"

"A few," she agreed.

"Where do you work?"

"In New York City, in Nashville," she told him. "All over. Wherever I can find work."

He ran his fingers up and down the keyboard. "How did you ever wind up here?"

"I needed a rest," she said. "My aunt is…a friend of Mr.

Durning. She asked him if I could borrow the cabin, and he said it was all right. I had to get away from work for a while."

"This doesn't bother you, does it? Teaching me to play, I mean?" he asked and looked concerned.

"No, Elliot, it doesn't bother me. I'm enjoying it." She ran a scale and taught it to him, then showed him the cadences of the chords that went with it.

"It's so complicated," he moaned.

"Of course it is. Music is an art form, and it's complex. But once you learn these basics, you can do anything with a chord. For instance..."

She played a tonic chord, then made an impromptu song from its subdominant and seventh chords and the second inversion of them. Elliot watched, fascinated.

"I guess you've studied for years," he said with a sigh.

"Yes, I have, and I'm still learning," she said. "But I love it more than anything. Music has been my whole life."

"No wonder you're so good at it."

She smiled. "Thanks, Elliot."

"Well, I'd better get my chores done before supper," he said, sighing. He handed Amanda the keyboard. "See you later."

She nodded. He went out. Harry was feeding the two calves that were still alive, so presumably he'd tell Elliot about the one that had died. Amanda hadn't had the heart to talk about it.

Her fingers ran over the keyboard lovingly and she

began to play a song that her group had recorded two years back, a sad, dreamy ballad about hopeless love that had won them a Grammy. She sang it softly, her pure, sweet voice haunting in the silence of the room as she tried to sing for the first time in weeks.

"Elliot, for Pete's sake, turn that radio down, I'm on the telephone!" came a pleading voice from the back of the house.

She stopped immediately, flushing. She hadn't realized that Harry had come back inside. Thank God he hadn't seen her, or he might have asked some pertinent questions. She put the keyboard down and went to the kitchen, relieved that her singing voice was back to normal again.

Elliot was morose at the supper table. He'd heard about the calf and he'd been as depressed as Amanda had. Quinn didn't look all that happy himself. They all picked at the delicious chili Harry had whipped up; nobody had much of an appetite.

After they finished, Elliot did his homework while Amanda put the last stitches into a chair cover she was making for the living room. Quinn had gone off to do his paperwork and Harry was making bread for the next day.

It was a long, lazy night. Elliot went to bed at eight-thirty and not much later Harry went to his room.

Amanda wanted to wait for Quinn to come back, but something in her was afraid of the new way he looked at her. He was much more a threat now than he had been before, because she was looking at him with new and interested eyes. She was drawn to him more than ever. But he didn't know who she really was, and she couldn't tell him. If she were persuaded into any kind of close relationship with him, it could lead to disaster.

So when Elliot went to bed, so did Amanda. She sat at the dresser and let down her long hair, brushing it with slow, lazy strokes, when there was a knock at the door.

She was afraid that it might be Quinn, and she hesitated. But surely he wouldn't make any advances toward her unless she showed that she wanted them. Of course he wouldn't.

She opened the door, but it wasn't Quinn. It was Elliot. And as he stared at her, wheels moved and gears clicked in his young mind. She was wearing a long granny gown in a deep beige, a shade that was too much like the color of the leather dress she wore onstage. With her hair loose and the color of the gown, Elliot made the connection he hadn't made the first time he saw her hair down.

"Yes?" she prompted, puzzled by the way he was looking at her. "Is something wrong, Elliot?"

"Uh, no," he stammered. "Uh, I forgot to say goodnight. Good night!" He grinned.

He turned, red-faced, and beat a hasty retreat, but not to his own room. He went to his father's and searched quickly through the hidden tapes until he found the one he wanted. He held it up, staring blankly at the cover.

There were four men who looked like vicious bikers surrounding a beautiful woman in buckskin with long, elegant, blond hair. The group was one of his favorites—Desperado. And the woman was Mandy. Amanda. His Amanda. He caught his breath. Boy, would she be in for it if his dad found out who she was! He put the tape into his pocket, feeling guilty for taking it when Quinn had told him not to. But these were desperate circumstances. He had to protect Amanda until he could figure out how to tell her that he knew the truth. Meanwhile, having her in the same house with him was sheer undiluted heaven! Imagine, a singing star that famous in his house. If only he could tell the guys! But that was too risky, because it might get back to Dad. He sighed. Just his luck, to find a rare jewel and have to hide it to keep someone from stealing it. He closed the door to Quinn's bedroom and went quickly back to his own.

Amanda slept soundly, almost missing breakfast. Outside, the sky looked blue for the first time in days, and she noticed that the snow had stopped.

"Chinook's coming," Harry said with a grin. "I knew it would."

Quinn's dark eyes studied Amanda's face. "Well, it will be a few days before they get the power lines back up again," he muttered. "So don't get in an uproar about it."

"I'm not in an uproar," Harry returned with a frown. "I just thought it was nice that we'll be able to get off the mountain and lay in some more supplies. I'm getting tired of beef. I want a chicken."

"So do I!" Elliot said fervently. "Or bear, or beaver or moose, anything but beef!"

Quinn glared at both of them. "Beef pays the bills around here," he reminded them.

They looked so guilty that Amanda almost laughed out loud.

"I'm sorry, Dad," Elliot sighed. "I'll tell my stomach to shut up about it."

Quinn's hard face relaxed. "It's all right. I wouldn't mind a chicken stew, myself."

"That's the spirit," Elliot said. "What are we going to do today? It's Saturday," he pointed out. "No school."

"You could go out with me and help me feed cattle," Quinn said.

"I'll stay here and help Harry," Amanda said, too quickly.

Quinn's dark eyes searched hers. "Harry can manage by himself. You can come with me and Elliot."

"You'll enjoy it," Elliot assured her. "It's a lot of fun. The cattle see us and come running. Well, as well as they can run in several feet of snow," he amended.

It was fun, too. Amanda sat on the back of the sled with Elliot and helped push the bales of hay off. Quinn cut the strings so the cattle could get to the hay. They did come running, reminding Amanda so vividly of women at a sale that she laughed helplessly until the others had to be told why she was laughing.

They came back from the outing in a new kind of harmony, and for the first time, Amanda understood what it felt like to be part of a family. She looked at Quinn and wondered how it would be if she never had to leave here, if she could stay with him and Elliot and Harry forever.

But she couldn't, she told herself firmly. She had to remember that this was a vacation, with the real world just outside the door.

Elliot was allowed to stay up later on Saturday night, so they watched a science-fiction movie together while Quinn grumbled over paperwork. The next morning they went to church on the sled, Amanda in the one skirt and blouse she'd packed, trying not to look too conspicuous as Quinn's few neighbors carefully scrutinized her.

When they got back home, she was all but shaking. She felt uncomfortable living with him, as if she really was a fallen woman now. He cornered her in the kitchen while she was washing dishes to find out why she was so quiet.

"I didn't think about the way people would react if you went with us this morning," he said quietly. "I wouldn't have subjected you to that if I'd just thought."

"It's okay," she said, touched by his concern. "Really. It was just a little uncomfortable."

He sighed, searching her face with narrowed eyes. "Most people around here know how I feel about women," he said bluntly. "That was why you attracted so much attention. People get funny ideas about woman haters who take in beautiful blondes."

"I'm not beautiful," she stammered shyly.

He stepped toward her, towering over her in his dress slacks and good white shirt and sedate gray tie. He looked handsome and strong and very masculine. She liked the spicy cologne he wore. "You're beautiful, all right," he murmured. His big hand touched her cheek, sliding down it slowly, his thumb brushing with soft abrasion over her full mouth.

Her breath caught as she looked up into his dark, soft eyes. "Quinn?" she whispered.

He drew her hands out of the warm, soapy water, still holding her gaze, and dried them on a dishcloth. Then he guided them, first one, then the other, up to his shoulders.

"Hold me," he whispered as his hands smoothed over her waist and brought her gently to him. "I want to kiss you."

She shivered from the sensuality in that soft whisper, lifting her face willingly.

He bent, brushing his mouth lazily over hers. "Isn't this how we did it before?" he breathed, parting his lips as they touched hers. "I like the way it feels to kiss you like this. My spine tingles."

"So…does mine." She slid her hands hesitantly into the thick, cool strands of hair at his nape and she went on tiptoe to give him better access to her mouth.

He accepted the invitation with quiet satisfaction, his mouth growing slowly rougher and hungrier as it fed on hers. He made a sound under his breath and all at once he bent, lifting her clear off the floor in a bearish embrace. His mouth bit hers, parting her lips, and she clung to him, moaning as the fever burned in her, too.

He let her go at once when Elliot called, "What?" from the living room. "Amanda, did you say something?"

"No... No, Elliot," she managed in a tone pitched a little higher than normal. Her answer appeared to satisfy him, because he didn't ask again. Harry was outside, but he probably wouldn't stay there long.

She looked up at Quinn, surprised by the intent stare he was giving her. He liked the way she looked, her face flushed, her mouth swollen from his kisses, her eyes wide and soft and faintly misty with emotion.

"I'd better get out of here," he said hesitantly.

"Yes." She touched her lips with her fingers and he watched the movement closely.

"Did I hurt your mouth?" he asked quietly.

She shook her head. "No. Oh, no, not at all," she said huskily.

Quinn nodded and sighed heavily. He smiled faintly and then turned and went back into the living room without another word.

It was a long afternoon, made longer by the strain Amanda felt being close to him. She found her eyes meeting his across the room and every time she flushed from the intensity of the look. Her body was hungry for him, and she imagined the reverse was equally true. He watched her openly now, with smoldering hunger in his eyes. They had a light supper and watched a little more television. But when Harry went to his room and Elliot called good-night and went up to bed, Amanda weakly stayed behind.

Quinn finished his cigarette with the air of a man who had all night, and then got up and reached for Amanda, lifting her into his arms.

"There's nothing to be afraid of," he said quietly, searching her wide, apprehensive eyes as he turned and carried her into his study and closed the door behind them.

It was a fiercely masculine room. The furniture was dark wood with leather seats, the remnants of more prosperous times. He sat down in a big leather armchair with Amanda in his lap.

"It's private here," he explained. His hand moved one of hers to his shirt and pressed it there, over the tie. "Even Elliot doesn't come in when the door's shut. Do you still want to take my shirt off?" he asked with a warm smile.

Amanda sighed. "Well, yes," she stammered. "I haven't done this sort of thing before...."

"Neither have I, honey," he murmured dryly. "I guess we'll learn it together, won't we?"

She smiled into his dark eyes. "That sounds nice." She

lowered her eyes to the tie and frowned when she saw how it was knotted.

"Here, I'll do it." He whipped it off with the ease of long practice and unlooped the collar button. "Now. You do the rest," he said deeply, and looked like a man anticipating heaven.

Her fingers, so adept on a keyboard, fumbled like two left feet while she worried buttons out of buttonholes. He was heavily muscled, tanned skin under a mass of thick, curling black hair. She remembered how it had looked that first night she'd been here, and how her hands had longed to touch it. Odd, because she'd never cared what was under a man's shirt before.

She pressed her hands flat against him, fascinated by the quick thunder of his heartbeat under them. She looked up into dark, quiet eyes.

"Shy?" he murmured dryly.

"A little. I always used to run a mile when men got this close."

The smile faded. His big hand covered hers, pressing them closer against him. "Wasn't there ever anyone you wanted?"

She shook her head. "The men I'm used to aren't like you. They're mostly rounders with a line a mile long. Everything is just casual to them, like eating mints." She flushed a little. "Intimacy isn't a casual thing to me."

"Or to me." His chest rose and fell heavily. He touched her bright head. "Now will you take your hair down, Amanda?" he asked gently. "I've dreamed about it for days."

Amanda smiled softly. "Have you, really? It's something of a nuisance to wash and dry, but I've gotten sort of used to it." She unbraided it and let it down, enchanted by Quinn's rapt fascination with it. His big hands tangled in it, as if he loved the feel of it. He brought his face down and kissed her neck through it, drawing her against his bare chest.

"It smells like flowers," he whispered.

"I washed it before church this morning," she replied. "Elliot loaned me his blow-dryer but it still took all of thirty minutes to get the dampness out." She relaxed with a sigh, nuzzling against his shoulder while her fingers tugged at the thick hair on his chest. "You feel furry. Like a bear," she murmured.

"You feel silky," he said against her hair. With his hand, Quinn tilted her face up to his and slid his mouth onto hers in the silent room. He groaned softly as her lips parted under his. His arms lifted and turned her, wrapped her up, so that her breasts were lying on his chest and her cheek was pressed against his shoulder by the force of the kiss.

He tasted of smoke and coffee, and if his mouth wasn't expert, it was certainly ardent. She loved kissing him. She curled her arms around his neck and turned a little more, hesitating when she felt the sudden stark arousal of his body.

Her eyes opened, looking straight into his, and she colored.

"I'm sorry," he murmured, starting to shift her, as if his physical reaction to her embarrassed him.

"No, Quinn," she said, resisting gently, holding his gaze as she relaxed into him, shivering a little. "There's nothing to apologize for. I…like knowing you want me," she whispered, lowering her eyes to his mouth. "It just takes a little getting used to. I've never let anyone hold me like this."

His chest swelled with that confession. His cheek rested on her hair as he settled into the chair and relaxed himself, taking her weight easily. "I'm glad about that," he said. "But it isn't just physical with me. I wanted you to know."

She smiled against his shoulder. "It isn't just physical with me, either." She touched his hard face, her fingers moving over his mouth, loving the feel of it, the smell of his body, the warmth and strength of it. "Isn't it incredible?" She laughed softly. "I mean, at our ages, to be so green…"

He laughed, too. It would have stung to have heard that from any other woman, but Amanda was different. "I've never minded less being inexperienced," he murmured.

"Oh, neither have I." She sighed contentedly.

His big hand smoothed over her shoulder and down her back to her waist and onto her rib cage. He wanted very much to run it over her soft breast, but that might be too much too soon, so he hesitated.

Amanda smiled to herself. She caught his fingers and, lifting her face to his eyes, deliberately pulled them onto her breast, her lips parting at the sensation that steely warmth imparted. The nipple hardened and she caught her breath as Quinn's thumb rubbed against it.

"Have you ever seen a woman…without her top on?" she whispered, her long hair gloriously tangled around her face and shoulders.

"No," he replied softly. "Only in pictures." His dark eyes watched the softness his fingers were tracing. "I want to see you that way. I want to touch your skin… like this."

She drew his hand to the buttons of her blouse and lay quietly against him, watching his hard face as he loosened the buttons and pulled the fabric aside. The bra seemed to fascinate him. He frowned, trying to decide how it opened.

"It's a front catch," she whispered. She shifted a little, and found the catch. Her fingers trembled as she loosened it. Then, watching him, she carefully peeled it away from the high, taut throb of her breasts and watched him catch his breath.

"My God," he breathed reverently. He touched her with trembling fingers, his eyes on the deep mauve of her nipples against the soft pink thrust of flesh, his body taut with sudden aching longing. "My God, I've never seen anything so beautiful."

He made her feel incredibly feminine. She closed her eyes and arched back against his encircling arm, moaning softly.

"Kiss me...there," she whispered huskily, aching for his mouth.

"Amanda..." He bent, delighting in her femininity, the obvious rapt fascination of the first time in her actions so that even if he hadn't suspected her innocence he would have now. His lips brushed over the silky flesh, and his hands lifted her to him, arched her even more. She tasted of flower petals, softly trembling under his warm, ardent mouth, her breath jerking past her parted lips as she lay with her eyes closed, lost in him.

"It's so sweet, Quinn," she whispered brokenly.

His lips brushed up her body to her throat, her chin, and then they locked against her mouth. He turned her slowly, so that her soft breasts lay against the muted thunder of his hair-roughened chest. He felt her shiver before her arms slid around his neck and she deliberately pressed closer, drawing herself against him and moaning.

"Am I hurting you?" he asked huskily, his mouth poised just above hers, a faint tremor in his arms. "Amanda, am I hurting you?"

"No." She opened her eyes and they were like black pools, soft and deep and quiet. With her blond hair waving at her temples, her cheeks, her shoulders, she was so beautiful that Quinn's breath caught.

He sat just looking at her, indulging his hunger for the sight of her soft breasts, her lovely face. She lay quietly in his arms without a protest, barely breathing as the spell worked on them.

"I'll live on this the rest of my life," he said roughly, his voice deep and soft in the room, with only an occasional crackle from the burning fire in the potbellied stove to break the silence.

"So will I," she whispered. She reached up to his face, touching it in silence, adoring its strength. "We shouldn't have done this," she said miserably. "It will make it...so much more difficult, when I have to leave. The thaw...!"

His fingers pressed against her lips. "One day at a time," he said. "Even if you leave, you aren't getting away from me completely. I won't let go. Not ever."

Tears stung her eyes. The surplus of emotion sent them streaming down her cheeks and Quinn caught his breath, brushing them away with his long fingers.

"Why?" he whispered.

"Nobody ever wanted to keep me before," she explained with a watery smile. "I've always felt like an extra person in the world."

He found that hard to imagine, as beautiful as she was. Perhaps her reticence made her of less value to sophisticated men, but not to him. He found her a pearl beyond price.

"You're not an extra person in my world," he replied. "You fit."

She sighed and nuzzled against him, closing her eyes as she drank in the exquisite pleasure of skin against skin, feeling his heart beat against her breasts. She shivered.

"Are you cold?" he asked.

"No. It's...so wonderful, feeling you like this," she whispered. "Quinn?"

He eased her back in his arm and watched her, understanding as she didn't seem to understand what was wrong.

His big, warm hand covered her breast, gently caressing it. "It's desire," he whispered softly. "You want me."

"Yes," she whispered.

"You can't have me. Not like this. Not in any honorable way." He sighed heavily and lifted her against him to hold her, very hard. "Now hold on, real tight. It will pass."

She shivered helplessly, drowning in the warmth of his body, in its heat against her breasts. But he was right. Slowly the ache began to ease away and her body stilled with a huge sigh.

"How do you know so much when you've...when you've never...?"

"I told you, I read a book. Several books." He chuckled, the laughter rippling over her sensitive breasts. "But, my God, reading was never like this!"

She laughed, too, and impishly bit his shoulder right through the cloth.

Then he shivered. "Don't," he said huskily.

She lifted her head, fascinated by the expression on his face. "Do you like it?" she asked hesitantly.

"Yes, I like it," he said with a rueful smile. "All too much." He gazed down at her bareness and his eyes darkened. "I like looking at your breasts, too, but I think we'd better stop this while we can."

He tugged the bra back around her with a grimace and hooked the complicated catch. He deftly buttoned her blouse up to her throat, his eyes twinkling as they met hers.

"Disappointed?" he murmured. "So am I. I have these dreams every night of pillowing you on your delicious hair while we make love until you cry out."

She could picture that, too, and her breath lodged in her throat as she searched his dark eyes. His body, bare and moving softly over hers on white sheets, his face above her…

She moaned.

"Oh, I want it, too," he whispered, touching his mouth with exquisite tenderness to hers. "You in my bed, your arms around me, the mattress moving under us." He lifted his head, breathing unsteadily. "I might have to hurt you a little at first," he said gruffly. "You understand?"

"Yes." She smoothed his shirt, absently drawing it back together and fastening the buttons with a sense of possession. "But only a little, and I could bear it for what would come afterward," she said, looking up. "Because you'd pleasure me then."

"My God, would I," he whispered. "Pleasure you until you were exhausted." He framed her face in his hands and kissed her gently. "Please go to bed, Amanda, before I double over and start screaming."

She smiled against his mouth and let him put her on her feet. She laughed when she swayed and he had to catch her.

"See what you do to me?" she mused. "Make me dizzy."

"Not half as dizzy as you make me." He smoothed down her long hair, his eyes adoring it. "Pretty little thing," he murmured.

"I'm glad you like me," she replied. "I'll do my best to stay this way for the next fifty years or so, with a few minor wrinkles."

"You'll be beautiful to me when you're an old lady. Good night."

She moved away from him with flattering reluctance, her dark eyes teasing his. "Are you sure you haven't done this before?" she asked with a narrow gaze. "You're awfully good at it for a beginner."

"That makes two of us," he returned dryly.

She liked the way he looked, with his hair mussed and his thin mouth swollen from her kisses, and his shirt disheveled. It made her feel a new kind of pride that she could disarrange him so nicely. After one long glance, she opened the door and went out.

"Lock your door," he whispered.

She laughed delightedly. "No, you lock yours the way you did the other night."

He shifted uncomfortably. "That was a low blow. I'm sorry."

"Oh, I was flattered," she corrected. "I've never felt so dangerous in all my life. I wish I had one of those long, black silk negligees…"

"Will you get out of here?" he asked pleasantly. "I think I did mention the urge to throw you on the floor and ravish you?"

"With Elliot right upstairs? Fie, sir, think of my reputation."

"I'm trying to, if you'll just go to bed!"

"Very well, if I must." She started up the staircase, her black eyes dancing as they met his. She tossed her hair back and smiled at him. "Good night, Quinn."

"Good night, Amanda. Sweet dreams."

"They'll be sweet from now on," she agreed. She turned reluctantly and went up the staircase. He watched her until she went into her room and closed the door.

It wasn't until she was in her own room that she realized just what she'd done.

She wasn't some nice domestic little thing who could fit into Quinn's world without any effort. She was Amanda Corrie Callaway, who belonged to a rock group with a worldwide reputation. On most streets in most cities, her face was instantly recognizable. How was Quinn going to take the knowledge of who she really was—and the fact that she'd deceived him by leading him to think she was just a vacationing keyboard player? She groaned as she put on her gown. It didn't bear thinking about. From sweet heaven to nightmare in one hour was too much.

Chapter Seven

Amanda hardly slept from the combined shock of Quinn's ardor and her own guilt. How could she tell him the truth now? What could she say that would take away the sting of her deceit?

She dressed in jeans and the same button-up pink blouse she'd worn the night before and went down to breakfast.

Quinn looked up as she entered the room, his eyes warm and quiet.

"Good morning," she said brightly.

"Good morning yourself," Quinn murmured with a smile. "Sleep well?"

"Barely a wink," she said, sighing, her own eyes holding his.

He chuckled, averting his gaze before Elliot became suspicious. "Harry's out feeding your calves," he said, "and I'm on my way over to Eagle Pass to help one of my neighbors feed some stranded cattle. You'll have to stay with Elliot—it's teacher workday."

"I forgot," Elliot wailed, head in hands. "Can you imagine that I actually forgot? I could have slept until noon!"

"There, there," Amanda said, patting his shoulder. "Don't you want to learn some more chords?"

"Is that what you do?" Quinn asked curiously, because now every scrap of information he learned about her was precious. "You said you played a keyboard for a living. Do you teach music?"

"Not really," she said gently. "I play backup for various groups," she explained. "That rock music you hate…" she began uneasily.

"That's all right," Quinn replied, his face open and kind. "I was just trying to get a rise out of you. I don't mind it all that much, I guess. And playing backup isn't the same thing as putting on those god-awful costumes and singing suggestive lyrics. Well, I'm gone. Stay out of trouble, you two," he said as he got to his feet in the middle of Amanda's instinctive move to speak, to correct his assumption that all she did was play backup. She wanted to tell him the truth, but he winked at her and Elliot and got into his outdoor clothes before she could find a way to break the news. By the time her mind was working again, he was gone.

She sat back down, sighing. "Oh, Elliot, what a mess," she murmured, her chin in her hands.

"Is that what you call it?" he asked with a wicked smile. "Dad's actually grinning, and when he looked at you, you blushed. I'm not blind, you know. Do you like him, even if he isn't Mr. America?"

"Yes, I like him," she said with a shy smile, lowering her eyes. "He's a pretty special guy."

"I think so, myself. Eat your breakfast. I want to ask you about some new chords."

"Okay."

They were working on the keyboard when the sound of an approaching vehicle caught Amanda's attention. Quinn hadn't driven anything motorized since the snow had gotten so high.

"That's odd," Elliot said, peering out the window curtain. "It's a four-wheel drive... Oh, boy." He glanced at Amanda. "You aren't gonna like this."

She lifted her eyebrows. "I'm not?" she asked, puzzled.

The knock at the back door had Harry moving toward it before Amanda and Elliot could. Harry opened it and looked up and up and up. He stood there staring while Elliot gaped at the grizzly-looking man who loomed over him in a black Western costume, complete with hat.

"I'm looking for Mandy Callaway," he boomed.

"Hank!"

Amanda ran to the big man without thinking, to be

lifted high in the air while he chuckled and kissed her warmly on one cheek, his whiskers scratching.

"Hello, peanut!" he grinned. "What are you doing up here? The old trapper down the hill said you hadn't been in Durning's cabin since the heavy snow came."

"Mr. Sutton took me in and gave me a roof over my head. Put me down," she fussed, wiggling.

He put her back on her feet while Harry and Elliot still gaped.

"This is Hank," she said, holding his enormous hand as she turned to face the others. "He's a good friend, and a terrific musician, and I'd really appreciate it if you wouldn't tell Quinn he was here just yet. I'll tell him myself. Okay?"

"Sure," Harry murmured. He shook his head. "You for real, or do you have stilts in them boots?"

"I used to be a linebacker for the Dallas Cowboys." Hank grinned.

"That would explain it," Harry chuckled. "Your secret's safe with me, Amanda." He excused himself and went to do the washing.

"Me, too," Elliot said, grinning, "as long as I get Mr. Shoeman's autograph before he leaves."

Amanda let out a long breath, her eyes frightened as they met Elliot's.

"That's right," Elliot said. "I already knew you were Mandy Callaway. I've got a Desperado tape. I took it out of Dad's drawer and hid it as soon as I recognized you. You'll tell him when the time's right. Won't you?"

"Yes, I will, Elliot," she agreed. "I'd have done it already except that…well, things have gotten a little complicated."

"You can say that again." Elliot led the way into the living room, watching Hank sit gingerly on a sofa that he dwarfed. "I'll just go make sure that tape's hidden," he said, leaving them alone.

"Complicated, huh?" Hank said. "I hear this Sutton man's a real woman hater."

"He was until just recently." She folded her hands in her lap. "And he doesn't approve of rock music." She sighed and changed the subject. "What's up, Hank?"

"We've got a gig at Larry's Lodge," he said. "I know, you don't want to. Listen for a minute. It's to benefit cystic fibrosis, and a lot of other stars are going to be in town for it, including a few pretty well-known singers." He named some of them and Amanda whistled. "See what I mean? It's strictly charity, or I wouldn't have come up here bothering you. The boys and I want to do it." His dark eyes narrowed. "Are you up to it?"

"I don't know. I tried to sing here a couple of times, and my voice seems to be good enough. No more lapses. But in front of a crowd…" She spread her hands. "I don't know, Hank."

"Here." He handed her three tickets to the benefit. "You think about it. If you can, come on up. Sutton might like

the singers even if he doesn't care for our kind of music."
He studied her. "You haven't told him, have you?"

She shook her head, smiling wistfully. "Haven't found
the right way yet. If I leave it much longer, it may be too
late."

"The girl's family sent you a letter," he said. "Thanking
you for what you tried to do. They said you were her
heroine...aw, now, Mandy, stop it!"

She collapsed in tears. He held her, rocking her, his face
red with mingled embarrassment and guilt.

"Mandy, come on, stop that," he muttered. "It's all over
and done with. You've got to get yourself together. You
can't hide out here in the Tetons for the rest of your life."

"Can't I?" she wailed.

"No, you can't. Hiding isn't your style. You have to face
the stage again, or you'll never get over it." He tilted her
wet face. "Look, would you want somebody eating her
guts out over you if you'd been Wendy that night? It
wasn't your fault, damn it! It wasn't anybody's fault; it was
an accident, pure and simple."

"If she hadn't been at the concert..."

"If, if, if," he said curtly. "You can't go back and change
things to suit you. It was her time. At the concert, on a
plane, in a car, however, it would still have been her time.
Are you listening to me, Mandy?"

She dabbed her eyes with the hem of her blouse. "Yes,
I'm listening."

"Come on, girl. Buck up. You can get over this if you set your mind to it. Me and the guys miss you, Mandy. It's not the same with just the four of us. People are scared of us when you aren't around."

That made her smile. "I guess they are. You do look scruffy, Hank," she murmured.

"You ought to see Johnson." He sighed. "He's let his beard go and he looks like a scrub brush. And Deke says he won't change clothes until you come back."

"Oh, my God," Amanda said, shuddering, "tell him I'll think hard about this concert, okay? You poor guys. Stay upwind of him."

"We're trying." He got up, smiling down at her. "Everything's okay. You can see the letter when you come to the lodge. It's real nice. Now stop beating yourself. Nobody else blames you. After all, babe, you risked your life trying to save her. Nobody's forgotten that, either."

She leaned against him for a minute, drawing on his strength. "Thanks, Hank."

"Anytime. Hey, kid, you still want that autograph?" he asked.

Elliot came back into the room with a pad and pen. "Do I!" he said, chuckling.

Hank scribbled his name and Desperado's curlicue logo underneath. "There you go."

"He's a budding musician," Amanda said, putting an arm around Elliot. "I'm teaching him the keyboard. One of these days, if we can get around Quinn, we'll have him playing backup for me."

"You bet." Hank chuckled, and ruffled Elliot's red hair. "Keep at it. Mandy's the very best. If she teaches you, you're taught."

"Thanks, Mr. Shoeman."

"Just Hank. See you at the concert. So long, Mandy."

"So long, pal."

"What concert?" Elliot asked excitedly when Hank had driven away.

Amanda handed him the three tickets. "To a benefit in Jackson Hole. The group's going to play there. Maybe. If I can get up enough nerve to get back onstage again."

"What happened, Amanda?" he asked gently.

She searched his face, seeing compassion along with the curiosity, so she told him, fighting tears all the way.

"Gosh, no wonder you came up here to get away," Elliot said with more than his twelve years worth of wisdom. He shrugged. "But like he said, you have to go back someday. The longer you wait, the harder it's going to be."

"I know that," she groaned. "But Elliot, I…" She took a deep breath and looked down at the floor. "I love your father," she said, admitting it at last. "I love him very much, and the minute he finds out who I am, my life is over."

"Maybe not," he said. "You've got another week until the concert. Surely in all that time you can manage to tell him the truth. Can't you?"

"I hope so," she said with a sad smile. "You don't mind who I am, do you?" she asked worriedly.

"Don't be silly." He hugged her warmly. "I think you're super, keyboard or not."

She laughed and hugged him back. "Well, that's half the battle."

"Just out of curiosity," Harry asked from the doorway, "who was the bearded giant?"

"That was Hank Shoeman," Elliot told him. "He's the drummer for Desperado. It's a rock group. And Amanda—"

"—plays backup for him," she volunteered, afraid to give too much away to Harry.

"Well, I'll be. He's a musician?" Harry shook his head. "Would have took him for a bank robber," he mumbled.

"Most people do, and you should see the rest of the group." She grinned. "Don't give me away, Harry, okay? I promise I'll tell Quinn, but I've got to do it the right way."

"I can see that," he agreed easily. "Be something of a shock to him to meet your friend after dark, I imagine."

"I imagine so," she said, chuckling. "Thanks, Harry."

"My pleasure. Desperado, huh? Suits it, if the rest of the group looks like he does."

"Worse," she said, and shuddered.

"Strains the mind, don't it?" Harry went off into the kitchen and Amanda got up after a minute to help him get lunch.

Quinn wasn't back until late that afternoon. Nobody

mentioned Hank's visit, but Amanda was nervous and her manner was strained as she tried not to show her fears.

"What's wrong with you?" he asked gently during a lull in the evening while Elliot did homework and Harry washed up. "You don't seem like yourself tonight."

She moved close to him, her fingers idly touching the sleeve of his red flannel shirt. "It's thawing outside," she said, watching her fingers move on the fabric. "It won't be long before I'll be gone."

He sighed heavily. His fingers captured hers and held them. "I've been thinking about that. Do you really have to get back?"

She felt her heart jump. Whatever he was offering, she wanted to say yes and let the future take care of itself. But she couldn't. She grimaced. "Yes, I have to get back," she said miserably. "I have commitments to people. Things I promised to do." Her fingers clenched his. "Quinn, I have to meet some people at Larry's Lodge in Jackson Hole next Friday night." She looked up. "It's at a concert and I have tickets. I know you don't like rock, but there's going to be all kinds of music." Her eyes searched his. "Would you go with me? Elliot can come, too. I…want you to see what I do for a living."

"You and your keyboard?" he mused gently.

"Sort of," she agreed, hoping she could find the nerve to tell him everything before next Friday night.

"Okay," he replied. "A friend of mine works there—I

used to be with the Ski Patrol there, too. Sure, I'll go with you." The smile vanished, and his eyes glittered down at her. "I'll go damned near anywhere with you."

Amanda slid her arms around him and pressed close, shutting her eyes as she held on for dear life. "That goes double for me, mountain man," she said half under her breath.

He bent his head, searching for her soft mouth. She gave it to him without a protest, without a thought for the future, gave it to him with interest, with devotion, with ardor. Her lips opened invitingly, and she felt his hands on her hips with a sense of sweet inevitability, lifting her into intimate contact with the aroused contours of his body.

"Frightened?" he whispered unsteadily just over her mouth when he felt her stiffen involuntarily.

"Of you?" she whispered back. "Don't be absurd. Hold me any way you want. I adore you…!"

He actually groaned as his mouth pressed down hard on hers. His arms contracted hungrily and he gave in to the pleasure of possession for one long moment.

Her eyes opened and she watched him, feeding on the slight contortion of his features, his heavy brows drawn over his crooked nose, his long, thick lashes on his cheek as he kissed her. She did adore him, she thought dizzily. Adored him, loved him, worshiped him. If only she could stay with him forever like this.

Quinn lifted his head and paused as he saw her

watching him. He frowned slightly, then bent again. This time his eyes stayed open, too, and she went under as he deepened the kiss. Her eyes closed in self-defense and she moaned, letting him see the same vulnerability she'd seen in him. It was breathlessly sweet.

"This is an education," he said, laughing huskily, when he drew slightly away from her.

"Isn't it, though?" she murmured, moving his hands from her hips up to her waist and moving back a step from the blatant urgency of his body. "Elliot and Harry might come in," she whispered.

"I wouldn't mind," he said unexpectedly, searching her flushed face. "I'm not ashamed of what I feel for you, or embarrassed by it."

"This from a confirmed woman hater?" she asked with twinkling eyes.

"Well, not exactly confirmed anymore," he confessed. He lifted her by the waist and searched her eyes at point-blank range until she trembled from the intensity of the look. "I couldn't hate you if I tried, Amanda," he said quietly.

"Oh, I hope not," she said fervently, thinking ahead to when she would have to tell him the truth about herself.

He brushed a lazy kiss across her lips. "I think I'm getting the hang of this," he murmured.

"I think you are, too," she whispered. She slid her arms around his neck and put her warm mouth hungrily against his, sighing when he caught fire and answered the kiss with feverish abandon.

A slight, deliberate cough brought them apart, both staring blankly at the small redheaded intruder.

"Not that I mind," Elliot said, grinning, "but you're blocking the pan of brownies Harry made."

"You can think of brownies at a time like this?" Amanda groaned. "Elliot!"

"Listen, he can think of brownies with a fever of a hundred and two," Quinn told her, still holding her on a level with his eyes. "I've seen him get out of a sickbed to pinch a brownie from the kitchen."

"I like brownies, too," Amanda confessed with a warm smile, delighted that Quinn didn't seem to mind at all that Elliot had seen them in a compromising position. That made her feel lighter than air.

"Do you?" Quinn smiled and brushed his mouth gently against hers, mindless of Elliot's blatant interest, before he put her back on her feet. "Harry makes his from scratch, with real baker's chocolate. They're something special."

"I'll bet they are. Here. I'll get the saucers," she volunteered, still catching her breath.

Elliot looked like the cat with the canary as she dished up brownies. It very obviously didn't bother him that Amanda and his dad were beginning to notice each other.

"Isn't this cozy?" he remarked as they went back into

the living room and Amanda curled up on the sofa beside his dad, who never sat there.

"Cozy, indeed," Quinn murmured with a warm smile for Amanda.

She smiled back and laid her cheek against Quinn's broad chest while they watched television and ate brownies. She didn't move even when Harry joined them. And she knew she'd never been closer to heaven.

That night they were left discreetly alone, and she lay in Quinn's strong arms on the long leather couch in his office while wood burned with occasional hisses and sparks in the potbellied stove.

"I've had a raw deal with this place," he said eventually between kisses. "But it's good land, and I'm building a respectable herd of cattle. I can't offer you wealth or position, and we've got a ready-made family. But I can take care of you," he said solemnly, looking down into her soft eyes. "And you won't want for any of the essentials."

Her fingers touched his lean cheek hesitantly. "You don't know anything about me," she said. "When you know my background, you may not want me as much as you think you do." She put her fingers against his mouth. "You have to be sure."

"Damn it, I'm already sure," he muttered.

But was he? She was the first woman he'd ever been intimate with. Couldn't that blind him to her real suitability? What if it was just infatuation or desire? She was afraid to take a chance on his feelings, when she didn't really know what they were.

"Let's wait just a little while longer before we make any plans, Quinn. Okay?" she asked softly, turning in his hard arms so that her body was lying against his. "Make love to me," she whispered, moving her mouth up to his. "Please…"

He gave in with a rough groan, gathering her to him, crushing her against his aroused body. He wanted her beyond rational thought. Maybe she had cold feet, but he didn't. He knew what he wanted, and Amanda was it.

His hands smoothed the blouse and bra away with growing expertise and he fought out of his shirt so that he could feel her soft skin against his. But it wasn't enough. He felt her tremble and knew that it was reflected in his own arms and legs. He moved against her with a new kind of sensuousness, lifting his head to hold her eyes while he levered her onto her back and eased over her, his legs between both of hers in their first real intimacy.

She caught her breath, but she didn't push him to try to get away.

"It's just that new for you, isn't it?" he whispered huskily as his hips moved lazily over hers and he groaned. "God, it burns me to…feel you like this."

"I know." She arched her back, loving his weight, loving the fierce maleness of his body. Her arms slid closer around him and she felt his mouth open on hers, his tongue softly searching as it slid inside, into an intimacy that made her moan. She began to tremble.

His lean hand slid under her, getting a firm grip, and he brought her suddenly into a shocking, shattering position that made her mindless with sudden need. She clutched him desperately, shuddering, her nails digging into him as the contact racked her like a jolt of raw electricity.

He pulled away from her without a word, shuddering as he lay on his back, trying to get hold of himself.

"I'm sorry," he whispered. "I didn't mean to let it go so far with us."

She was trembling, too, trying to breathe while great hot tears rolled down her cheeks. "Gosh, I wanted you," she whispered tearfully. "Wanted you so badly, Quinn!"

"As badly as I wanted you, honey," he said heavily. "We can't let things get that hot again. It was a close call. Closer than you realize."

"Oh, Quinn, couldn't we make love?" she asked softly, rolling over to look down into his tormented face. "Just once…?"

He framed his face in his hands and brought her closed eyes to his lips. "No. I won't compromise you."

She hit his big, hair-roughened chest. "Goody Two-Shoes…!"

"Thank your lucky stars that I am," he chuckled. His eyes dropped to her bare breasts and lingered there before he caught the edges of her blouse and tugged them together. "You sex-crazed female, haven't you ever heard about pregnancy?"

"That condition where I get to have little Quinns?"

"Stop it, you're making it impossible for me," he said huskily. "Here, get up before I lose my mind."

She sat up with a grimace. "Spoilsport."

"Listen to you," he muttered, putting her back into her clothes with a wry grin. "I'll give you ten to one that you'd be yelling your head off if I started taking off your jeans."

She went red. "My jeans…!"

His eyebrows arched. "Amanda, would you like me to explain that book I read to you? The part about how men and women…"

She cleared her throat. "No, thanks, I think I've got the hang of it now," she murmured evasively.

"We might as well add a word about birth control," he added with a chuckle when he was buttoning up his own shirt. "You don't take the Pill, I assume?"

She shook her head. The whole thing was getting to be really embarrassing!

"Well, that leaves prevention up to me," he explained. "And that would mean a trip into town to the drugstore, since I never indulged, I never needed to worry about prevention. *Now* do you get the picture?"

"Boy, do I get the picture." She grimaced, avoiding his knowing gaze.

"Good girl. That's why we aren't lying down anymore."

She sighed loudly. "I guess you don't want children."

"Sure I do. Elliot would love brothers and sisters, and I'm crazy about kids." He took her slender hands in his and smoothed them over with his thumbs. "But kids should be born inside marriage, not outside it. Don't you think so?"

She took a deep breath, and her dark eyes met his. "Yes."

"Then we'll spend a lot of time together until you have to meet your friends at this concert," he said softly. "And afterward, you and I will come in here again and I'll ask you a question."

"Oh, Quinn," she whispered with aching softness.

"Oh, Amanda," he murmured, smiling as his lips softly touched hers. "But right now, we go to bed. Separately. Quick!"

"Yes, sir, Mr. Sutton." She got up and let him lead her to the staircase.

"I'll get the lights," he said. "You go on up. In the morning after we get Elliot off to school you can come out with me, if you want to."

"I want to," she said simply. She could hardly bear to be parted from him even overnight. It was like an addiction, she thought as she went up the staircase. Now if only she could make it last until she had the nerve to tell Quinn the truth....

The next few days went by in a haze. The snow began

to melt and the skies cleared as the long-awaited chinook blew in. In no time at all it was Friday night and Amanda was getting into what Elliot would recognize as her stage costume. She'd brought it, with her other things, from the Durning cabin. She put it on, staring at herself in the mirror. Her hair hung long and loose, in soft waves below her waist, in the beige leather dress with the buckskin boots that matched, she was the very picture of a sensuous woman. She left off the headband. There would be time for that if she could summon enough courage to get onstage. She still hadn't told Quinn. She hadn't had the heart to destroy the dream she'd been living. But tonight he'd know. And she'd know if they had a future. She took a deep breath and went downstairs.

Chapter Eight

Amanda sat in the audience with Quinn and Elliot at a far table while the crowded hall rang with excited whispers. Elliot was tense, like Amanda, his eyes darting around nervously. Quinn was frowning. He hadn't been quite himself since Amanda came down the staircase in her leather dress and boots, looking expensive and faintly alien. He hadn't asked any questions, but he seemed as uptight as she felt.

Her eyes slid over him lovingly, taking in his dark suit. He looked out of place in fancy clothes. She missed the sight of him in denim and his old shepherd's coat, and wondered fleetingly if she'd ever get to see him that way again after tonight—if she'd ever lie in his arms on the big sofa and warm to his kisses while the fire burned in the stove. She almost groaned. Oh, Quinn, she thought, I love you.

Elliot looked uncomfortable in his blue suit. He was watching for the rest of Desperado while a well-known Las Vegas entertainer warmed up the crowd and sang his own famous theme song.

"What are you looking for, son?" Quinn asked.

Elliot shifted. "Nothing. I'm just seeing who I know."

Quinn's eyebrows arched. "How would you know any-body in this crowd?" he muttered, glancing around. "My God, these are show people. Entertainers. Not people from our world."

That was a fact. But hearing it made Amanda heartsick. She reached out and put her hand over Quinn's.

"Your fingers are like ice," he said softly. He searched her worried eyes. "Are you okay, honey?"

The endearment made her warm all over. She smiled sadly and slid her fingers into his, looking down at the contrast between his callused, work-hardened hand and her soft, pale one. His was a strong hand, hers was artistic. But despite the differences, they fit together perfectly. She squeezed her fingers. "I'm fine," she said. "Quinn…"

"And now I want to introduce a familiar face," the Las Vegas performer's voice boomed. "Most of you know the genius of Desperado. The group has won countless awards for its topical, hard-hitting songs. Last year, Desperado was given a Grammy for 'Changes in the Wind,' and Hank

Shoeman's song 'Outlaw Love' won him a country music award and a gold record. But their fame isn't the reason we're honoring them tonight."

To Amanda's surprise, he produced a gold plaque. "As some of you may remember, a little over a month ago, a teenage girl died at a Desperado concert. The group's lead singer leaped into the crowd, disregarding her own safety, and was very nearly trampled trying to protect the fan. Because of that tragedy, Desperado went into seclusion. We're proud to tell you tonight that they're back and they're in better form than ever. This plaque is a token of respect from the rest of us in the performing arts to a very special young woman whose compassion and selflessness have won the respect of all."

He looked out toward the audience where Amanda sat frozen. "This is for you—Amanda Corrie Callaway. Will you come up and join the group, please? Come on, Mandy!"

She bit her lower lip. The plaque was a shock. The boys seemed to know about it, too, because they went to their instruments grinning and began to play the downbeat that Desperado was known for, the deep throbbing counter rhythm that was their trademark.

"Come on, babe!" Hank called out in his booming voice, he and Johnson and Deke and Jack looking much more like backwoods robbers than musicians with their huge bulk and outlaw gear.

Amanda glanced at Elliot's rapt, adoring face, and then

looked at Quinn. He was frowning, his dark eyes searching the crowd. She said a silent goodbye as she got to her feet. She reached into her pocket for her headband and put it on her head. She couldn't look at him, but she felt his shocked stare as she walked down the room toward the stage, her steps bouncing as the rhythm got into her feet and her blood.

"Thank you," she said huskily, kissing the entertainer's cheek as she accepted the plaque. She moved in between Johnson and Deke, taking the microphone. She looked past Elliot's proud, adoring face to Quinn's. He seemed to be in a state of dark shock. "Thank you all. I've had a hard few weeks. But I'm okay now, and I'm looking forward to better times. God bless, people. This one is for a special man and a special boy, with all my love." She turned to Hank, nodded, and he began the throbbing drumbeat of "Love Singer."

It was a song that touched the heart, for all its mad beat. The words, in her soft, sultry, clear voice caught every ear in the room. She sang from the heart, with the heart, the words fierce with meaning as she sang them to Quinn. "Love you, never loved anybody but you, never leave me lonely, love…singer."

But Quinn didn't seem to be listening to the words. He got to his feet and jerked Elliot to his. He walked out in the middle of the song and never looked back once.

Amanda managed to finish, with every ounce of will-power she had keeping her onstage. She let the last few notes hang in the air and then she bowed to a standing ovation. By the time she and the band did an encore and she got out of the hall, the truck they'd come in was long gone. There was no note, no message. Quinn had said it all with his eloquent back when he walked out of the hall. He knew who she was now, and he wanted no part of her. He couldn't have said it more clearly if he'd written it in blood.

She kept hoping that he might reconsider. Even after she went backstage with the boys, she kept hoping for a phone call or a glimpse of Quinn. But nothing happened.

"I guess I'm going to need a place to stay," Amanda said with a rueful smile, her expression telling her group all they needed to know.

"He couldn't handle it, huh?" Hank asked quietly. "I'm sorry, babe. We've got a suite, there's plenty of room for one more. I'll go up and get your gear tomorrow."

"Thanks, Hank." She took a deep breath and clutched the plaque to her chest. "Where's the next gig?"

"That's my girl," he said gently, sliding a protective arm around her. "San Francisco's our next stop. The boys and I are taking a late bus tomorrow." He grimaced at her knowing smile. "Well, you know how I feel about airplanes."

"Chicken Little," she accused. "Well, I'm not going to sit on a bus all day. I'll take the first charter out and meet you guys at the hotel."

"Whatever turns you on," Hank chuckled. "Come on. Let's get out of here and get some rest."

"You did good, Amanda," Johnson said from behind her. "We were proud."

"You bet," Deke and Jack seconded.

She smiled at them all. "Thanks, group. I shocked myself, but at least I didn't go dry the way I did last time." Her heart was breaking in two, but she managed to hide it. Quinn, she moaned inwardly. Oh, Quinn, was I just an interlude, an infatuation?

She didn't sleep very much. The next morning Amanda watched Hank start out for Ricochet then went down to a breakfast that she didn't even eat while she waited for him to return.

He came back three hours later, looking ruffled.

"Did you get my things?" she asked when he came into the suite.

"I got them." He put her suitcase down on the floor. "Part at Sutton's place, part at the Durning cabin. Elliot sent you a note." He produced it.

"And...Quinn?"

"I never saw him," he replied tersely. "The boy and the old man were there. They didn't mention Sutton and I didn't ask. I wasn't feeling too keen on him at the time."

"Thanks, Hank."

He shrugged. "That's the breaks, kid. It would have been a rough combination at best. You're a bright-lights girl."

"Am I?" she asked, thinking how easily she'd fit into Quinn's world. But she didn't push it. She sat down on the couch and opened Elliot's scribbled note.

> Amanda,
> I thought you were great. Dad didn't say anything all the way home and last night he went into his study and didn't come out until this morning. He went hunting, he said, but he didn't take any bullets. I hope you are okay. Write me when you can. I love you.
>
> Your friend, Elliot.

She bit her lip to keep from crying. Dear Elliot. At least he still cared about her. But her fall from grace in Quinn's eyes had been final, she thought bitterly. He'd never forgive her for deceiving him. Or maybe it was just that he'd gotten over his brief infatuation with her when he found out who she really was. She didn't know what to do. She couldn't remember ever feeling so miserable. To have discovered something that precious, only to lose it forever. She folded Elliot's letter and put it into her purse. At least it would be something to remember from her brief taste of heaven.

For the rest of the day, the band and Jerry, the road manager, got the arrangements made for the San Francisco concert, and final travel plans were laid. The boys were to board the San Francisco bus the next morning. Amanda was to fly out on a special air charter that specialized in flights for business executives. They'd managed to fit her in at the last minute when a computer-company executive had canceled his flight.

"I wish you'd come with us," Hank said hesitantly. "I guess I'm overreacting and all, but I hate airplanes."

"I'll be fine," she told him firmly. "You and the boys have a nice trip and stop worrying about me. I'll be fine."

"If you say so," Hank mumbled.

"I do say so." She patted him on the shoulder. "Trust me."

He shrugged and left, but he didn't look any less worried. Amanda, who'd gotten used to his morose predictions, didn't pay them any mind.

She went to the suite and into her bedroom early that night. Her fingers dialed the number at Ricochet. She had to try one last time, she told herself. There was at least the hope that Quinn might care enough to listen to her explanation. She had to try.

The phone rang once, twice, and she held her breath, but on the third ring the receiver was lifted.

"Sutton," came a deep weary-sounding voice.

Her heart lifted. "Oh, Quinn," she burst out. "Quinn, please let me try to explain—"

"You don't have to explain anything to me, Amanda," he said stiffly. "I saw it all on the stage."

"I know it looks bad," she began.

"You lied to me," he said. "You let me think you were

just a shy little innocent who played a keyboard, when you were some fancy big-time entertainer with a countrywide following."

"I knew you wouldn't want me if you knew who I was," she said miserably.

"You knew I'd see right through you if I knew," he corrected, his voice growing angrier. "You played me for a fool."

"I didn't!"

"All of it was a lie. Nothing but a lie! Well, you can go back to your public, Miss Callaway, and your outlaw buddies, and make some more records or tapes or whatever the hell they are. I never wanted you in the first place except in bed, so it's no great loss to me." He was grimacing, and she couldn't see the agony in his eyes as he forced the words out. Now that he knew who and what she was, he didn't dare let himself weaken. He had to make her go back to her own life, and stay out of his. He had nothing to give her, nothing that could take the place of fame and fortune and the world at her feet. He'd never been more aware of his own inadequacies as he had been when he'd seen Amanda on that stage and heard the applause of the audience. It ranked as the worst waking nightmare of his life, putting her forever out of his reach.

"Quinn!" she moaned. "Quinn, you don't mean that!"

"I mean it," he said through his teeth. He closed his eyes. "Every word. Don't call here again, don't come by, don't write. You're a bad influence on Elliot now that he knows who you are. I don't want you. You've worn out your welcome at Ricochet." He hung up without another word.

Amanda stared at the telephone receiver as if it had sprouted wings. Slowly she put it back in the cradle just as the room splintered into wet crystal around her.

She put on her gown mechanically and got into bed, turning out the bedside light. She lay in the dark and Quinn's words echoed in her head with merciless coolness. *Bad influence. Don't want you. Worn out your welcome. Never wanted you anyway except in bed.*

She moaned and buried her face in her pillow. She didn't know how she was going to go on, with Quinn's cold contempt dogging her footsteps. He hated her now. He thought she'd been playing a game, enjoying herself while she made a fool out of him. The tears burned her eyes. How quickly it had all ended, how finally. She'd hoped to keep in touch with Elliot, but that wouldn't be possible anymore. She was a bad influence on Elliot, so he wouldn't be allowed to contact her. She sobbed her hurt into the cool linen. Somehow, being denied contact with Elliot was the last straw. She'd grown so fond of the boy during those days she'd spent at Ricochet, and he cared about her, too. Quinn was being unnecessarily harsh. But perhaps he was right, and it was for the best. Maybe she could learn to think that way eventually. Right now she had a concert to get to, a sold-out one from what the boys and Jerry had said. She couldn't let the fans down.

Amanda got up the next morning, looking and feeling as if it were the end of the world. The boys took her suitcase downstairs, not looking too closely at her face without makeup, her long hair arranged in a thick, haphazard bun. She was wearing a dark pantsuit with a cream-colored blouse, and she looked miserable.

"We'll see you in San Francisco," Jerry told her with a smile. "I have to go nursemaid these big, tough guys, so you make sure the pilot of your plane has all his marbles, okay?"

"I'll check him out myself," she promised. "Take care of yourselves, guys. I'll see you in California."

"Okay. Be good, babe," Hank called. He and the others filed into the bus Jerry had chartered and Jerry hugged her impulsively and went in behind them.

She watched the bus pull away, feeling lost and alone, not for the first time. It was cold and snowy, but she hadn't wanted her coat. It was packed in her suitcase, and had already been put on the light aircraft. With a long sigh, she went back to the cab and sat disinterestedly in it as it wound over the snowy roads to the airport.

Fortunately the chinook had thawed the runways so that the planes were coming and going easily. She got out at the air charter service hangar and shook hands with the pilot.

"Don't worry, we're in great shape," he promised

Amanda with a grin. "In fact, the mechanics just gave us another once-over to be sure. Nothing to worry about."

"Oh, I wasn't worried," she said absently and allowed herself to be shepherded inside. She slid into an empty aisle seat on the right side and buckled up. Usually she preferred to sit by the window, but today she wasn't in the mood for sightseeing. One snow-covered mountain looked pretty much like another to her, and her heart wasn't in this flight or the gig that would follow it. She leaned back and closed her eyes.

It seemed to take forever for all the businessmen to get aboard. Fortunately there had been one more cancellation, so she had her seat and the window seat as well. She didn't feel like talking to anyone, and was hoping she wouldn't have to sit by some chatterbox all the way to California.

She listened to the engines rev up and made sure that her seat belt was properly fastened. They would be off as soon as the tower cleared them, the pilot announced. Amanda sighed. She called a silent goodbye to Quinn Sutton, and Elliot and Harry, knowing that once this plane lifted off, she'd never see any of them again. She winced at the thought. Oh, Quinn, she moaned inwardly, why wouldn't you *listen?*

The plane got clearance and a minute later, it shot down the runway and lifted off. But it seemed oddly sluggish. Amanda was used to air travel, even to charter flights, and she opened her eyes and peered forward worriedly as she listened to the whine become a roar.

She was strapped in, but a groan from behind took her mind off the engine. The elderly man behind her was clutching his chest and groaning.

"What's wrong?" she asked the worried businessman in the seat beside the older man.

"Heart attack, I think." He grimaced. "What can we do?"

"I know a little CPR," she said. She unfastened her seat belt; so did the groaning man's seat companion. But just as they started to lay him on the floor, someone shouted something. Smoke began to pour out of the cockpit, and the pilot called for everyone to assume crash positions. Amanda turned, almost in slow motion. She could feel the force of gravity increase as the plane started down. The floor went out from under her and her last conscious thought was that she'd never see Quinn again....

Elliot was watching television without much interest, wishing that his father had listened when Amanda had phoned the night before. He couldn't believe that he was going to be forbidden to even speak to her again, but Quinn had insisted, his cold voice giving nothing away as he'd made Elliot promise to make no attempt to contact her.

It seemed so unfair, he thought. Amanda was no wild party girl, surely his father knew that? He sighed heavily and munched on another potato chip.

The movie he was watching was suddenly interrupted as the local station broke in with a news bulletin. Elliot listened for a minute, gasped and jumped up to get his father.

Quinn was in the office, not really concentrating on what he was doing, when Elliot burst in. The boy looked odd, his freckles standing out in an unnaturally pale face.

"Dad, you'd better come here," he said uneasily. "Quick!"

Quinn's first thought was that something had happened to Harry, but Elliot stopped in front of the television. Quinn frowned as his dark eyes watched the screen. They were showing the airport.

"What's this all—" he began, then stopped to listen.

"…plane went down about ten minutes ago, according to our best information," the man, probably the airport manager, was saying. "We've got helicopters flying in to look for the wreckage, but the wind is up, and the area the plane went down in is almost inaccessible by road."

"What plane?" Quinn asked absently.

"To repeat our earlier bulletin—" the man on television seemed to oblige "—a private charter plane has been reported lost somewhere in the Grand Teton Mountains just out of Jackson Hole. One eyewitness interviewed by KWJC-TV newsman Bill Donovan stated that he saw flames shooting out of the cockpit of the twin-engine aircraft and that he watched it plummet into the mountains and vanish. Aboard the craft were prominent San

Francisco businessmen Bob Doyle and Harry Brown, and the lead singer of the rock group Desperado, Mandy Callaway."

Quinn sat down in his chair hard enough to shake it. He knew his face was as white as Elliot's. In his mind, he could hear his own voice telling Mandy he didn't want her anymore, daring her to ever contact him again. Now she was dead, and he felt her loss as surely as if one of his arms had been severed from his body.

That was when he realized how desperately he loved her. When it was too late to take back the harsh words, to go after her and bring her home where she belonged. He thought of her soft body lying in the cold snow, and a sound broke from his throat. He'd sent her away because he loved her, not because he'd wanted to hurt her, but she wouldn't have known that. Her last memory of him would have been a painful, hateful one. She'd have died thinking he didn't care.

"I don't believe it," Elliot said huskily. He was shaking his head. "I just don't believe it. She was onstage Friday night, singing again—" His voice broke and he put his face in his hands.

Quinn couldn't bear it. He got up and went past a startled Harry and out the back door in his shirtsleeves, so upset that he didn't even feel the cold. His eyes went to the barn, where he'd watched Amanda feed the calves, and around the back where she'd run from him that snowy afternoon and he'd had to save her from McNaber's bear traps. His big fists clenched by his sides and he shuddered with the force of the grief he felt, his face contorting.

"Amanda!" He bit off the name.

A long time later, he was aware of someone standing nearby. He didn't turn because his face would have said too much.

"Elliot told me," Harry said hesitantly. He stuck his hands into his pockets. "They say where she is, they may not be able to get her out."

Quinn's teeth clenched. "I'll get her out," he said huskily. "I won't leave her out there in the cold." He swallowed. "Get my skis and my boots out of the storeroom, and my insulated ski suit out of the closet. I'm going to call the lodge and talk to Terry Meade."

"He manages Larry's Lodge, doesn't he?" Harry recalled.

"Yes. He can get a chopper to take me up."

"Good thing you've kept up your practice," Harry muttered. "Never thought you'd need the skis for something this awful, though."

"Neither did I." He turned and went back inside. He might have to give up Amanda forever, but he wasn't giving her up to that damned mountain. He'd get her out somehow.

He grabbed the phone, ignoring Elliot's questions, and called the lodge, asking for Terry Meade in a tone that got instant action.

"Quinn!" Terry exclaimed. "Just the man I need. Look, we've got a crash—"

"I know," Quinn said tightly. "I know the singer. Can you get me a topo map of the area and a chopper? I'll need a first-aid kit, too, and some flares—"

"No sooner said than done," Terry replied tersely. "Although I don't think that first-aid kit will be needed, Quinn, I'm sorry."

"Well, pack it anyway, will you?" He fought down nausea. "I'll be up there in less than thirty minutes."

"We'll be waiting."

Quinn got into the ski suit under Elliot's fascinated gaze.

"You don't usually wear that suit when we ski together," he told his father.

"We don't stay out that long," Quinn explained. "This suit is a relatively new innovation. It's such a tight weave that it keeps out moisture, but it's made in such a way that it allows sweat to get out. It's like having your own heater along."

"I like the boots, too," Elliot remarked. They were blue, and they had a knob on the heel that allowed them to be tightened to fit the skier's foot exactly. Boots had to fit tight to work properly. And the skis themselves were equally fascinating. They had special brakes that unlocked when the skier fell, which stopped the ski from sliding down the hill.

"Those sure are long skis," Elliot remarked as his father took precious time to apply hot wax to them.

"Longer than yours, for sure. They fit my height," Quinn said tersely. "And they're short compared to jumping skis."

"Did you ever jump, Dad, or did you just do downhill?"

"Giant slalom," he replied. "Strictly Alpine skiing. That's going to come in handy today."

Elliot sighed. "I don't guess you'll let me come along?"

"No chance. This is no place for you." His eyes darkened. "God knows what I'll find when I get to the plane."

Elliot bit his lower lip. "She's dead, isn't she, Dad?" he asked in a choked tone.

Quinn's expression closed. "You stay here with Harry, and don't tie up the telephone. I'll call home as soon as I know anything."

"Take care of yourself up there, okay?" Elliot murmured as Quinn picked up the skis and the rest of his equipment, including gloves and ski cap. "I don't say it a lot, but I love you, Dad."

"I love you, too, son." Quinn pulled him close and gave him a quick, rough hug. "I know what I'm doing. I'll be okay."

"Good luck," Harry said as Quinn went out the back door to get into his pickup truck.

"I'll need it," Quinn muttered. He waved, started the truck, and pulled out into the driveway.

Terry Meade was waiting with the Ski Patrol, the helicopter pilot, assorted law enforcement officials and the civil defense director and trying to field the news media gathered at Larry's Lodge.

"This is the area where we think they are," Terry said grimly, showing Quinn the map. "What you call Ironside peak, right? It's not in our patrol area, so we don't have anything to do with it officially. The helicopter tried and failed to get into the valley below it because of the wind. The trees are dense down there and visibility is limited by blowing snow. Our teams are going to start here," he pointed at various places on the map. "But this hill is a killer." He grinned at Quinn. "You cut your teeth on it when you were practicing for the Olympics all those years ago, and you've kept up your practice there. If anyone can ski it, you can."

"I'll get in. What then?"

"Send up a flare. I'm packing a cellular phone in with the other stuff you asked for. It's got a better range than our walkie-talkies. Everybody know what to do? Right. Let's go."

He led them out of the lodge. Quinn put on his goggles, tugged his ski cap over his head and thrust his hands into his gloves. He didn't even want to think about what he might have to look at if he was lucky enough to find the downed plane. He was having enough trouble living with what he'd said to Amanda the last time he'd talked to her.

He could still hear her voice, hear the hurt in it when he'd told her he didn't want her. Remembering that was like cutting open his heart. For her sake, he'd sent her away. He was a poor man. He had so little to offer such a famous, beautiful woman. At first, at the lodge, his pride had been cut to ribbons when he discovered who she was, and how she'd fooled him, how she'd deceived him. But her adoration had been real, and when his mind was functioning again, he realized that. He'd almost phoned her back, he'd even dialed the number. But her world was so different from his. He couldn't let her give up everything she'd worked all her life for, just to live in the middle of nowhere. She deserved so much more. He sighed wearily. If she died, the last conversation would haunt him until the day he died. He didn't think he could live with it. He didn't want to have to try. She had to be alive. Oh, dear God, she had to be!

Chapter Nine

The sun was bright, and Quinn felt its warmth on his face as the helicopter set him down at the top of the mountain peak where the plane had last been sighted.

He was alone in the world when the chopper lifted off again. He checked his bindings one last time, adjusted the lightweight backpack and stared down the long mountainside with his ski poles restless in his hands. This particular slope wasn't skied as a rule. It wasn't even connected with the resort, which meant that the Ski Patrol didn't come here, and that the usual rescue toboggan posted on most slopes wouldn't be in evidence. He was totally on his own until he could find the downed plane. And he knew that while he was searching this untamed area, the Ski

Patrol would be out in force on the regular slopes looking for the aircraft.

He sighed heavily as he stared down at the rugged, untouched terrain, which would be a beginning skier's nightmare. Well, it was now or never. Amanda was down there somewhere. He had to find her. He couldn't leave her there in the cold snow for all eternity.

He pulled down his goggles, suppressed his feelings and shoved the ski poles deep as he propelled himself down the slope. The first couple of minutes were tricky as he had to allow for the slight added weight of the backpack. But it took scant time to adjust, to balance his weight on the skis to compensate.

The wind bit his face, the snow flew over his dark ski suit as he wound down the slopes, his skis throwing up powdered snow in his wake. It brought back memories of the days when he'd maneuvered through the giant slalom in Alpine skiing competition. He'd been in the top one percent of his class, a daredevil skier with cold nerve and expert control on the slopes. This mountain was a killer, but it was one he knew like the back of his hand. He'd trained on this peak back in his early days of competition, loving the danger of skiing a slope where no one else came. Even for the past ten years or so, he'd honed his skill here every chance he got.

Quinn smiled to himself, his body leaning into the turns, not too far, the cutting edge of his skis breaking his speed as he maneuvered over boulders, down the fall line, around trees and broken branches or over them, whichever seemed more expedient.

His dark eyes narrowed as he defeated the obstacles. At least, thank God, he was able to do something instead of going through hell sitting at home waiting for word. That in itself was a blessing, even if it ended in the tragedy everyone seemed to think it would. He couldn't bear to imagine Amanda dead. He had to think positively. There were people who walked away from airplane crashes. He had to believe that she could be one of them. He had to keep thinking that or go mad.

He'd hoped against hope that when he got near the bottom of the hill, under those tall pines and the deadly updrafts and downdrafts that had defeated the helicopter's reconnoitering, that he'd find the airplane. But it wasn't there. He turned his skis sideways and skidded to a stop, looking around him. Maybe the observer had gotten his sighting wrong. Maybe it was another peak, maybe it was miles away. He bit his lower lip raw, tasting the lip balm he'd applied before he came onto the slope. If anyone on that plane was alive, time was going to make the difference. He had to find it quickly, or Amanda wouldn't have a prayer if she'd managed to survive the initial impact.

He started downhill again, his heartbeat increasing as the worry began to eat at him. On an impulse, he shot across the fall line, parallel to it for a little while before he maneuvered back and went down again in lazy S patterns. Something caught his attention. A sound. Voices!

He stopped to listen, turning his head. There was wind, and the sound of pines touching. But beyond it was a voice, carrying in the silence of nature. Snow blanketed most sound, making graveyard peace out of the mountain's spring noises.

Quinn adjusted his weight on the skis and lifted his hands to his mouth, the ski poles dangling from his wrists. "Hello! Where are you?" he shouted, taking a chance that the vibration of his voice wouldn't dislodge snow above him and bring a sheet of it down on him.

"Help!" voices called back. "We're here! We're here!"

He followed the sound, praying that he wasn't following an echo. But no, there, below the trees, he saw a glint of metal in the lowering sun. The plane! Thank God, there were survivors! Now if only Amanda was one of them...

He went the rest of the way down. As he drew closer, he saw men standing near the almost intact wreckage of the aircraft. One had a bandage around his head, another was nursing what looked like a broken arm. He saw one woman, but she wasn't blond. On the ground were two still forms, covered with coats. Covered up.

Please, God, no, he thought blindly. He drew to a stop.

"I'm Sutton. How many dead?" he asked the man who'd called to him, a burly man in a gray suit and white shirt and tie.

"Two," the man replied. "I'm Jeff Coleman, and I sure am glad to see you." He shook hands with Quinn. "I'm the pilot. We had a fire in the cockpit and it was all I could do to set her down at all. God, I feel bad! For some reason, three of the passengers had their seat belts off when we hit." He shook his head. "No hope for two of them. The third's concussed and looks comatose."

Quinn felt himself shaking inside as he asked the question he had to ask. "There was a singer aboard," he said. "Amanda Callaway."

"Yeah." The pilot shook his head and Quinn wanted to die, he wanted to stop breathing right there… "She's the concussion."

Quinn knew his hand shook as he pushed his goggles up over the black ski cap. "Where is she?" he asked huskily.

The pilot didn't ask questions or argue. He led Quinn past the two bodies and the dazed businessmen who were standing or sitting on fabric they'd taken from the plane, trying to keep warm.

"She's here," the pilot told him, indicating a makeshift stretcher constructed of branches and pillows from the cabin, and coats that covered the still body.

"Amanda," Quinn managed unsteadily. He knelt beside her. Her hair was in a coiled bun on her head. Her face was alabaster white, her eyes closed, long black lashes lying still on her cheekbones. Her mouth was as pale as the rest of her face, and there was a bruise high on her forehead at the right temple. He stripped off his glove and felt the artery at her neck. Her heart was still beating, but slowly and not very firmly. Unconscious. Dying, perhaps. "Oh, God," he breathed.

He got to his feet and unloaded the backpack as the pilot and two of the other men gathered around him.

"I've got a modular phone," Quinn said, "which I hope to God will work." He punched buttons and waited, his dark eyes narrowed, holding his breath.

It seemed to take forever. Then a voice, a recognizable voice, came over the wire. "Hello."

"Terry!" Quinn called. "It's Sutton. I've found them."

"Thank God!" Terry replied. "Okay, give me your position."

Quinn did, spreading out his laminated map to verify it, and then gave the report on casualties.

"Only one unconscious?" Terry asked again.

"Only one," Quinn replied heavily.

"We'll have to airlift you out, but we can't do it until the wind dies down. You understand, Quinn, the same downdrafts and updrafts that kept the chopper out this morning are going to keep it out now."

"Yes, I know, damn it," Quinn yelled. "But I've got to get her to a hospital. She's failing already."

Terry sighed. "And there you are without a rescue toboggan. Listen, what if I get Larry Hale down there?"

he asked excitedly. "You know Larry; he was national champ in downhill a few years back, and he's a senior member of the Ski Patrol now. We could airdrop you the toboggan and some supplies for the rest of the survivors by plane. The two of you could tow her to a point accessible by chopper. Do you want to risk it, Quinn?"

"I don't know if she'll be alive in the morning, Terry," Quinn said somberly. "I'm more afraid to risk doing nothing than I am of towing her out. It's fairly level, if I remember right, all the way to the pass that leads from Caraway Ridge into Jackson Hole. The chopper might be able to fly down Jackson Hole and come in that way, without having to navigate the peaks. What do you think?"

"I think it's a good idea," Terry said. "If I remember right, they cleared that pass from the Ridge into Jackson Hole in the fall. It should still be accessible."

"No problem," Quinn said, his jaw grim. "If it isn't cleared, I'll clear it, by hand if necessary."

Terry chuckled softly. "Hale says he's already on the way. We'll get the plane up—hell of a pity he can't land where you are, but it's just too tricky. How about the other survivors?"

Quinn told him their conditions, along with the two bodies that would have to be airlifted out.

"Too bad," he replied. He paused for a minute to talk to somebody. "Listen, Quinn, if you can get the woman to

Caraway Ridge, the chopper pilot thinks he can safely put down there. About the others, can they manage until morning if we drop the supplies?"

Quinn looked at the pilot. "Can you?"

"I ate snakes in Nam and Bill over there served in Antarctica." He grinned. "Between us, we can keep these pilgrims warm and even feed them. Sure, we'll be okay. Get that little lady out if you can."

"Amen," the man named Bill added, glancing at Amanda's still form. "I've heard her sing. It would be a crime against art to let her die."

Quinn lifted the cellular phone to his ear. "They say they can manage, Terry. Are you sure you can get them out in the morning?"

"If we have to send the snowplow in through the valley or send in a squad of snowmobiles and a horse-drawn sled, you'd better believe we'll get them out. The Ski Patrol is already working out the details."

"Okay."

Quinn unloaded his backpack. He had flares and matches, packets of high protein dehydrated food, the first-aid kit and some cans of sterno.

"Paradise," the pilot said, looking at the stores. "With that, I can prepare a seven-course meal, build a bonfire and make a house. But those supplies they're going to drop will come in handy, just the same."

Quinn smiled in spite of himself. "Okay."

"We can sure use this first-aid kit, but I've already set a broken arm and patched a few cuts. Before I became a pilot, I worked in the medical corps."

"I had rescue training when I was in the Ski Patrol," Quinn replied. He grinned at the pilot. "But if I ever come down in a plane, I hope you're on it."

"Thanks. I hope none of us ever come down again." He glanced at the two bodies. "God, I'm sorry about them." He glanced at Amanda. "I hope she makes it."

Quinn's jaw hardened. "She's a fighter," he said. "Let's hope she cares enough to try." He alone knew how defeated she'd probably felt when she left the lodge. He'd inflicted some terrible damage with his coldness. Pride had forced him to send her away, to deny his own happiness. Once he knew how famous and wealthy she was in her own right, he hadn't felt that he had the right to ask her to give it all up to live with him and Elliot in the wilds of Wyoming. He'd been doing what he thought was best for her. Now he only wanted her to live.

He took a deep breath. "Watch for the plane and Hale, will you? I'm going to sit with her."

"Sure." The pilot gave him a long look that he didn't see before he went back to talk to the other survivors.

Quinn sat down beside Amanda, reaching for one cold little hand under the coats that covered her. It was going to be a rough ride for her, and she didn't need any more jarring. But if they waited until morning, without medical help, she could die. It was much riskier to do nothing than it was to risk moving her. And down here in the valley, the snow was deep and fairly level. It would be like Nordic skiing; cross-country skiing. With luck, it would feel like a nice lazy sleigh ride to her.

"Listen to me, honey," he said softly. "We've got a long way to go before we get you out of here and to a hospital. You're going to have to hold on for a long time." His hand tightened around hers, warming it. "I'll be right with you every step of the way. I won't leave you for a second. But you have to do your part, Amanda. You have to fight to stay alive. I hope that you still want to live. If you don't, there's something I need to tell you. I sent you away not because I hated you, Amanda, but because I loved you so much. I loved you enough to let you go back to the life you needed. You've got to stay alive so that I can tell you that," he added, stopping because his voice broke.

He looked away, getting control back breath by breath. He thought he felt her fingers move, but he couldn't be sure. "I'm going to get you out of here, honey, one way or the other, even if I have to walk out with you in my arms. Try to hold on, for me." He brought her hand to his mouth and kissed the palm hungrily. "Try to hold on, because if you die, so do I. I can't keep going unless you're some-where in the world, even if I never see you again. Even if you hate me forever."

He swallowed hard and put down her hand. The sound

of an airplane in the distance indicated that supplies were on the way. Quinn put Amanda's hand back under the cover and bent to brush his mouth against her cold, still one.

"I love you," he whispered roughly. "You've got to hold on until I can get you out of here."

He stood, his face like the stony crags above them, his eyes glittering as he joined the others.

The plane circled and seconds later, a white parachute appeared. Quinn held his breath as it descended, hoping against hope that the chute wouldn't hang up in the tall trees and that the toboggan would soft-land so that it was usable. A drop in this kind of wind was risky at best.

But luck was with them. The supplies and the sled made it in one piece. Quinn and the pilot and a couple of the sturdier survivors unfastened the chute and brought the contents back to the wreckage of the commuter plane. The sled was even equipped with blankets and a pillow and straps to keep Amanda secured.

Minutes later, the drone of a helicopter whispered on the wind, and not long after that, Hale started down the mountainside.

It took several minutes. Quinn saw the flash of rust that denoted the distinctive jacket and white waist pack of the Ski Patrol above, and when Hale came closer, he could see the gold cross on the right pocket of the jacket—a duplicate of the big one stenciled on the jacket's back. He smiled, remembering when he'd worn that same type of jacket during a brief stint as a ski patrolman. It was a special kind of occupation, and countless skiers owed their lives to those brave men and women. The National Ski Patrol had only existed since 1938. It was created by Charles Dole of Connecticut, after a skiing accident that took the life of one of his friends. Today, the Ski Patrol had over 10,000 members nationally, of whom ninety-eight percent were volunteers. They were the first on the slopes and the last off, patrolling for dangerous areas and rescuing injured people. Quinn had once been part of that elite group and he still had the greatest respect for them.

Hale was the only color against the whiteness of the snow. The sun was out, and thank God it hadn't snowed all day. It had done enough of that last night.

Quinn's nerves were stretched. He hadn't had a cigarette since he'd arrived at the lodge, and he didn't dare have one now. Nicotine and caffeine tended to constrict blood vessels, and the cold was dangerous enough without giving it any help. Experienced skiers knew better than to stack the odds against themselves.

"Well, I made it." Hale grinned, getting his breath. "How are you, Quinn?" He extended a hand and Quinn shook it.

The man in the Ski Patrol jacket nodded to the others, accepted their thanks for the supplies he'd brought with him, which included a makeshift shelter and plenty of food and water and even a bottle of cognac. But he didn't waste time. "We'd better get moving if we hope to get Miss Callaway out of here by dark."

"She's over here," Quinn said. "God, I hate doing this," he added heavily when he and Hale were standing over the unconscious woman. "If there was any hope, any at all, that the chopper could get in here…"

"You can feel the wind for yourself," Hale replied, his eyes solemn. "We're the only chance she has. We'll get her to the chopper. Piece of cake," he added with a reassuring smile.

"I hope so," Quinn said somberly. He bent and nodded to Hale. They lifted her very gently onto the long sled containing the litter. It had handles on both ends, because it was designed to be towed. They attached the towlines, covered Amanda carefully and set out, with reassurances from the stranded survivors.

There was no time to talk. The track was fairly straightforward, but it worried Quinn, all the same, because there were crusts that jarred the woman on the litter. He towed, Hale guided, their rhythms matching perfectly as they made their way down the snow-covered valley. Around them, the wind sang through the tall firs and lodgepole pines, and Quinn thought about the old trappers and mountain men who must have come through this valley a hundred, two hundred years before. In those days of poor sanitation and even poorer medicine, Amanda wouldn't have stood a chance.

He forced himself not to look back. He had to concen-

trate on getting her to the Ridge. All that was important
now, was that she get medical help while it could still do
her some good. He hadn't come all this way to find her
alive, only to lose her.

It seemed to take forever. Once, Quinn was certain that
they'd lost their way as they navigated through the narrow
pass that led to the fifty-mile valley between the Grand
Tetons and the Wind River Range, an area known as
Jackson Hole. But he recognized landmarks as they went
along, and eventually they wound their way around the
trees and along the sparkling river until they reached the
flats below Caraway Ridge.

Quinn and Hale were both breathing hard by now.
They'd changed places several times, so that neither got
too tired of towing the toboggan, and they were both in
peak condition. But it was still a difficult thing to do.

They rested, and Quinn reached down to check
Amanda's pulse. It was still there, and even seemed to be,
incredibly, a little stronger than it had been. But she was
pale and still and Quinn felt his spirits sink as he looked
down at her.

"There it is," Hale called, sweeping his arm over the
ridge. "The chopper."

"Now if only it can land," Quinn said quietly, and he
began to pray.

The chopper came lower and lower, then it seemed to
shoot up again and Quinn bit off a hard word. But the pilot

corrected for the wind, which was dying down, and eased the helicopter toward the ground. It seemed to settle inch by inch until it landed safe. The pilot was out of it before the blades stopped.

"Let's get out of here," he called to the men. "If that wind catches up again, I wouldn't give us a chance in hell of getting out. It was a miracle that I even got in!"

Quinn released his bindings in a flash, leaving his skis and poles for Hale to carry, along with his own. He got one side of the stretcher while the pilot, fortunately no lightweight himself, got the other. They put the stretcher in the back of the broad helicopter, on the floor, and Quinn and Hale piled in—Hale in the passenger seat up front, Quinn behind with Amanda, carefully laying ski equipment beside her.

"Let's go!" the pilot called as he revved up the engine.

It was touch and go. The wind decided to play tag with them, and they almost went into a lodgepole pine on the way up. But the pilot was a tenacious man with good nerves. He eased down and then up, down and up until he caught the wind off guard and shot up out of the valley and over the mountain.

Quinn reached down and clasped Amanda's cold hand in his. Only a little longer, honey, he thought, watching her with his heart in his eyes. Only a little longer, for God's sake, hold on!

It was the longest ride of his entire life. He spared one

thought for the people who'd stayed behind to give Amanda her chance and he prayed that they'd be rescued without any further injuries. Then his eyes settled on her pale face and stayed there until the helicopter landed on the hospital lawn.

The reporters, local, state and national, had gotten word of the rescue mission. They were waiting. Police kept them back just long enough for Amanda to be carried into the hospital, but Quinn and Hale were caught. Quinn volunteered Hale to give an account of the rescue and then he ducked out, leaving the other man to field the enthusiastic audience while he trailed quickly behind the men who'd taken Amanda into the emergency room.

He drank coffee and smoked cigarettes and glared at walls for over an hour until someone came out to talk to him. Hale had to go back to the lodge, to help plan the rescue of the rest of the survivors, but he promised to keep in touch. After he'd gone, Quinn felt even more alone. But at last a doctor came into the waiting room, and approached him.

"Are you related to Miss Callaway?" the doctor asked with narrowed eyes.

Quinn knew that if he said no, he'd have to wait for news of her condition until he could find somebody who was related to her, and he had no idea how to find her aunt.

"I'm her fiancé," he said without moving a muscle in his face. "How is she?"

"Not good," the doctor, a small wiry man, said bluntly. "But I believe in miracles. We have her in intensive care, where she'll stay until she regains consciousness. She's badly concussed. I gather she hasn't regained consciousness since the crash?" Quinn shook his head. "That sleigh ride and helicopter lift didn't do any good, either," he added firmly, adding when he saw the expression on Quinn's tormented face, "but I can understand the necessity for it. Go get some sleep. Come back in the morning. We won't know anything until then. Maybe not until much later. Concussion is tricky. We can't predict the outcome, as much as we'd like to."

"I can't rest," Quinn said quietly. "I'll sit out here and drink coffee, if you don't mind. If this is as close to her as I can get, it'll have to do."

The doctor took a slow breath. "We keep spare beds in cases like this," he said. "I'll have one made up for you when you can't stay awake any longer." He smiled faintly. "Try to think positively. It isn't medical, exactly, but sometimes it works wonders. Prayer doesn't hurt, either."

"Thank you," Quinn said.

The doctor shrugged. "Wait until she wakes up. Good night."

Quinn watched him go and sighed. He didn't know what to do next. He phoned Terry at the lodge to see if Amanda's band had called. Someone named Jerry and a man called Hank had been phoning every few minutes, he was told. Quinn asked for a phone number and Terry gave it to him.

He dialed the area code. California, he figured as he waited for it to ring.

"Hello?"

"This is Quinn Sutton," he began.

"Yes, I recognize your voice. It's Hank here. How is she?"

"Concussion. Coma, I guess. She's in intensive care and she's still alive. That's about all I know."

There was a long pause. "I'd hoped for a little more than that."

"So had I," Quinn replied. He hesitated. "I'll phone you in the morning. The minute I know anything. Is there anybody we should notify...her aunt?"

"Her aunt is a scatterbrain and no help at all. Anyway, she's off with Blalock Durning in the Bahamas on one of those incommunicado islands. We couldn't reach her if we tried."

"Is there anybody else?" Quinn asked.

"Not that I know of." There was a brief pause. "I feel bad about the way things happened. I hate planes, you know. That's why the rest of us went by bus. We stopped here in some hick town to make sure Amanda got her plane, and Terry told us what happened. We got a motel room and we're waiting for a bus back to Jackson. It will probably be late tomorrow before we get there. We've already canceled the gig. We can't do it without Amanda."

"I'll book a room for you," Quinn said.

"Make it a suite," Hank replied, "and if you need anything, you know, anything, you just tell us."

"I've got plenty of cigarettes and the coffee machine's working. I'm fine."

"We'll see you when we get there. And Sutton—thanks. She really cares about you, you know?"

"I care about her," he said stiffly. "That's why I sent her away. My God, how could she give all that up to live on a mountain in Wyoming?"

"Amanda's not a city girl, though," Hank said slowly. "And she changed after those days she spent with you. Her heart wasn't with us anymore. She cried all last night…"

"Oh, God, don't," Quinn said.

"Sorry, man," Hank said quietly. "I'm really sorry, that's the last thing I should have said. Look, go smoke a cigarette. I think I'll tie one on royally and have the boys put me to bed. Tomorrow we'll talk. Take care."

"You, too."

Quinn hung up. He couldn't bear to think of Amanda crying because of what he'd done to her. He might lose her even yet, and he didn't know how he was going to go on living. He felt so alone.

He was out of change after he called the lodge and booked the suite for Hank and the others, but he still had to talk to Elliot and Harry. He dialed the operator and called collect. Elliot answered the phone immediately.

"How is she?" he asked quickly.

Quinn went over it again, feeling numb. "I wish I knew more," he concluded. "But that's all there is."

"She can't die," Elliot said miserably. "Dad, she just can't!"

"Say a prayer, son," he replied. "And don't let Harry teach you any bad habits while I'm gone."

"No, sir, I won't," Elliot said with a feeble attempt at humor. "You're going to stay, I guess?"

"I have to," Quinn said huskily. He hesitated. "I love her."

"So do I," Elliot said softly. "Bring her back when you come."

"If I can. If she'll even speak to me when she wakes up," Quinn said with a total lack of confidence.

"She will," Elliot told him. "You should have listened to some of those songs you thought were so horrible. One of hers won a Grammy. It was all about having to give up things we love to keep from hurting them. She always seemed to feel it when somebody was sad or hurt, you know. And she risked her own life trying to save that girl at the concert. She's not someone who thinks about getting even with people. She's got too much heart."

Quinn drew deeply from his cigarette. "I hope so, son," he said. "You get to bed. I'll call you tomorrow."

"Okay. Take care of yourself. Love you, Dad."

"Me, too, son," Quinn replied. He hung up. The waiting area was deserted now, and the hospital seemed to have gone to sleep. He sat down with his foam cup of black coffee and finished his cigarette. The room looked like he felt—empty.

Chapter Ten

It was late morning when the nurse came to shake Quinn gently awake. Apparently around dawn he'd gone to sleep sitting up, with an empty coffee cup in his hand. He thought he'd never sleep at all.

He sat up, drowsy and disheveled. "How is Amanda?" he asked immediately.

The nurse, a young blonde, smiled at him. "She's awake and asking for you."

"Oh, thank God," he said heavily. He got quickly to his feet, still a little groggy, and followed her down to the intensive-care unit, where patients in tiny rooms were monitored from a central nurses' station and the hum and click and whir of life-supporting machinery filled the air.

If she was asking for him, she must not hate him too much. That thought sustained him as he followed the nurse into one of the small cubicles where Amanda lay.

Amanda looked thinner than ever in the light, her face pinched, her eyes hollow, her lips chapped. They'd taken her hair down somewhere along the way and tied it back with a pink ribbon. She was propped up in bed, still with the IV in position, but she'd been taken off all the other machines.

She looked up and saw Quinn and all the weariness and pain went out of her face. She brightened, became beautiful despite her injuries, her eyes sparkling. Her last thought when she'd realized in the plane what was going to happen had been of Quinn. Her first thought when she'd regained consciousness had been of him. The pain, the grief of having him turn away from her was forgotten. He was here, now, and that meant he had to care about her.

"Oh, Quinn!" she whispered tearfully, and held out her arms.

He went to her without hesitation, ignoring the nurses, the aides, the whole world. His arms folded gently around her, careful of the tubes attached to her hand, and his head bent over hers, his cheek on her soft hair, his eyes closed as he shivered with reaction. She was alive. She was going to live. He felt as if he were going to choke to death on his own rush of feeling.

"My God," he whispered shakily. "I thought I'd lost you."

That was worth it all, she thought, dazed from the emotion in his voice, at the tremor in his powerful body as he held her. She clung to him, her slender arms around his neck, drowning in pleasure. She'd wondered if he hadn't sent her away in a misguided belief that it was for her own good. Now she was sure of it. He couldn't have looked that haggard, that terrible, unless she mattered very much to him. Her aching heart soared. "They said you brought me out."

"Hale and I did," he said huskily. He lifted his head, searching her bright eyes slowly. "It's been the longest night of my life. They said you might die."

"Oh, we Callaways are tough birds," she said, wiping away a tear. She was still weak and sore and her headache hadn't completely gone away. "You look terrible, my darling," she whispered on a choked laugh.

The endearment fired his blood. He had to take a deep breath before he could even speak. His fingers linked with hers. "I felt pretty terrible when we listened to the news report, especially when I remembered the things I said to you." He took a deep breath. "I didn't know if you'd hate me for the rest of your life, but even if you did, I couldn't just sit on my mountain and let other people look for you." His thumb gently stroked the back of her pale hand. "How do you feel, honey?"

"Pretty bad. But considering it all, I'll do. I'm sorry about the men who died. One of them was having a heart attack," she explained. "The other gentleman who was sitting with him alerted me. We both unfastened our seat belts to try and give CPR. Just after I got up, the plane started down," she said. "Quinn, do you believe in predestination?"

"You mean, that things happen the way they're meant to in spite of us?" He smiled. "I guess I do." His dark eyes slid over her face hungrily. "I'm so glad it wasn't your time, Amanda."

"So am I." She reached up and touched his thin mouth with just the tips of her fingers. "Where is it?" she asked with an impish smile as a sudden delicious thought occurred to her.

He frowned. "Where's what?"

"My engagement ring," she said. "And don't try to back out of it," she added firmly when he stood there looking shocked. "You told the doctor and the whole medical staff that I was your fiancée, and you're not ducking out of it now. You're going to marry me."

His eyebrows shot up. "I'm what?" he said blankly.

"You're going to marry me. Where's Hank? Has anybody phoned him?"

"I did. I was supposed to call him back." He checked his watch and grimaced. "I guess it's too late now. He and the band are on the way back here."

"Good. They're twice your size and at least as mean." Her eyes narrowed. "I'll tell them you seduced me. I could be pregnant." She nodded, thinking up lies fast while Quinn's face mirrored his stark astonishment. "That's right, I could."

"You could not," he said shortly. "I never…!"

"But you're going to," she said with a husky laugh. "Just wait until I get out of here and get you alone. I'll wrestle you down and start kissing you, and you'll never get away in time."

"Oh, God," he groaned, because he knew she was right. He couldn't resist her that way, it was part of the problem.

"So you'll have to marry me first," she continued. "Because I'm not that kind of girl. Not to mention that you aren't that kind of guy. Harry likes me and Elliot and I are already friends, and I could even get used to McNaber if he'll move those traps." She pursed her lips, thinking. "The concert tour is going to be a real drag, but once it's over, I'll retire from the stage and just make records and tapes and CDs with the guys. Maybe a video now and again. They'll like that, too. We're all basically shy and we don't like live shows. I'll compose songs. I can do that at the house, in between helping Harry with the cooking and looking after sick calves, and having babies," she added with a shy smile.

He wanted to sit down. He hadn't counted on this. All that had mattered at the time was getting her away from the wreckage and into a hospital where she could be cared for. He hadn't let himself think ahead. But she obviously had. His head spun with her plans.

"Listen, you're an entertainer," he began. His fingers curled around hers and he looked down at them with a hard, grim sigh. "Amanda, I'm a poor man. All I've got is a broken-down ranch in the middle of nowhere. You'd have a lot of hardships, because I won't live on your money. I've got a son, even if he isn't mine, and…"

She brought his hand to her cheek and held it there, nuzzling her cheek against it as she looked up at him with dark, soft, adoring eyes. "I love you," she whispered.

He faltered. His cheeks went ruddy as the words penetrated, touched him, excited him. Except for his mother and Elliot, nobody had ever said that to him before Amanda had. "Do you?" he asked huskily. "Still? Even after the way I walked off and left you there at the lodge that night? After what I said to you on the phone?" he added, because he'd had too much time to agonize over his behavior, even if it had been for what he thought was her own good.

"Even after that," she said gently. "With all my heart. I just want to live with you, Quinn. In the wilds of Wyoming, in a grass shack on some island, in a mansion in Beverly Hills—it would all be the same to me—as long as you loved me back and we could be together for the rest of our lives."

He felt a ripple of pure delight go through him. "Is that what you really want?" he asked, searching her dark eyes with his own.

"More than anything else in the world," she confessed. "That's why I couldn't tell you who and what I really was. I loved you so much, and I knew you wouldn't want me…" Her voice trailed off.

"I want you, all right," he said curtly. "I never stopped. Damn it, woman, I was trying to do what was best for you!"

"By turning me out in the cold and leaving me to starve to death for love?" she asked icily. "Thanks a bunch!"

He looked away uncomfortably. "It wasn't that way and you know it. I thought maybe it was the novelty. You know, a lonely man in the backwoods," he began.

"You thought I was having the time of my life playing you for a fool," she said. Her head was beginning to hurt, but she had to wrap it all up before she gave in and asked for some more medication. "Well, you listen to me, Quinn Sutton, I'm not the type to go around deliberately trying to hurt people. All I ever wanted was somebody to care about me—just me, not the pretty girl on the stage."

"Yes, I know that now," he replied. He brought her hand to his mouth and softly kissed the palm. The look on his face weakened her. "So you want a ring, do you? It will have to be something sensible. No flashy diamonds, even if I could give you something you'd need sunglasses to look at."

"I'll settle for the paper band on a King Edward cigar if you'll just marry me," she replied.

"I think I can do a little better than that," he murmured

dryly. He bent over her, his lips hovering just above hers. "And no long engagement," he whispered.

"It takes three days, doesn't it?" she whispered back. "That is a long engagement. Get busy!"

He stifled a laugh as he brushed his hard mouth gently over her dry one. "Get well," he whispered. "I'll read some books real fast."

She colored when she realized what kind of books he was referring to, and then smiled under his tender kiss. "You do that," she breathed. "Oh, Quinn, get me out of here!"

"At the earliest possible minute," he promised.

The band showed up later in the day while Quinn was out buying an engagement ring for Amanda. He'd already called and laughingly told Elliot and Harry what she'd done to him, and was delighted with Elliot's pleasure in the news and Harry's teasing. He did buy her a diamond, even if it was a moderate one, and a gold band for each of them. It gave him the greatest kind of thrill to know that he was finally marrying for all the right reasons.

When he got back to the hospital, the rest of the survivors had been airlifted out and all but one of them had been treated and released. The news media had tried to get to Amanda, but the band arrived shortly after Quinn left and ran interference. Hank gave out a statement and stopped them. The road manager, as Quinn found out, had gone on to San Francisco to make arrangements for canceling the concert.

The boys were gathered around Amanda, who'd been moved into a nice private room. She was sitting up in bed, looking much better, and her laughing dark eyes met Quinn's the minute he came in the door.

"Hank brought a shotgun," she informed him. "And Deke and Johnson and Jack are going to help you down the aisle. Jerry's found a minister, and Hank's already arranged a blood test for you right down the hall. The license—"

"Is already applied for," Quinn said with a chuckle. "I did that myself. Hello, boys," he greeted them, shaking hands as he was introduced to the rest of the band. "And you can unload the shotgun. I'd planned to hold it on Amanda, if she tried to back out."

"Me, back out? Heaven forbid!" she exclaimed, smiling as Quinn bent to kiss her. "Where's my ring?" she whispered against his hard mouth. "I want it on, so these nurses won't make eyes at you. There's this gorgeous redhead…"

"I can't see past you, pretty thing," he murmured, his eyes soft and quiet in a still-gaunt face. "Here it is." Quinn produced it and slid it on her finger. He'd measured the size with a small piece of paper he'd wrapped around her finger, and he hoped that the method worked. He needn't have worried, because the ring was a perfect fit, and she acted as if it were the three-carat monster he'd wanted to get her. Her face lit up, like her pretty eyes, and she beamed as she showed it to the band.

"Did you sleep at all?" Hank asked him while the others gathered around Amanda.

"About an hour, I think," Quinn murmured dryly. "You?"

"I couldn't even get properly drunk," Hank said, sighing, "so the boys and I played cards until we caught the bus. We slept most of the way in. It was a long ride. From what I hear," he added with a level look, "you and that Hale fellow had an even longer one, bringing Amanda out of the mountains."

"You'll never know." Quinn looked past him to Amanda, his dark eyes full of remembered pain. "I had to decide whether or not to move her. I thought it was riskier to leave her there until the next morning. If we'd waited, we had no guarantee that the helicopter would have been able to land even then. She could have died. It's a miracle she didn't."

"Miracles come in all shapes and sizes," Hank mused, staring at her. "She's been ours. Without her, we'd never have gotten anywhere. But being on the road has worn her out. The boys and I were talking on the way back about cutting out personal appearances and concentrating on videos and albums. I think Amanda might like that. She'll have enough to do from now on, I imagine, taking care of you and your boy," he added with a grin. "Not to mention all those new brothers and sisters you'll be adding. I grew up on a ranch," he said surprisingly. "I have five brothers."

Quinn's eyebrows lifted. "Are they all runts like you?" he asked with a smile.

"I'm the runt," Hank corrected.

Quinn just shook his head.

Amanda was released from the hospital two days later. Every conceivable test had been done, and fortunately there were no complications. The doctor had been cautiously optimistic at first, but her recovery was rapid—probably due, the doctor said with a smile, to her incentive. He gave Amanda away at the brief ceremony, held in the hospital's chapel just before she was discharged, and one of the nurses was her matron of honor. There were a record four best men; the band. But for all its brevity and informality, it was a ceremony that Amanda would never forget. The Methodist minister who performed it had a way with words, and Amanda and Quinn felt just as married as if they'd had the service performed in a huge church with a large crowd present.

The only mishap was that the press found out about the wedding, and Amanda and Quinn and the band were mobbed as they made their way out of the hospital afterward. The size of the band members made them keep well back. Hank gave them his best wildman glare while Jack whispered something about the bandleader becoming homicidal if he was pushed too far. They escaped in two separate cars. The driver of the one taking Quinn and

Amanda to the lodge managed to get them there over back roads, so that nobody knew where they were.

Terry had given them the bridal suite, on the top floor of the lodge, and the view of the snowcapped mountains was exquisite. Amanda, still a little shaky and very nervous, stared out at them with mixed feelings.

"I don't know if I'll ever think of them as postcards again," she remarked to Quinn, who was trying to find places to put everything from their suitcase. He'd had to go to Ricochet for his suit and a change of clothing.

"What, the mountains?" he asked, smiling at her. "Well, it's not a bad thing to respect them. But airplanes don't crash that often, and when you're well enough, I'm going to teach you to ski."

She turned and looked at him for a long time. Her wedding outfit was an off-white, a very simple shirtwaist dress with a soft collar and no frills. But with her long hair around her shoulders and down to her waist, framed in the light coming through the window, she looked the picture of a bride. Quinn watched her back and sighed, his eyes lingering on the small sprig of lily of the valley she was wearing in her hair—a present from a member of the hospital staff.

"One of the nurses brought me a newspaper," Amanda said. "It told all about how you and Mr. Hale got me out." She hesitated. "They said that only a few men could ski that particular mountain without killing themselves."

"I've been skiing it for years," he said simply. He took off the dark jacket of his suit and loosened his tie with a long sigh. "I knew that the Ski Patrol would get you out, but they usually only work the lodge slopes—you know, the ones with normal ski runs. The peak the plane landed on was off the lodge property and out-of-the-way. It hadn't even been inspected. There are all sorts of dangers on slopes like that—fallen trees, boulders, stumps, debris, not to mention the threat of avalanche. The Ski Patrol marks dangerous runs where they work. They're the first out in the morning and the last off the slopes in the afternoon."

"You seem to know a lot about it," Amanda said.

"I used to be one of them," he replied with a grin. "In my younger days. It's pretty rewarding."

"There was a jacket Harry showed me," she frowned. "A rust-colored one with a big gold cross on the back…"

"My old patrol jacket." He chuckled. "I wouldn't part with it for the world. If I'd thought of it, I'd have worn it that day." His eyes darkened as he looked at her. "Thank God I knew that slope," he said huskily. "Because I'd bet money that you wouldn't have lasted on that mountain overnight."

"I was thinking about you when the plane went down," she confessed. "I wasn't sure that I'd ever see you again."

"Neither was I when I finally got to you." He took off his tie and threw it aside. His hand absently unfastened the top buttons of his white shirt as he moved toward her.

"I was trying so hard to do the right thing," he murmured. "I didn't think I could give you what you needed, what you were used to."

"I'm used to you, Mr. Sutton," she murmured with a smile. Amanda slid her arms under his and around him, looking up at him with her whole heart in her dark eyes. "Bad temper, irritable scowl and all. Anything you can't give me, I don't want. Will that do?"

His broad chest rose and fell slowly. "I can't give you much. I've lost damned near everything."

"You have Elliot and Harry and me," she pointed out. "And some fat, healthy calves, and in a few years, Elliot will have a lot of little brothers and sisters to help him on the ranch."

A faint dusky color stained his high cheekbones. "Yes."

"Why, Mr. Sutton, honey, you aren't shy, are you?" she whispered dryly as she moved her hands back around to his shirt and finished unbuttoning it down his tanned, hair-roughened chest.

"Of course I'm shy," he muttered, heating up at the feel of her slender hands on his skin. He caught his breath and shuddered when she kissed him there. His big hands slid into her long, silky hair and brought her even closer. "I like that," he breathed roughly. "Oh, God, I love it!"

She drew back after a minute, her eyes sultry, drowsy. "Wouldn't you like to do that to me?" she whispered. "I like it, too."

He fumbled with buttons until he had the dress out of the way and she was standing in nothing except a satin teddy. He'd never seen one before, except in movies, and he stared at her with his breath stuck somewhere in his chest. It was such a sexy garment low on her lace-covered breasts, nipped at her slender waist, hugging her full hips. Below it were her elegant silk-clad legs, although he didn't see anything holding up her hose.

"It's a teddy," she whispered. "If you want to slide it down," she added shyly, lowering her eyes to his pulsating chest, "I could step out of it."

He didn't know if he could do that and stay on his feet. The thought of Amanda unclothed made his knees weak. But he slid the straps down her arms and slowly, slowly, peeled it away from her firm, hard-tipped breasts, over her flat stomach, and then over the panty hose she was wearing. He caught them as well and eased the whole silky mass down to the floor.

She stepped out of it, so much in love with him that all her earlier shyness was evaporating. It was as new for him as it was for her, and that made it beautiful. A true act of love.

She let him look at her, fascinated by the awe in his hard face, in the eyes that went over her like an artist's brush, capturing every line, every soft curve before he even touched her.

"Amanda, you're the most beautiful creature I've ever

seen," he said finally. "You look like a drawing of a fairy I saw in an old-time storybook...all gold and ivory."

She reached up and leaned close against him, shivering a little when her breasts touched his bare chest. The hair was faintly abrasive and very arousing. She moved involuntarily and gasped at the sensation.

"Do you want to help me?" he whispered as he stripped off his shirt and his hands went to his belt.

"I..." She hesitated, her nerve retreating suddenly at the intimacy of it. She grimaced. "Oh, Quinn, I'm such a coward!" She hid her face against his chest and felt his laughter.

"Well, you're not alone," he murmured. "I'm not exactly an exhibitionist myself. Look, why don't you get under the covers and close your eyes, and we'll pretend it's dark."

She looked up at him and laughed. "This is silly."

"Yes, I know." He sighed. "Well, honey, we're married. I guess it's time to face all the implications of sharing a bed."

He sat down, took off his boots and socks, stood to unbuckle his belt, holding her eyes, and slid the zip down. Everything came off, and seconds later, she saw for herself all the differences between men and women.

"You've gone scarlet, Mrs. Sutton," he observed.

"You aren't much whiter yourself, Mr. Sutton," she replied.

He laughed and reached for her and she felt him press against her. It was incredible, the feel of skin against skin, hair-rough flesh against silky softness. He bent and found her mouth and began to kiss her lazily, while his big, rough hands slid down her back and around to her hips. His mouth opened at the same time that his fingers pulled her thighs against his, and she felt for the first time the stark reality of arousal.

He felt her gasp and lifted his head, searching her flushed face. "That has to happen before anything else can," he whispered. "Don't be afraid. I think I know enough to make it easy for you."

"I love you, Quinn," she whispered back, forcing her taut muscles to relax, to give in to him. She leaned her body into his with a tiny shiver and lifted her mouth. "However it happens between us, it will be all right."

He searched her eyes and nodded. His mouth lowered to hers. He kissed her with exquisite tenderness while his hands found the softness of her breasts. Minutes later, his mouth traced them, covered the hard tips in a warm, moist suction that drew new sounds from her. He liked that, so he lifted her and put her on the big bed, and found other places to kiss her that made the sounds louder and more tormented.

The book had been very thorough and quite explicit, so he knew what to do in theory. Practice was very different. He hadn't known that women could lose control, too. That their bodies were so soft, or so strong. That their eyes grew wild and their faces contorted as the pleasure built in them, that they wept with it. Her pleasure became his only goal in the long, exquisite oblivion that followed.

By the time he moved over her, she was more than ready for him, she was desperate for him. He whispered to her, gently guided her body to his as he fought for control of his own raging need so that he could satisfy hers first.

There was one instant when she stiffened and tried to pull away, but he stopped then and looked down into her frightened eyes.

"It will only hurt for a few seconds," he whispered huskily. "Link your hands in mine and hold on. I'll do it quickly."

"All...all right." She felt the strength in his hands and her eyes met his. She swallowed.

He pushed, hard. She moaned a little, but her body accepted him instantly and without any further difficulty.

Her eyes brightened. Her lips parted and she breathed quickly and began to smile. "It's gone," she whispered. "Quinn, I'm a woman now...."

"My woman," he whispered back. The darkness grew in his eyes. He bent to her mouth and captured it, held it as he began to move, his body dancing above hers, teaching it the rhythm. She followed where he led, gasping as the cadence increased, as the music began to grow in her mind and filtered through her arms and legs. She held on to him with the last of her strength, proud of his stamina, of the power in his body that was taking hers from reality and into a place she'd never dreamed existed.

She felt the first tremors begin, and work into her like fiery pins, holding her body in a painful arch as she felt the tension build. It grew to unbearable levels. Her head thrashed on the pillow and she wanted to push him away, to make him stop, because she didn't think she could live through what was happening to her. But just as she began to push him the tension broke and she fell, crying out, into a hot, wild satisfaction that convulsed her. Above her, Quinn saw it happen and finally gave in to the desperate fever of his own need. He drove for his own satisfaction and felt it take him, his voice breaking on Amanda's name as he went into the fiery depths with her.

Afterward, he started to draw away, but her arms went around him and refused to let go. He felt her tears against his hot throat.

"Are you all right?" he asked huskily.

"I died," she whispered brokenly. Her arms contracted. "Don't go away, please don't. I don't want to let you go," she moaned.

He let his body relax, giving her his full weight. "I'll crush you, honey," he whispered in her ear.

"No, you won't." She sighed, feeling his body pulse with every heartbeat, feeling the dampness of his skin on her own, the glory of his flesh touching hers. "This is nice."

He laughed despite his exhaustion. "There's a new word for it," he murmured. He growled and bit her shoulder gently. "Wildcat," he whispered proudly. "You bit me. Do you remember? You bit me and dug your nails into my hips and screamed."

"So did you," she accused, flushing. "I'll have bruises on my thighs…"

"Little ones," he agreed. He lifted his head and searched her dark, quiet eyes. "I couldn't help that, at the last. I lost it. Really lost it. Are you as sated as I am?" he mused. "I feel like I've been walking around like half a person all my life, and I've just become whole."

"So do I." Her eyes searched his, and she lifted a lazy hand to trace his hard, thin lips. After a few seconds, she lifted her hips where they were still joined to his and watched his eyes kindle. She drew in a shaky breath and did it again, delighting in the sudden helpless response of his body.

"That's impossible," he joked. "The book said so."

Amanda pulled his mouth down to hers. "Damn the book," she said and held on as he answered her hunger with his own.

They slept and finally woke just in time to go down to dinner. But since neither of them wanted to face having to get dressed, they had room service send up a tray. They drank champagne and ate thick steaks and went back to bed. Eventually they even slept.

The next morning, they set out for Ricochet, holding hands all the way home.

Chapter Eleven

Elliot and Harry were waiting at the door when Quinn brought Amanda home. There was a big wedding cake on the table that Harry had made, and a special present that Elliot had made Harry drive him to town in the sleigh to get—a new Desperado album with a picture of Amanda on the cover.

"What a present," Quinn murmured, smiling at Amanda over the beautiful photograph. "I guess I'll have to listen to it now, won't I?"

"I even got Hank Shoeman's autograph," Elliot enthused. "Finally I can tell the guys at school! I've been going nuts ever since I realized who Amanda was…."

"You knew?" Quinn burst out. "And you didn't tell me? So that's why that tape disappeared."

"You were looking for it?" Elliot echoed.

"Sure, just after we got home from the lodge that night I deserted Amanda," Quinn said with a rueful glance at her. "I was feeling pretty low. I just wanted to hear her voice, but the tape was missing."

"Sorry, Dad," Elliot said gently. "I'll never do it again, but I was afraid you'd toss her out if you knew she was a rock singer. She's really terrific, you know, and that song that won a Grammy was one of hers."

"Stop, you'll make me blush," Amanda groaned.

"I can do that," Quinn murmured dryly and the look he gave Amanda brought scarlet color into her hot cheeks.

"You were in the paper, Dad," Elliot continued excitedly. "And on the six-o'clock news, too! They told all about your skiing days and the Olympic team. Dad, why didn't you keep going? They said you were one of the best giant slalom skiers this country ever produced, but that you quit with a place on the Olympic team in your pocket."

"It's a long story, Elliot," he replied.

"It was because of my mother, wasn't it?" the boy asked gravely.

"Well, you were on the way and I didn't feel right about deserting her at such a time."

"Even though she'd been so terrible to you?" he probed.

Quinn put his hands on his son's shoulders. "I'll tell you for a fact, Elliot, you were mine from the day I knew about your existence. I waited for you like a kid waiting for a Christmas present. I bought stuff and read books about babies and learned all the things I'd need to know to help your mother raise you. I'd figured, you see, that she might eventually decide that having you was pretty special. I'm sorry that she didn't."

"That's okay," Elliot said with a smile. "You did."

"You bet I did. And do."

"Since you like kids so much, you and Amanda might have a few of your own," Elliot decided. "I can help. Me and Harry can wash diapers and make formula…"

Amanda laughed delightedly. "Oh, you doll, you!" She hugged Elliot. "Would you really not mind other kids around?"

"Heck, no," Elliot said with genuine feeling. "All the other guys have little brothers and sisters. It gets sort of lonely, being the only one." He looked up at her admiringly. "And they'd be awful pretty, if some of them were girls."

She grinned. "Maybe we'll get lucky and have another redhead, too. My mother was redheaded. So was my grandmother. It runs in the family."

Elliot liked that, and said so.

"Hank Shoeman has a present for you, by the way," she told Elliot. "No, there's no use looking in the truck, he ordered it."

Elliot's eyes lit up. "What is it? An autographed photo of the group?"

"It's a keyboard," Amanda corrected gently, smiling at his awe. "A real one, a Moog like I play when we do instrumentals."

"Oh, my gosh!" Elliot sat down. "I've died and gone to heaven. First I get a great new mother and now I get a Moog. Maybe I'm real sick and have a high fever," he frowned, feeling his forehead.

"No, you're perfectly well," Quinn told him. "And I guess it's all right if you play some rock songs," he added with a grimace. "I got used to turnips, after all, that time when Harry refused to cook any more greens. I guess I can get used to loud music."

"I refused to cook greens because we had a blizzard and canned turnips was all I had," Harry reminded him, glowering. "Now that Amanda's here, we won't run out of beans and peas and such, because she'll remember to tell me we're out so I can get some more."

"I didn't forget to remind you," Quinn muttered.

"You did so," Elliot began. "I remember—"

"That's it, gang up on me," Quinn glowered at them.

"Don't you worry, sweet man, I'll protect you from ghastly turnips and peas and beans," she said with a quick glance at Harry and Elliot. "I like asparagus, so I'll make sure that's all we keep here. Don't you guys like asparagus?"

"Yes!" they chorused, having been the culprits who told Amanda once that Quinn hated asparagus above all food in the world.

Quinn groaned.

"And I'll make liver and onions every night," Amanda added. "We love that, don't we, gang?"

"We sure do!" they chorused again, because they knew it was the only meat Quinn wouldn't eat.

"I'll go live with McNaber," he threatened.

Amanda laughed and slid her arms around him. "Only if we get to come, too." She looked up at him. "It's all right. We all really hate asparagus and liver and onions."

"That's a fact, we do," Elliot replied. "Amanda, are you going to go on tour with the band?"

"No," she said quietly. "We'd all gotten tired of the pace. We're going to take a well-earned rest and concentrate on videos and albums."

"I've got this great idea for a video," Elliot volunteered.

She grinned. "Okay, tiger, you can share it with us when Hank and the others come for a visit."

His eyes lit up. "They're all coming? The whole group?"

"My aunt is marrying Mr. Durning," she told him, having found out that tidbit from Hank. "They're going to live in Hawaii, and the band has permission to use the cabin whenever they like. They've decided that if I like the mountains so much, there must be something special about them. Our next album is going to be built around a mountain theme."

"Wow." Elliot sighed. "Wait'll I tell the guys."

"You and the guys can be in the video," Amanda

promised. "We'll find some way to fit you into a scene or two." She studied Harry. "We'll put Harry in, too."

"Oh, no, you won't!" he said. "I'll run away from home first."

"If you do, we'll starve to death." Amanda sighed. "I can't do cakes and roasts. We'll have to live on potatoes and fried eggs."

"Then you just make a movie star out of old Elliot and I'll stick around," he promised.

"Okay," Amanda said, "but what a loss to women everywhere. You'd have been super, Harry."

He grinned and went back to the kitchen to cook. Elliot eventually wandered off, too, and Quinn took Amanda into the study and closed the door.

They sat together in his big leather armchair, listening to the crackling of the fire in the potbellied stove.

"Remember the last time we were in here together?" he asked lazily between kisses.

"Indeed, I do," she murmured with a smile against his throat. "We almost didn't stop in time."

"I'm glad we did." He linked her fingers with his. "We had a very special first time. A real wedding night. That's marriage the way it was meant to be; a feast of first times."

She touched his cheek lightly and searched his dark eyes. "I'm glad we waited, too. I wanted so much to go to my husband untouched. I just want you to know that it was worth the wait. I love you, really love you, you know?" She sighed shakily. "That made it much more than my first intimate experience."

He brought his mouth down gently on hers. "I felt just that way about it," he breathed against her lips. "I never asked if you wanted me to use anything…?"

"So I wouldn't get pregnant?" She smiled gently. "I love kids."

"So do I." He eased back and pulled her cheek onto his chest, smoothing her long, soft hair as he smiled down into her eyes. "I never dreamed I'd find anyone like you. I'd given up on women. On life, too, I guess. I've been bitter and alone for such a long time, Amanda. I feel like I was just feverish and dreaming it all."

"You aren't dreaming." She pulled him closer to her and kissed him with warm, slow passion. "We're married and I'm going to love you for the rest of my life, body and soul. So don't get any ideas about trying to get away. I've caught you fair and square and you're all mine."

He chuckled. "Really? If you've caught me, what are you going to do with me?"

"Have I got an answer for that," she whispered with a sultry smile. "You did lock the door, didn't you?" she murmured, her voice husky as she lifted and turned so that she was facing him, her knees beside him on the chair. His heart began to race violently.

"Yes, I locked the door. What are you…Amanda!"

She smiled against his mouth while her hands worked

at fastenings. "That's my name, all right," she whispered. She nipped his lower lip gently and laughed delightedly when she felt him helping her. "Life is short. We'd better start living it right now."

"I couldn't possibly agree more," he whispered back, and his husky laugh mingled with hers in the tense silence of the room.

Beside them, the burning wood crackled and popped in the stove while the snow began to fall again outside the window. Amanda had started it, but almost immediately Quinn took control and she gave in with a warm laugh. She knew already that things were done Sutton's way around Ricochet. And this time, she didn't really mind at all.

* * * * *